Rose Piddington

The Last of the Cavaliers

Vol. I

SALZWASSER
VERLAG

Rose Piddington

The Last of the Cavaliers

Vol. I

Reprint of the original, first published in 1859.

1st Edition 2022 | ISBN: 978-3-37512-923-1

Verlag (Publisher): Salzwasser Verlag GmbH, Zeilweg 44, 60439 Frankfurt, Deutschland
Vertretungsberechtigt (Authorized to represent): E. Roepke, Zeilweg 44, 60439 Frankfurt, Deutschland
Druck (Print): Books on Demand GmbH, In de Tarpen 42, 22848 Norderstedt, Deutschland

THE

LAST OF THE CAVALIERS.

Fare thee well, great heart!
Ill-weaved ambition, how much art thou shrunk!
* * * * * * *
Thy ignomy sleep with thee in the grave,
But not remembered in thy epitaph.
KING HENRY THE FOURTH, Part I.

IN THREE VOLUMES.

VOL. I.

RICHARD BENTLEY, NEW BURLINGTON STREET

1859.

THE

LAST OF THE CAVALIERS.

CHAPTER I.

ALICE.

> Her household motions light and free,
> Her steps of virgin liberty;
> A countenance in which did meet
> Sweet records, promises as sweet;
> A creature not too bright or good
> For human nature's daily food;
> For transient pleasúres, simple wiles,
> Praise, blame, love, kisses, tears, and smiles.

THE scene of our tale opens in Edinburgh, in the early part of the year 1688.

The winter had been unusually long and severe in Scotland, and at the time of which we speak (the middle of March) the weather did not appear soon likely to break up. The frost had lasted without intermission since the beginning of February, and the earth lay parched and white as beneath a torrid sky; the keen north-east wind swept over the country biting and ceaseless; the meridian warmth of day had scarcely power to produce a momentary thaw; and, as night after night the sun went down in a firmament of intense and cloudless blue and rose-colour, it seemed as though spring had been for ever banished from the face of the earth.

In one of the narrow lanes which run northwards from the lower extremity of the Canongate, in the direction of the Calton Hill, there was (and for aught we know there may be still) a small narrow house jammed up between its larger and broader neighbours, and which, to a fanciful eye, would suggest the idea of having been thereby stunted in its growth. It was only five stories high, and, containing but two rooms on each flat, was let to such persons as were glad to find accommodation suited to their limited means, without being obliged to seek it in the lower and poorer quarters of the crowded city.

On one of the brightest and coldest afternoons of that rigorous season, two women, a mother and daughter, were sitting in a front room on the very highest story of this house. It was small, but exceedingly neat, and showed signs of comfort and care rarely to be met with among the humbler classes in Scotland, and presented certain articles of furniture which seemed to announce a slight superiority, if not of fortune, at least of station and habit—such as some pieces of thick old tapestry, one or two large chairs, a carved closet or almry of dark oak, and table of the same. The window was curtained with coarse but warm stuff, and the whole aspect of the room, although poor, bore no tokens of want.

The elder of the two inmates, a delicate-looking grey-haired woman of fifty, was sitting in a high-backed chair on one side of the window. She seemed in ill health, and her thin figure, uneasy movement, and frequent dry cough, told too plainly the nature of her disease. She was speaking in a quick and irritable, but by no means unkind, tone to her daughter, who, seated on the broad window ledge, with a small basket full of implements of feminine industry beside her, was plying her needle busily on some delicate piece of ornamental work.

She was an exceedingly pretty girl—between seventeen and eighteen years of age—of a somewhat small but very graceful figure, with a complexion whose sunny freshness, not yet blanched by the close air of the city, betrayed a country life; large tender hazel eyes, and a quantity of golden chestnut curls tastefully fastened up by a broad black snood, which, together with her mourning dress and the quiet saddened expression of a face which seemed made to glow with smiles, proclaimed some recent loss.

Alice Scott was indeed an orphan. Her father, a minister of the moderate Presbyterian sect, had died suddenly some months previously, leaving his widow totally unprovided for. The mother and daughter had come to Edinburgh in the hope of turning to account the skill which both possessed in embroidery of every description, then so much in vogue among the higher classes of both sexes, and also in order to be near an only son and brother who was in the employment of a bookseller and printer. But the widow's health, never strong, had completely broken down after the shock of her husband's death, and almost the whole burden of their support fell upon Alice. Her brother Norman, although older than herself, was unable to assist them, and in truth was but little comfort to the lonely women. They saw him but rarely, and then with pain, for a cold and gloomy fanaticism was settling down upon him, by no means uncommon even at his early age during that period of exaggerated passions, but which was neither the result of education nor an inheritance from his father, a very superior man, and one whose benevolent toleration and truly Christian charity had been the distinguishing feature of his life.

"Alice, hinnie! ye maun certainly gang,—I fear ye maun,—and yet I am laith to let ye," said the widow. "If Norman would but come, may be he would take ye, but he'll no be here the night, nor may be the morn, and I'm sure I kenna where to find him."

"Never fear, mother," said Alice cheerfully, "I have been there before, and ye mind how often I have gone on worse errands than yon, at home; I'll be back early, if ye can want me so long."

"I'd want ye longer than ye'll be awa', suner than that the puir creature suld die without a soul to speak comfort till her. Eh, Elsie! think o' her sae sick, without a Christian by to read her a verse, or a screed o' sound doctrine frae the Word, that may be would yet turn her to the right path; and the minister no there. And to think o' that hard-hearted auld cummer that cam speiring for us, saying that for a' the gowd that was in the Temple at Jerusalem she wadna bide wi' puir Lucky Wilson alane: that she was feared o' her because she spake scraps o' unknown tongues in her light-headed talk, forbye that she had ance been a Papist. Heard ye ever the like o' that, Alice?"

"No, indeed, mother," replied Alice, half laughing:

"but I shouldna laugh," she added, checking herself, "for it is nae jesting matter. I must go to her. I would be but an ill daughter of my dear father if I could be kept away by such daft sayings as that."

"Go, then, my doo," said her mother; "take a' ye can spare for her, and God's blessin be wi' ye. I hae little fear for ye, Alice—ye were aye a discreet and courageous lassie, though I say it to yer face; but come back, love, as airly as ye can. Dinna forsake the puir body while ye can be ony use to her till the minister comes, only mind that ye're in Edinburgh, and no in wer ain bonnie clachan, where a' men kenned and lo'ed ye. And if while ye're crossing the links ye feel a wee feared for spunkies or worricows, or thae uncanny things,"—here she prudently sunk her voice a little—"keep some gude words in yer mind, and haud up yer heart; for I canna believe that evil would ha' power to touch ye while ye are on yer Master's business, my dearie! Fain would I gang mysel; but it's just a dispensation, and we maun submit."

"Go yourself, mother!" said Alice, as she put by her work and began to prepare for her expedition; "and do you think your little Elsie would allow you? Nay, indeed! I shall be back by eight o'clock, and, if I am a wee bit behind time, hold up your heart too. I know the road, and the frost must have made it good. I wish Norman had been with me, for a' that," she murmured to herself, as she fetched her large plaid muffler and proceeded to envelope herself in it, smiling as she did so to reassure her invalid mother, although her own intrepidity was somewhat diminished by the remembrance of a large piece of open downs or moor she would have to cross at night on her way home.

"But I'm on a gude errand," thought she, "and surely no ill will come to me." So, collecting what little matters she proposed to carry to her poor old pensioner, she kissed her mother, promised an early return, and left her.

"Alice," said the widow, calling after her, "take the muckle key wi' ye, hinnie. Dinna ye mind how ill to please auld Janet is when she needs to open the yett after nightfall?"

Alice laughed merrily at the fear her mother entertained of displeasing their old portress, but complied with her desire, and a minute or two more saw her fairly on her road.

The poor woman whom she was going to visit lived in a cottage, or rather a mere hovel, at some distance from the town in a south-western direction, in an unfrequented place, which, according to the superstitious fancies of the times, had been peopled with a great variety of spiritual inhabitants in default of human. It might be that the circumstance of her living in this "uncanny" spot had something to do with the dislike in which Lucky Wilson was held—not absolutely amounting to an accusation of witchcraft, but quite sufficient to render the harmless, unhappy old female a subject of malicious whispering, and to account for the repugnance to being left in charge of her expressed by the person who had carried her supplicating request for help and comfort to the kind widow Scott and her daughter.

It may perhaps be as well to inform the reader that the "unknown tongues" consisted simply of scraps of French acquired in her early days in the service of a noble Scottish family, exiled for many years during the great Civil Wars; and these once familiar words, uttered unconsciously in the semi-delirium of weakness and old age, were the cabalistic sounds which had scared her ignorant neighbours. Alice fortunately was not so easily alarmed. She was a girl of much natural sense and nerve—healthy in mind as in body, and trained by her father to assist him in all the varied, and often painful, duties of his ministration. I do not mean to say that she was superior to such superstitions as were then positive articles of belief; but they had not upon her mind the enervating effect they might have produced upon a more feebly constituted character. Her sound judgment preserved her from slavish fear, and her perception of the ludicrous enabled her to laugh at much that sounded terrific in the ears of credulous gossips, who will often credit a thing because it is incredible, while they pervert, mis-state, or disbelieve facts which have passed before their own eyes. Such individuals abound everywhere, but most of all did they abound in Edinburgh, and Scotland generally, in the year of grace 1688.

It was now nearly five o'clock in the afternoon, and the busy crowd that all day long had thronged the streets was beginning to thin; but enough still remained to present a very brilliant appearance. Edinburgh, possessing at that time a local government, and being the head-quarters of a considerable standing force, the recognised capital of the North, vied on a small scale with the metropolis itself in splendour and gaiety. The uneasy state of the greater part of the Lowlands had induced numbers of wealthy and noble families to resort thither instead of remaining upon their estates; large bodies of troops were quartered in and near it, adding all the attractions of military show to the more sober richness of civilian attire and equipage; while the confined space into which the population was crowded contributed, by bringing it into a comparatively small compass, to enhance the gaiety of the scene. All up the long suburb of the Canongate, along the High-street—both then the residence of the highest classes—almost to the Castle Hill, the view was one shifting panorama of bright colours and lively animation, lighted up by the cold but glittering rays of the declining sun—a cheerful, bustling, pleasant sight. But Alice, a true country girl, had very little sympathy with all the shopping, gossiping, promenading, and flirting in which the beaux and belles of the capital found such enjoyment; the crowd annoyed and hindered her so much that she wished herself out on the open downs, and felt quite delighted at the thought that there would be no one in the streets as she returned. She could scarcely conquer her vexation when she was stopped and accosted by the stately old dowager of Libberton, who somewhat patronised the young needlewoman, and now inquired with majestic condescension after her mother's health, and the success of a remedy for a cough and pain in the side, which she (the Lady Libberton) believed infallible. Alice listened with all due submission to the excellent dame's well-meant advice and recommendations; but when released she sped away like an arrow from a tight-strung bow, leaving the dowager to look after her and lament the giddiness of "young folk o' this generation—even the vera best and discreetest o' them, whilk sure ye might count the bairn Scott to be."

Fate had, however, decreed that even then Alice was not to proceed on her journey unmolested. As ill luck would have it, she came full upon the sedan-chair of my Lady Jean Gordon, a very celebrated belle of that time, who was just issuing from the mansion of the Duke of Queensberry. She beckoned Alice to come and speak to her about some work the latter had in hand for her, and, with an inconsiderateness by no means confined to ladies of rank in those days, but quite as prevalent in our own, kept the girl standing talking, in spite of her visible impatience to proceed. Alice strove to answer with her usual good temper, although extremely worried by her ladyship's contradictory orders and useless repetitions—still more so by the evident and insolent admiration of a gentleman in the uniform of the Scots Life Guards who escorted her. He was not plain in person, but the expression of his features was coarse and disagreeable; and not all the tasteful elegance of his dress could alleviate an air of vulgar rakishness, rare amongst the officers of his regiment, who, whatever their conduct and character might too often be, were nearly all remarkable for courtliness of demeanour and distinction of appearance.

It was not by any means the first time that the pretty embroideress had been subjected to such, and still more offensive, attentions on the part of this same individual; she had only too much reason to dislike him, and perhaps might have felt some satisfaction could she have heard the sharp reprimand which the offender drew down upon himself from the beautiful coquette whose devoted slave he had declared himself *pro tem.*

At last she was free, and plunging into the labyrinth of lanes and closes which lay between the High Street and the Portsburgh entrance, reached the open country, which then extended nearly up to the city gates. She stopped for an instant to look at the splendid spectacle which the town and castle presented from thence, the casements glowing like crimson flames, the edges of the buildings sharply tinged and defined, every angle and fracture of the Castle Rock rosy with the red beams. Not a cloud speckled the intensely blue sky, a purple mist lay over the distant country, but the dazzling purity and clearness of the atmosphere did not prognosticate any relenting from the bitter frost, which made the ground like marble, and the keen air almost unfit to breathe. Trembling with cold, Alice drew her plaid more closely round her, and walked on faster than ever.

CHAPTER II.

THE PROPHECY.

> Say from whence
> You owe this strange intelligence, or why
> Upon this blasted heath you stop our way
> With strange, prophetic greeting?
>
> MACBETH.

SHE reached at last the place of her destination—a poor hut containing only one room, in which, on a bed as poor, lay her patient, a woman of advanced years and miserable appearance. She seemed asleep, or in a species of torpor, and Alice, as she lifted the latch, and stealing in, saw the failing fire, the thin covering, and the wretched appearance of the whole place, could not help marvelling at the degrading effects which superstition and ignorance will have in hardening even naturally kind hearts.

"How glad I am that I came!" she said to herself, as she sat cheerfully to work to make up the fire, by help of a few peats and some dried thorn-branches, and began to warm some milk posset, which she had brought with her. She moved very lightly, not to disturb the sleeper, and, when all was ready, pulled out her little Bible and sat down by the bedside on a wooden stool, waiting for her to wake. The woman who had gone to Edinburgh to summon Alice had assured them that the minister would come as soon as he returned home, probably about eight o'clock, so she felt pretty easy on that score, and, after doing all in her power, read on peacefully as long as daylight lasted.

But the clear gloaming faded soon, and shadows crept darkly over the rough walls and bare rafters of the hut. The poor woman moaned and tossed in her fevered sleep, but without waking; and Alice, finding the time pass and no human foot approach, grew undecided, and rather uncomfortable. With a restless impatience of sitting unoccupied, natural to one whose life was so busy, she searched about until she found a small iron lamp, which she trimmed and lighted, and began to read afresh, as the most efficacious means of quieting herself.

She was, nevertheless, still trying to listen for the sound of steps, or some sign of the minister's arrival, when through the frosty night-air came the clang of St. Giles's bells ringing out eight o'clock.

"And mother will be waiting on me; how unfortunate! what can I do?" she thought, as she went back to her seat, with something of natural tremor at her loneliness and responsibility. "Oh, that my mother were here!"

"Is that you, Alice Scott?" said a feeble broken voice.

"Yes, it is I," said Alice gently, bending over the sick woman. "My mother is ill herself, and so I came."

"Blessins on ye, my sweet bairn, for a gude Christian, as ye are! How dark it is, Alice! Can this be death? I didna dream he would come sae sune."

"Oh no, no! I hope you are better now, you have slept so soundly," replied Alice, quite glad that she had awoke; anything was better than that solitary moveless watching.

She bestirred herself, and brought her the food she had prepared; but the invalid could not swallow it, and Alice perceived, with much alarm, that she was far worse than she had at first thought her. The wasted features were pinched and ghastly; the eyes open and wild; the hands agitated by a convulsive motion; the voice was unnaturally shrill, and she talked almost incoherently.

"Didna I say it was Death, Alice? and sae it is. But I dinna fear him! I dinna fear him! he 's a welcome guest to an aching heart and weary head, and they hae been my company for mony a year. Ay, I kenned it whenever I woke, and a' seemed mirk around me. I kenned then that it couldna lang delay. Is the minister ne'er comin'?"

"He will come, certainly, he has promised," answered Alice, exerting all her self-possession to speak very quietly and composedly; "but let me say a prayer and read to you now, shall I?"

"Ay, read—read the aughty-aughth Psalm; mony a time hae I read it, and weel may ye do sae too, puir bairn, for He above kens it fits ye but too close. Oh, Alice, dearie! but my heart's sair for ye!"

She stopped, gasping for breath, and with an expression of such unspeakable distress on her withered countenance, that Alice shuddered at her words and look.

"Pray for me, and for yersel, forbye that ye may hae strength gien ye frae abuve to thole the weird ye'll need to dree. Oh why, why was I bound to see ye the night? why am I to greet for anither's woes when I suld greet for my ain sins and sorrows? Why couldna my grey hairs gang down to the grave in peace?"

"What can you mean? you are raving, my poor woman! Think rather of yourself than of me, and if you have any heavy grief tell it to Him who calls the weary and heavy laden to His bosom," said Alice, as she tenderly raised her patient on the hard bed, arranged the flock pillow, and then knelt down. She repeated, in her soft trembling voice, but with fervent sincerity, the prayers her father had often used by a sick bed; growing calmer from the very urgency of her situation, and pleading with earnest faith and charity for the poor departing spirit. When at last she fancied that the patient had grown somewhat more composed, she rose, and, opening her Bible, read every comforting and helpful passage that her memory could suggest, hoping thereby to still the excitement which preyed upon the dying woman, and inwardly supplicating meanwhile for succour and support. To abandon the poor creature was impossible, and, even if Alice had known where to seek assistance, the sufferer might expire during her absence. It was growing very late, and the young girl, terrified and bewildered, knew not what course to pursue. She was silently praying with clasped hands, and lips just moving, when she was startled by seeing the dying woman sit upright in her bed with a strength perfectly unnatural, and a burning lustre in her faded eyes that spoke of delirium or insanity.

"Alice Scott, hearken till me! I maun speak, or I canna die in peace! The fire burns in my heart, and I maun speak wi' my tongue! I luve ye, puir lassie, and my heart aches, aches for ye!" and she pressed her skeleton hands upon it; "for it's gien me to see what mortals rarely see, the ill that's to come on ane anither."

"For God's sake, dinna talk so wildly!" exclaimed Alice, turning deadly pale. "You cannot know aught of my fate; and, whatever it may be, He will give me patience to thole it. Oh, that the minister would but come!" she murmured to herself.

"And if he came, what mair could he do for me than ye hae dune?" said the sick woman, who had overheard the scarcely breathed desire. "I am deeing fast now, Alice; but, auld as I am, and near the grave, ye are well nigh as near—I read it in your face. Sair, sair sall ye greet, and weary sall ye be, till, like auld Helen Wilson, ye will be blythe to ca' corruption mither, and the worm yer sister. Sair shall ye weep the saut tears frae yer e'en, and the heart's drap o' yer bluid, for the loss of ane your heart loves, and for the sin of ane whose flesh and bane are yours, and, bitterest, dreariest of a'! for the sake o' ane wha will never love ye! and the better for ye, the better for the doo that she canna mate wi' the kestrel! Ye are young and gay and bonnie noo, but the kindest wish auld Helen can wish ye is, that, ere the spring-tide she will never see mair hath passed thrice ower yer brown locks, they may lie low beneath the green sod, as her grey hairs will to-morrow!"

The cold drops stood on Alice's brow. A sickening chill ran through her veins at the utterance of this wild language, vague as it was; and the sayings of the poor neighbours regarding Lucky Wilson's unlawful dealings recurred to her mind with a degree of probability that almost unmanned her. Nothing but the most unusual self-control kept her steady to her unwelcome task; she was trembling all over.

With every calm word and caressing gesture she could employ, she answered and soothed the excited sufferer, who had seized her hand, and was gazing with wild earnestness into her face.

"Hush! dinna speak thus! why should ye try to scare me? Don't ye mind me—little Alice Scott, that you always seemed to like so much? You cannot wish to make me believe such horrible tales; you are surely dreaming still!"

"Oh, that I were! but na, na! it's nae dream, Alice! my gudesire had the gift, and my father foretelled me on his ain deathbed, the life that was set for me—that was the gift—the life of the last mortal their een beheld. And ye are the last I'll ever see, Alice—for the mirk night is come, the warld is departing, the Valley o' the Shadow is very near at hand—oh God!" And, with a long shudder and a faint moan, she sank back upon her pillow, and moved not again.

The lamp burned low and dimly; its feeble light fell unsteadily on the ghastly figure of the dead, and the face, almost as pale, of poor Alice, who bent over the couch, trying to revive her by bathing her brow with ice-cold water—the only thing at hand. No sound could be distinguished without save the keen whistling of the blast and the distant sound of the city bells chiming nine. To the excited fancy of the solitary girl, the howling of the wind, the mournful tolling of the far-off peal, were the very "dirge of the departing soul." Like one in a fearful dream, chained to some spot from which every natural longing, every impulse of human fear and weakness, conspire to force him away—cold, pale, and half-fainting, Alice stood firm to her post. It was not the first time she had seen Death; at such a period, few ever attained her age without having witnessed its terrors; but now, alone, unbefriended, far from aid and sympathy, her nerves already unstrung by the terrible and apparently involuntary prophecy of the unhappy old woman—Alice was very young, and she almost gave way. Unable to endure any longer the awe and solitude of the place, she sank on her knees, and, hiding her face in the tattered bed-clothes, cried, half aloud, "Will no one ever come to help me? Oh, what *will* I do?"

The latch grated and turned, and a figure presented itself at the door. The help she desired was come—yet Alice almost shrieked as the new arrival—the episcopal curate of a neighbouring parish—entered hastily, and came up to the bed-side.

"Poor child! is it possible that you are here all alone? Has no one been with you?" he exclaimed, as his eye fell on Alice.

"No," she said faintly, and burst into tears.

"Have you been long here? Has no one come near the poor creature but yourself?" he asked. "She is dead." And, as he took up the icy hand, it dropped heavily again in the abandonment of death. "I learned only to-day that she was sick and wished to see me. I am this moment returned from a long day's journey, and came hither straightway."

"Every one was afraid of her," faltered Alice; "and I could not bear to think of her being left, perhaps to die alone—or to starve for want of food and care; so I came, and have been here since five o'clock, or thereby."

The minister, who had been carefully examining whether any remains of life yet lingered in the emaciated frame, now said, with a sigh,

"She must have been dead some short time; I wish I had come sooner, for her sake and for yours, but it was impossible."

"I will go home, then, if I can do nothing more," said Alice.

"Are you not the widow Scott's daughter?" asked the curate, who remembered having met Alice and her mother once before at the cottage on their errand of charity.

"Ay, sir, and my own dear mother is sick; that is why I am alone. It is very, very late, and she will want me sadly; I *must* go."

"It is, indeed, very late, and a fearfully cold night; are you not afraid to venture so far alone?"

"Afraid or no, it must not hinder me, sir," replied

Alice, as the remembrance of her mother's intense anxiety on her account presented itself vividly to her mind. "Besides, how could I stay here?"

"Farewell, my poor girl, and God speed you! You have done a truly Christian work," said the kind minister, laying his hand, as if in blessing, on Alice's fair head. "It is, indeed, a bleak and mirk night; but darkness is the same as day to Him who protects those that love His will, and walk in His footsteps. Fare ye well."

He accompanied her to the door, and remained there, as she stood for an instant shivering on the threshold, like a bird on the edge of its nest, then darted off as lightly upon the white frozen road, which wound away towards the dark irregular mass of the city, towering up in the distance against the deep blue starry sky—then murmuring to himself, "A far walk and a weary for the young thing,—and so late too!"—went back to sit until morning by the side of the body.

CHAPTER III.

A RENCONTRE.

Proteus.—Nay, if the gentle spirit of moving words
Can no way change you to a milder form,
I'll woo you like a soldier, at arm's end.
TWO GENTLEMEN OF VERONA.

WEARY and frightened as she was, the thought of her invalid mother gave Alice wings. She flew along, finding the road almost by instinct, until compelled by the excessive cold to slacken her pace and gasp for breath—then, after a moment's rest, she would dart forward again, until, just as the ten o'clock drum began to beat, she reached the city gates. The guard was being relieved for the night, and there was a slight confusion beneath the archway, under cover of which, and favoured by her dark garb, she contrived to slip through, and to turn unnoticed into the entrance of the first close that presented itself. Rejoicing at finding herself once more fairly within the town, and especially at having passed the port unperceived, she stopped to consider the shortest and most unfrequented way home, deeming that necessarily the safest; an error by no means unusual with those unaccustomed to a city life.

But, unfortunately, as is also by no means unusual, her extreme desire for speed thwarted her intentions. Whether from a want of a familiar knowledge of that portion of the city, or from the perturbation of mind caused by the sad scene which she had just witnessed, joined to the absence of any light in the now deserted streets, which looked more like gaps in a wall of black rock than human habitations, certain it is that she missed her road, and, stopping for an instant to right herself, perceived with dismay that she was not where she expected to be.

She could not even guess in what direction the end of her journey lay, for the great height of the houses completely prevented her from catching sight of any familiar edifice or spire which could serve as a landmark; the faint glimmer of here and there an oil-lamp was insufficient to enable her to recognise her position, so that, after a short indulgence of angry impatience at her own carelessness, she determined upon continuing straight forward, trusting thus to strike some main thoroughfare from which she might easily reach the Canongate.

But she had not gone a couple of hundred yards before she found herself in what appeared to be a long closed court, with no outlet at the further end. She turned back, wishing that she could hear the Cathedral bell toll or clock strike, that the sound of the chime might give her some conception of whither she had best turn her steps, when another and less welcome sound met her ear—that of human voices. Her first impression had been one of satisfaction, and the exclamation, "Now I shall find my way!" flashed through her mind, but this instantly changed to a feeling of extreme alarm, for the voices were those of three individuals, and the sounds those of a Bacchanalian chorus, unsteady in tune and rhythm. It came nearer and nearer, and the singers thereof, evidently fresh from some roystering evening entertainment, turned into the close.

Alice's first natural impulse was to fly, but flight seemed out of the question; arm-in-arm they came on, occupying the entire width of the passage; no thoroughfare was perceptible at the bottom, and any attempt to meet and pass them must have been a signal for instant discovery. Her sole resource, and that she took, was to creep into the hollow archway of a door, and, shrinking into the deepest shadow, wait until they had passed.

"Drummond's always so horribly sulky," said one of the revellers; "he won't submit to be held up, and he *can't* stand. Lucky Barnard ought to be warned not to waste her capital claret upon him, it never makes *him* a cheerful companion, but a most infernal cross one! Now I'm the most amiable fellow in the world in my cups——"

"Hold your confounded folly!" retorted Drummond, who was the one nearest to Alice. "I'm no more drunk than——"

"Than our colonel, eh? ah! ah! ah!" laughed out the middle singer. "The taverns of Auld Reekie might put on mourning if we were *his* dutiful and exemplary disciples."

"Curse him! I say," muttered Drummond between his teeth, "with his pale face and girl's habits. I hate a soldier who won't take his tankard like a gentleman; poor, sneaking, white-livered, carpet-knight——"

"Halloa! that's for swearing and cursing at the colonel!" said the first speaker, as Drummond, unable to keep his footing, stumbled over the execrable pavement, and fell very heavily. Both the hair-brained youths burst into inextinguishable fits of laughter at their fallen comrade, while he, with an angry volley of oaths, which only served to increase their hilarity, tried to struggle up again.

"Hay! Dalmeny! help me, can't you? instead of staring and braying there like a couple of asses!" he exclaimed furiously, and staggering stupidly forwards felt about for the hat which he had dropped in his tumble. Groping in the darkness, and feeling himself unsteady, he clutched forwards at what he imagined to be the wall. He missed his grasp, which fell direct upon the trembling girl crouching in the corner of the archway.

"Treasure trove! treasure trove!" he cried, while Alice with a scream of terror sprang away; but his hold was too firm, and he dragged her back with a shout of drunken laughter.

"Ha! ha! pretty nightingale!" said Hay; "whom wert thou waiting for? What gallant cavalier will be disappointed to-night? Tell us, sweet bird of eve."

"He sha'nt get all the luck, by Jove! I'll have some kisses too! Don't weep, little one, I'm the youngest and best looking of the lot——"

"Hands off, Dalmeny! she's my prize," said Drummond, dealing him a thrust in the breast as he attempted to make good his words. Then, pulling Alice, in spite of her struggles and cries, under the only lamp in the gloomy alley, he tore off the plaid from her head, and looked at her all over with an insolent curiosity that drove her nearly wild.

"Help! help!" she shrieked again; but her voice was stifled by a large muscular hand over her mouth.

"Who is she?" asked Hay.

"Never mind, I know her well enough, and never was better luck! Aha! my Lady Jean, if you could be here to see! Come, come, pretty mistress, don't show fight that way, you'll only hurt yourself and do no good; I'm not a cannibal, and besides I've supped already."

"Don't be a fool, Drummond, and let her go," said Dalmeny. "I'm in a hurry to be at quarters, for there's the very devil's own wind cutting down here."

"Let her go? faith, yes!" replied Drummond with a brutal sneer; "may I have my ears cut off and nailed up at the Tron for those of an ass if I do! All's fair in love and war. To quarters, if you will; but hang me if I abandon so charming a damsel to the inclemency of the weather. We'll have up Mary Gourlay and black Isabel Campbell, and finish the night with such a rouse as we've not had since Sedgemoor!"

"Agreed! agreed!" shouted the reckless young men; "only don't hurt her so, Drummond; you are too rough with such a dainty blossom. Tell us your name, sweet one, it must certainly be as pretty as your face."

"I will not! I will not! let me go!" moaned Alice; "I am an honest girl; kill me if you like, rather than treat me so. Oh mother, mother!"

She was crouching together, striving to hide her face with her hands, but Drummond pulled them away, saying with a sort of brutal gallantry,

"Kill you? no, no, indeed, we're not so cruel; you're too charming to be killed, my adored one! You shall come along with me, and shall have lights and fire, and such wine as you have rarely tasted, to put some life into your pretty limbs, and some fire into your bright eyes—better than waiting here in the dark and cold for a faithless lover who has forgotten his tryst! One gallant is as good as another, any day, or night, if you like, ha! ha!"

In an ecstacy of shame, disgust, and indignation, Alice struggled and screamed so violently that her tormentor's coarse passions were roused.

"This won't do, fair one!" said he, angrily. "I'm not going to be baulked that way!" and pulling off his large cravat, he forcibly bound it over her mouth. He then took her up in his arms, and followed his companions, who, in a state of wild jollity, had gone on before, renewing their chorus, and turned down a passage leading from the foot of the steep lane, which had Alice perceived, or been acquainted with, it would have saved her from her present disastrous situation. But in a very few minutes Drummond began to discover that he had quite sufficient difficulty in preserving his equilibrium without the incumbrance of an additional burden, and setting Alice down, grasped both her little wrists in his powerful hand, bidding her come along quietly.

Stupified by terror, exhausted by her own struggles for freedom, half torpid too with the intensity of the cold, for her plaid had been torn from her shoulders, and left behind by her captors, the young girl was hurried on, more dead than alive,—capable only of one sensation, the loathing inspired by the insulting admiration and coarse speeches of Drummond. He was one of those men who rarely lose the consciousness of their actions even in the lowest depths of intoxication, but in whom excess only serves to bring out in full force all the evil of their natures, and assumes the form of a species of insanity. The repulsion and abhorrence of Alice had long ago served to aggravate the unmanly obstinacy with which he was now bent upon tormenting her, mingling ever and anon with his discourse such phrases and epithets of gallantry and attempted tenderness as he fancied calculated to soothe and reconcile her, but which only tended to increase her anguish.

"Five minutes more, and we shall be under shelter—it's a devilish cold night, and I'm sorry I had no carriage at hand for your service, pretty bird!"

CHAPTER IV.

A SILVER LINING TO THE CLOUD.

"Madam, this service have I done for you;
To hazard life, and rescue you from him
That would have forced your honour and your love."

TWO GENTLEMEN OF VERONA.

WITH a dim sense of danger and misery, but little real comprehension of her position left in the chaos of ideas that whirled through her brain, Alice felt herself dragged along—not insensible, however, sustained as she was by the might of one remaining thought, the almost hopeless hope of escape. As the party, silent now, passed through the several streets and wynds, they met two or three belated citizens, who lifted their lanterns and glanced suspiciously at them, but being very prudent men, and dreading to adventure their persons in a contest with three military gentlemen, the respectable burghers "kept a calm sough," shook their heads over the depravity of mankind, and pursued their ways homeward, glad to escape notice themselves.

The last chance seemed gone, and despair was taking absolute possession of her mind, when suddenly, at a little distance in front of the party, a dark figure emerged into the narrow street from a side alley narrower still, and proceeded at a leisurely pace along the side of the wynd lighted by the moon, which had now risen, and poured a stream of rays directly down the lane. A desperate resolve sprang up in the girl's soul with this glimmer of hope—regardless of the pain it gave her, she wrenched her delicate wrists from the vice-like grip of Drummond, who, rendered careless by impunity, had somewhat loosened his hold—with a strength which nothing but despair could have bestowed, and snatching away the thick cravat which stifled her, shrieked aloud until the street rang,

"Help me! save me! for God's sake!"

The whole thing occurred so suddenly, that, before Drummond knew where she was, Alice had rushed forwards, repeating her screams, towards the stranger. As the first cry fell upon his ear, he turned and looked behind him, then sprang with the agility of a bloodhound upon Drummond, and dashed him back, just as he had again clutched Alice by her dress.

"Unhand the girl, ruffian!" he exclaimed, as Alice, still shrieking, clung to him, and glided to the ground at his feet; "Dare to touch her again!" but Hay and Dalmeny, seizing him both together by the collar of his richly-furred cloak, pulled him off roughly.

"Fair play, fair play!" cried they; "an open field, and no favour shown—here's the happy lover, come to rescue his mistress! Draw, gallants both! and let us see a brave camisado; she's worth it!"

"Fools! the first that touches me is a dead man!" was the stranger's answer, delivered in an accent which made the young rioters start back as from the thrust of a rapier.

"The great devil has put his cloven hoof into this gear!" muttered Hay; "what's going to become of us now? here's a precious clanjamfrey!"

"What signifies all this?" asked the new comer, imperiously; "this disgraceful brawling in the very streets of Edinburgh? what outrage have you been committing?"

There was a dead silence. Drummond, grasping Alice by the wrist as she lay prostrate on the ground, stood a step or two apart. Hay and the young Dalmeny, very much sobered by the shock of this undesirable rencontre, murmured some unintelligible excuses in reply.

"Am I to be answered?" demanded the stranger again.

"I'll answer you!" exclaimed Drummond. "The girl's mine, and I intend to keep her—in the teeth of you and all the other meddling vagabonds in Edinburgh!"

"Good God! Drummond is mad!" exclaimed Hay in a low voice, as the stranger, with an ironical laugh, bent down over the senseless figure of the unhappy young girl.

"Will you let her go, I say!" cried Drummond, stamping, and blinded by rage as well as intoxication; "and hold your blasted tongue, Hay; what care I for man or devil?—I'm a gentleman, and what right has any ruffler of them all to cross my path? I'll have his life-blood, were he Claverhouse himself!"

"Indeed!" said the stranger, very composedly, rising from his stooping attitude. As he did so, a furious thrust from Drummond's rapier passed harmlessly over his right shoulder.

"I will not be held!" panted Drummond, in a paroxysm of exasperation, while his two friends vainly endeavoured to restrain him. "Were he King James himself, he should pay for this insolence with his life!"

"A most pleasing and creditable affair—quite an honour to His Majesty's Life Guard!" said the gentleman, who was in fact no less a personage than the colonel of that regiment, the celebrated Grahame of Claverhouse himself—"a most worthy amusement for gentlemen—brawling in the open streets at dead of night, and insulting helpless women! *Gentlemen*, forsooth!"

He had drawn his rapier, and was holding it before him, and without assuming any posture of regular attack or defence, parried with admirable skill and coolness the frantic attempts which Drummond made to reach him; for, considerably more intoxicated than his companions, the latter had not recognised, or chose to defy, his commanding officer.

"Drummond, you are demented! you will ruin yourself!" cried Hay and Dalmeny; but advice was useless, fury and disappointment had swept away all remains of caution.

"Draw, draw! defend thyself, or I will strike thee in the face, braggart and meddler!"

"By St. Andrew! this passes all patience!" exclaimed Claverhouse, with contemptuous indignation. "Gentlemen, if you have not abandoned all common sense, along with all self-respect, and really wish to save your friend from a court-martial, take charge of him, and get him to quarters as soon as may be. He's amazingly drunk!"

The stinging sarcasm of the tone goaded Hay and Dalmeny beyond endurance. They flung themselves together upon their comrade—disarmed, and succeeded in forcing him off, swearing and foaming.

"Return to quarters forthwith," said Colonel Grahame, in the same voice of calm superiority, as he restored his rapier to its sheath: "You, Hay and Dalmeny, will wait upon me the first thing to-morrow morning; and, if this insubordination and disorder be not explained somewhat more to my satisfaction, you will be at no loss to imagine the consequences, I suppose."

He touched his hat haughtily as he spoke, and turned away.

"But Drummond—what of Drummond?" asked Hay, very much crest-fallen, and divided between the desire to assert his independence and the overpowering influence which bore him down.

"That is my concern, not yours, sir," was the cool reply.

Chafing, yet unable to vent his temper in any visible form, the young officer was about to follow his friends, when Colonel Grahame's voice recalled him.

"One moment, sir,—do you know this girl?"

"Not I; and I beg you to believe, Colonel Grahame, that I have not the slightest intention of becoming in any way responsible for Mr. Drummond's drunken frolics."

"Frolics!" retorted Claverhouse, his lip curling; "you, an officer and Scottish gentleman, call such cowardly and gratuitous brutality as this a *frolic?* Have the kindness to reply to my question without any further attempt at qualifying your friend's behaviour by another name than that which it deserves. Do you know who this girl is, or where she lives?"

"I believe her to be an honest girl enough," replied Hay, sullenly; "but know neither her name nor place of abode."

"That is sufficient."

And a slight motion of the hand dismissed him to rejoin, in no very pleasant mood, Dalmeny and the still unmanageable Drummond, who had by this time reached the bottom of the street.

Left alone with the poor girl, whom his opportune arrival had rescued from a violence which in our more orderly days seems hardly credible, Claverhouse stooped to raise her from the ground. She had fainted at the moment when the hope of safety had all at once destroyed the unnatural tension of every nerve which had until then sustained her faculties, and now lay in his arms without giving one sign of life. Her slight figure bent helplessly as he lifted her, the head fell backwards, then rested on his shoulder; the face, almost hidden by the tangled ruffled curls, was perfectly white, and the deathly coldness of her stiff hands, together with the total absence of any pulsation, startled him with the idea that she might be really dead. He seated her on the low stone step of a door, and looked about for some gleam of light in a neighbouring house that might offer a chance of assistance and shelter; but at that hour all was dark and silent as the grave. He next tried every means he could think of to bring her to her senses; but cold, terror, and fatigue had done their work too well, and Alice continued hopelessly immovable.

Considerably embarrassed, Colonel Grahame stood for some instants hesitating, but he was not a man much given to indecision. His resolution was soon taken, and, murmuring to himself, "There at least I can *command* discretion—or buy it; one thing is certain, no time must be lost," he unfastened his ample cloak, lined and faced with fur, wrapped it round Alice, and lifting her as easily as if she had been an infant, set off in the direction from which he had so suddenly appeared upon the scene of action.

CHAPTER V.

AN UNKNOWN FRIEND.

Portia. Yes, yes, it was Bassanio, as I think ; so was he called.

Nerissa. True, madam ; of all men that ever my foolish eyes looked upon, he was the best deserving a fair lady.

MERCHANT OF VENICE.

THERE existed in Edinburgh, at the period of which we write, a number of what were then called taverns, which served in some measure the compound purposes of the hotels, clubs, and coffee-houses of our more favoured epoch, and were the general resort of even the highest classes. Blair's coffee-house was—if we may be allowed the term—the highest expression of this almost forgotten species of establishment ; but there were also others which, if less renowned, were quite as flourishing and popular. The King's Head, near Bristo Port, was one of these—Lucky Jamieson's another, which, in virtue of a central position and first-rate entertainment, had become a place of rendezvous for all the cavalier gentlemen in the capital. It so happened that on the night in question a small but important political meeting had been held there, by some of the most influential men of rank in Edinburgh; the *réunion* had broken up late, and it was on his way home that Claverhouse had fallen in with the adventure which brought him back to the house within half an hour of his quitting it.

It was just as closed and obscure now as its neighbours, and at first gave no response to the tremendous appeal of the heavy risp; but, upon the summons being repeated still more impatiently, a slow, unwilling step was heard, and a shrill voice exclaiming—

"What's a' this clanjamfrey aboot? Gang awa'! gang awa! do ye think I'm gaun to open the yett at siccan ungodly hours? Aff wi' ye, I say!"

"Open the door instantly!" was the answer.

There was an exclamation of surprise, a muttering—a falling of chains—a withdrawal of ponderous bolts—the door moved back, displaying within an untidy looking elderly woman, with her soiled mutch all awry on her disordered grey locks, and without—to her blinking, sleepy, eyes, the elegant and richly attired figure of her visitor, bearing in his arms the half-concealed form of Alice Scott.

"Eh, sirs! Gude be wi' us a'!" was the first ejaculation of the bewildered hostess, but her speech was unceremoniously cut short by Colonel Grahame.

"Shut the door, and keep silence. Is every one away?" he said, as she obeyed, and then stood staring, unable to believe her own eyesight.

"Ou ay! and the hail hoose sleepin' sweetly! I doubt they'll a' be waken up wi' the clatter, though. Hech, but I'm just clean confounded to see ye . . . ."

"Hush!" said Claverhouse, sharply; "have you light and fire?"

"Ay, ay; there'll be some fire still, and light is easy come by. Eh, sirs! to think o' this!" she muttered again and again to herself as she followed her guest up two or three stone steps into a large room on the ground story to the left of the entry. It was dark, save for the flickering gleams which escaped from the half-extinguished embers of the wood fire on the hearth.

"Lights, quick! and make up a blaze," said Colonel Grahame, depositing his burden in a large high-backed chair. Burning with curiosity, yet not daring to interrogate, the woman hastily obeyed. She drew down from the ceiling a large brass lamp with three branches, and its light soon showed a rather handsome and spacious room, which had apparently been used by a number of persons that very evening. It was, in fact, the apartment where the afore-mentioned meeting had been held. The hostess next proceeded to blow up the gathering peat, and supply the flames with fresh dry fuel, wasting, however, as much time as possible in the process, in the hope of discovering something which might help to clear up this remarkable occurrence.

"Make haste, unless you want to see a fellow-creature die of cold," exclaimed Colonel Grahame, irritated at her wilful prolixity. "There, leave all that alone! give me some sort of spirit, and then make ready, as fast as you can, some hot wine, spiced—the very best—do you hear me?"

"I'll just cry upon Maggie, it's her that makes a' thae thing; she'll do't better than me, and quicker too."

"No such thing; do it yourself, and that as quietly as may be; I do'nt choose to have the whole house roused," replied Colonel Grahame, who had drawn Alice close to the hearth, and was looking rather anxiously at her motionless features.

"Eh, eh! Gude sain us!" muttered Lucky Jamieson, as she slowly descended the stairs leading to the lower regions; "Whatna gate is this for ye to gang to the de'il? Ain wad ha' thocht ye had enough to answer for without sic like follies! Gif ony ither body had telled me, I wadna ha' believed it. Him, Claver'se—him sae cauld that beauty couldna win him—him sae proud, that the red wine couldna tempt him—him that I ha' seen sittin' like a marble image in the midst o' a' the roystering and drinkin', wi' ne'er a smile on his bonny face, and his toom bicker aye before him! Eh, sirs! to see him come hither at the deid hours o' night wi' a winsome damsel in his arms, speirin' for spiced wines, and sic like. Hech! but we mortals is frail creatures whenever we're left to owrsells! and whenever the enemy gets a grip o' ye at the tae end (here she nodded her head mysteriously), there's nae kenning how sune ye may be grippit at the tither. But I wadna hae believed it o' *him*," she concluded, sensible of the necessity for executing her orders with some decent degree of promptitude, and wild to be again within sight and hearing of what was going on above.

Colonel Grahame's first care, when the hostess had departed, was to fetch some water from a little tap or fountain in the wall, an accommodation frequently met with at that period in public as well as private dining rooms, and, after mixing a few drops of spirit with it, to administer it, as well as he could, to Alice; then, sitting down beside her, he took her small icy fingers in his warm hands, and began to chafe them with almost a woman's tenderness, watching, as he did so, the effect of the remedy he had applied.

It was some time before Alice showed any symptoms of returning animation, but at last, whether from the warmth of the fire, the action of the cordial, or the fact that nature was beginning to exert herself afresh, probably from all three causes combined, a transient shade that was hardly colour yet, crept over her face —her features, without moving, became less rigid, and as her protector bent forward to look at her, he felt the first faint breath caress his cheek. He continued to hold and rub her hands until Alice moved slightly in her seat, and saying, half audibly, "Mother!" opened her eyes. She closed them again instantly, without perceiving where she was, and remained quite still, two or three large tears springing from under her eyelashes, adding to the expression of weariness and pain that was stamped upon her innocent young face. Nevertheless it was evident that her senses were returning, and Colonel Grahame, with an almost chivalrous fear of alarming her, retired to a seat on the opposite side of the fire-place, and sat ready to render any further assistance she might require.

Little by little, as the blazing fire dissipated the stupor of cold that numbed her, and the dormant brain resumed its lost powers, Alice slowly became conscious of a change in her situation. She did not move at first, lest the quiet and warmth should prove only a delusion; her mind was still struggling in a dreamy torpor, across which floated fragments of half-remembered troubles, unmingled with much sense of personal interest in them; her heavy eyelids felt as though they would never unclose again, and indeed she made no effort to awaken herself from the delicious rest which she could hardly believe to be real. Then came the fancy that she must be at home—that soft touch was surely her own mother's hand, as surely as it was *not* the cruel grasp which was her last clear memory of the night. What *could* have passed since? She shivered all over, and involuntarily drew around her the cloak in which she was wrapped. The luxurious touch of the fur startled her; she languidly opened her eyes,—glanced down at it, —then, raising them, they fell full upon the brilliant figure of Claverhouse, seated directly opposite to her.

In that single instant, like a flash of lightning, the remembrance of all that had occurred rushed in upon her. Forgetful of her hoped-for rescue, ignorant of everything that had taken place since her call for aid had been so promptly responded to, she only thought of this—that she was alone, in an unknown place, in the absolute power of an utter stranger; and starting up with momentary energy, she exclaimed,

"What is this place? Where have you brought me? Oh, sir! if you are a Christian, if you are a gentleman, let me go home to my poor mother!"

"Hush! hush!" said Colonel Grahame, gravely and kindly; "there is no cause for such alarm. You are quite safe now."

He had risen as she rose and laid his hand upon her arm. The light yet steady pressure seemed to calm the agitated girl, for she only repeated in a lower, more trembling voice, "Let me go! I only want to go home!"

"You shall indeed. Sit down, sit down; you are not fit to stand," he added very gently.

Alice was fain to comply; her limbs failed her, her head swam round, and she sat, or rather sank down into her chair. It required all Colonel Grahame's attentions to prevent her from fainting a second time.

"What has become of them? Where am I now? I don't understand this," she said, when she at last recovered sufficiently to look around her; "Where are they?"

"If you mean your assailants, not here, certainly," he answered, smiling. "As to yourself, believe me you have nothing more to fear. You are safe, and under my protection."

From the lips of many men such an assurance would have been rather alarming than agreeable, and it was quite natural that Alice should glance hurriedly up at him as he bent over her, arranging the cloak which had fallen from her shoulders, so as to form a comfortable resting place for her head. But not even her frightened, timid look could read anything alarming on that handsome face—aught but truth in the clear serenity of the calm eyes that met hers so frankly; and, although her breath came faster, and a quick flush eddied up over her pale cheeks, her heart was lighter from that moment.

"And you will let me go home, sir?" she asked, eagerly.

"Most undoubtedly; as soon as ever you are fit and able."

"But I am quite able now; indeed, indeed I am!" said Alice, trembling at the very thought of being detained.

"You must give me leave to differ from you there," said Colonel Grahame. "Will you tell me your name, and where you live? Had I been able to discover that, I would have taken you home at once, rather than bring you here."

"I thank you, sir; my name is Alice Scott, and I live with my mother, who is a widow, at the bottom of the Canongate."

"The end of the Canongate! you would not reach one-tenth of the distance, even if I could persuade myself to let you set out just now."

"But I should ha' been at home three hours syne; my mother will be half dead wi' fear, sir!" faltered Alice.

"And you would be *more* than half dead if you were to attempt anything so ill-advised," replied Claverhouse, with another of his grave smiles. "Nay, be ruled; wait until you are refreshed and rested, then, I give you my word of honour, you shall go as soon as you please. You will not, I am very sure, do me the injury of suspecting that I would detain you one instant longer than was for your own good?"

"No, sir, indeed!" she replied with great sincerity, for in truth it was difficult to disbelieve such words, so spoken. "I have too much reason to be grateful to you to wish to offend; but ——"

"But you are nervous and frightened yet. I can quite understand *that.* Sit still now, and make yourself quite easy."

So after replenishing the fire, Claverhouse, who saw that no assurances of respect or protection would avail to inspire confidence so much as leaving her completely to herself, with delicate tact made no further attempts at conversation, but began to walk up and down the room revolving in his mind the consequences of this curious adventure.

The most serious part of it was the collision into which he had been thrown with one of the men of his own regiment, and that, too, an individual whom he heartily disliked, and had long wished to get rid of. In fact, the only thing which had hitherto prevented his doing so was, that Drummond, in spite of the reckless profligacy of his general conduct, had not as yet rendered himself positively amenable to the military discipline of a system infinitely more lax than that which has obtained in later periods; although nothing less than the iron hand and indomitable will of Claverhouse could have sufficed to repress the insolent impatience of all control which distinguished the young rake. But the present affair was quite important enough to justify any steps he might choose to take against the offender, whose insubordination and violence against his commanding officer had been such as to warrant the application of the strictest penalties authorised by military law. The case called for some consideration; more especially as Drummond was a near relation of the

Earl of Perth, Colonel Grahame's own colleague in the Privy Council, a man known to be even more forward than the generality of Scottish heads of families in pushing and supporting those in any way connected with himself. As regarded Alice, however, no decision could be taken without some acquaintance with what had occurred before their meeting; and this he resolved to elicit from the young girl as soon as he found means of conversing freely with her.

He had been perfectly correct in supposing that Alice would be more tranquillised by his silence and apparent inattention, than by anything else he could have done to re-assure her. Her fears were decreasing every minute, and, as her confidence of reaching home in safety increased in like proportion, she perceived, for the first time, how much fatigue and exertion were beginning to tell even upon her active frame and healthy nerves—she was very well pleased to take her companion's advice, and sit with her chair drawn close to the hearth—resting. Her curiosity as to who this high-bred, graceful man could possibly be—so very unlike the *gentlemen* at whose hands she had suffered so much—was becoming excessive; yet she could not summon up courage to put a direct question, and he, on his part, gave her no clue. She followed him with her eyes as far as she could, while he paced backwards and forwards, in and out of the circle of rays from the lamp, not with the restless hurry of an unsettled mind, but with a step so light, elastic, and regular, that it fell almost pleasantly in the silence. Who *could* he be? "I never saw him before, I am very sure," thought Alice; "but still—"

But still, face, voice, and step came upon her with that soothing sense of agreeable familiarity which seems like a reminiscence of some former state of existence. She did *not* know him, and had really never seen him; but she experienced in all its force that attraction of confidence and good will which is the exact reverse of that equally instinctive repugnance with which some persons inspire us. All these speculations, however, did not enlighten her in the least—watching tired, and thinking puzzled her; gradually, as the minutes went by, all began again to grow indistinct before her eyes, her head drooped a little on one side, her lips parted, the long brown lashes fell, and she fairly dropped asleep from sheer weariness, to repeat over in a confused dream the various incidents of that eventful evening.

Her soft, regular breathing caught the quick ear of Colonel Grahame, who stopped in his walk, and came lightly up to the fire-place. Unobservant as he had seemed, not one variation of her countenance had passed unnoticed by him. He had been struck from the very first by a certain refinement in the girl's look and manner, indicating a rank superior to that denoted by her plain, almost coarse dress; the tone of her voice, the absence of any vulgarity of accent, confirmed this impression, and now, as he contemplated the slight figure nestled in its wrapper of velvet and fur, the child-like simplicity of the very youthful face hushed in its trusting sleep, sorrowful still, and with an expression of trouble lingering round the corners of the lips—as he saw all this, it brought vividly to his mind the image of his own young wife—one of the few tender ideas that gilded the stern and agitated life of this extraordinary man.

"Poor child!" he said, half aloud, and a sigh rose to his lips, but was instantly stifled—"Poor young thing! thank God that it was a loyal and true man into whose hands she was thrown, else the remedy might have been as bad as, or worse than, the disease. This is a new thing for me," he murmured, half smiling, "to play the squire of dames, especially under such circumstances; but, luckily, I can afford to defy evil speakers, liars, and slanderers."

His meditations were interrupted by the entrance of the hostess, bearing a small tray, on which stood a silver tankard and two of the tall, slender drinking-glasses then in fashion. Raising his finger to enforce silence, Claverhouse beckoned her into a distant corner of the room.

Their whispered conference had not the power to disturb Alice—she remained perfectly and happily oblivious, exciting afresh thereby the astonishment and suspicions of Mrs. Jamieson, who vainly tried to worm out from her guest some information respecting her—but a granite rock would have been about as communicative.

"Aweel, sir," she said, in answer to one of his short questions, "gif ye say onything woud serve yer turn, ye can just get the minister o' Dirleton's, that he left wi' my ain mither eight-and-thirty years syne, mair by token it was the day my lord o' Montrose lost his head."

The handsome face of her auditor grew dark at the words, but the talkative dame never even hesitated.

"He was a vera zealous man and a godly—he just cam' up to Edinbro' to behold the grand show—I mind it weel mysell, though I was but a bit lassie then—and couldna pay the lawin' by reason he had tint his purse in the hurley-burley—and as my mither, wha was a lane woman like mysell, couldna bide the loss, he just left his cloak in pledge—it was a bonnie bit o' braid claith then. And indeed sae is it noo,—though no just sae free frae moths as ye could wuss."

"You may go," said Colonel Grahame, who had not heard a single word of this dissertation, "and return when you hear me ring."

"Will ye be wanting naething mair, sir?"

"Nothing whatever."

"Nor the young leddy?" she asked in a coaxing tone, and making a step or two forwards in order to get a better view of Alice. "Nor the bonnie young leddy? are ye quite sure she'll be needin' naething?"

"I *think* I said you might leave the room," replied Colonel Grahame, turning coolly round upon her.

It was not in human nature—not even the nature of an inquisitive Scotch gossip—to stand this little speech, and the look which gave it emphasis. Lucky Jamieson retired, routed and in great disorder, and, as was very natural, feeling more than usually spiteful in consequence. The loud bang with which she closed the door startled Alice from her doze; she opened her eyes with a long sigh and saw Colonel Grahame standing beside her, holding one of the tall Leith glasses.

"I am glad to see your colour come back again," he said; but it suddenly deepened to such a shade that he almost regretted having spoken. "Here, take this; it will do *you* good in spite of the harm it has done so many others."

Her first shy impulse was to refuse.

"You are not afraid of it—of me?"

If Alice could have blushed more deeply she must have done so, as she again met his eyes, and felt a pang of absolute shame at having doubted him. She took the wine from his hand unhesitatingly.

"What is that on your arm?" he asked, all at once.

Her face answered him as she held out the other; both were marked just above the wrist with a broad purple bar like the trace of fetters. An exclamation of disgust and anger half broke from his lips; but he suppressed it, and turning to the table filled a few drops into the other glass for himself.

"Your health, Mistress Alice," he said, with as much courtly grace as if he had saluted a duchess; then, merely touching the wine with his lips, he drew a seat to the table and began to talk to her.

He found some difficulty at first in inducing Alice to relate the circumstances which had brought them so singularly together; but the peculiar tact and ease which nothing but familiarity with the highest society, joined to natural penetration, can bestow, overcame finally even her timid reserve. Very modestly, and with a propriety of language and manner which impressed her fastidious listener most favourably, she related the occurrences of the night, dwelling upon the unfortunate accident which had caused her to be so far from home at so unseemly an hour, with an anxious particularity that made her new friend smile. He listened with great attention, only putting now and then some question calculated to lead her into more minute detail than she had at first seemed inclined to give, or detect any inconsistency in the narrative should such exist. But Alice, strong in her truth and unconsciousness, came through this species of cross-examination triumphantly.

"Thank you," said he, "I have much interest in hearing your story, and if I could serve you in the way of punishing those who have offended you I should be delighted. Good faith, Mistress Alice! if such things were common amongst us, I should blush to write myself gentleman."

He rose as he spoke, and took from her the cup she had moved to replace upon the table.

"Was I not a true prophet?" he resumed with a glance at her brightening face; "I am no bad physician when I choose, I assure you. Now for a quarter of an hour's rest, and then, Eastward ho!"

Alice, anxious for her mother, would willingly have argued this latter stipulation; but, in spite of the gentleness of her companion's manner, it somewhat overawed her; she forbore, and, all distrust having long vanished from her thoughts, she made up her mind to the delay, settled herself comfortably in the large old chair, and resigned herself to wait contentedly, looking shyly from under her eyelashes at Colonel Grahame, who, apparently absorbed in some distant train of thought, had resumed his former seat and attitude.

Poor Alice! better had it been for her happiness that the rich fragrant wine which was infusing life and warmth into every fibre of her chilled limbs had been a cup of deadly nightshade! She had no idea—nor indeed could she have—that her protector was the man whose very name had so long been a sound of fear and aversion to her ears; could she have suspected it, her dismay would probably have been quite as great as at any previous period of her night's troubles. But in happy ignorance of her friend's quality, conscious only of a feeling of comfort and security which an hour before she would have deemed it impossible ever to experience again, she sat innocently drinking in long draughts of that admiration he was so eminently fitted to inspire, and of that confiding gratitude, beneath which a woman's heart so often expands to love, as a bud in sunshine.

And here we may pause, and offer some slight sketch of the personal appearance of this singular man, whose name, in good or evil repute, must live as long as Scottish story endures.

He was, as we have already said, richly attired in the costume of the period, which, even degenerated as it then was from the artistic picturesqueness of the "Vandyke style," still formed so humiliating a contrast to the funereal garments in which we moderns are compelled to array ourselves. His dress was composed entirely of white velvet, with a plain but rich lacing of gold; a broad scarlet silk sash crossed his breast, supporting his long rapier in its velvet sheath; his stockings were of white silk, and his boots of fine Spanish leather, accoutred with small gold spurs. The wide cuffs of his coat, fastened back by gold loops and buttons, showed his cambric sleeves and ruffles of priceless Alençon lace, which, with a magnificent cravat of the same material, formed the only ornaments of a dress, peculiar from its extreme simplicity, at a time when jewels and ribbons, embroidery and gauds of every description seemed quite as much the property of one sex as the other. The white feather, which drooped from his hat, was fastened by a perfectly plain band; he wore neither chain, medal, nor order, and, except one large signet, apparently a family relic, no ring broke the outline of the long, slight, muscular hand, which, by its aristocratic form and colour, would, in default of any other indication, have declared him a man of high rank and ancient descent.

But this attire, which, elegant and becoming as it was, would have appeared simply ridiculous if assumed by a vulgar, awkward, or insignificant wearer, was on him only the suitable setting to personal attractions so remarkable as to have been almost unrivalled amongst the men of his time.

He seemed in the very prime and flower of manhood—perhaps some five or six and thirty years of age—and was not tall, certainly not above the middle height; but the well-proportioned shoulders, deep square chest, and exact symmetry of limb, would have given to an experienced eye a promise of strength and activity far exceeding what might have seemed possible in so slight a frame, of which grace, not vigour, was at first sight the most prominent characteristic. In spite of the hideous fashion of enormous wigs, then so universally prevalent, Colonel Grahame wore his own dark hair, which, curled and perfumed with the care gentlemen of that age were wont to bestow on every detail of their personal equipment, fell round his face and over his shoulders, long and thick, with the gloss and sheen of satin. The head was small, the brow white and fair as a woman's, the eyebrows somewhat too much arched and raised, perhaps, for masculine beauty; but this defect, if defect it could be termed, only served to impart a still more striking expression of sad and thoughtful earnestness to the large eyes which lay beneath—full, limpid, and dark, through whose rich lashes the rays of the lamp flashed back with a fiery tremulous radiance quite indescribable. The nose, although straight, regular, and finely lined, could not have been termed classical: its open sensitive nostril and delicate palpitating muscles, which the slightest emotion could dilate, betrayed a temperament too keenly nervous, too acutely impressionable, to have found its fitting expression in the calmer elegance of the Greek type. The mouth and chin, on the contrary, were thoroughly antique, and constituted perhaps the rarest charm of this singular countenance. The mouth was small, the upper lip short, arched, and sharply dimpled, the corners deep set in the smooth oval cheek, the under one rather full, meeting its fellow in one wavy line, as clear and fine as if the lovely curves had been chiseled in marble; the chin round and firm, marked with that slight hollow near the centre, which gives such a stamp of resolution to the lower portion of the face—all so soft, yet so decided; so manly, yet so delicate; so haughty, yet capable of such womanly fascination and sweetness, that the most imaginative artist could not have copied shade, tint, or line without in some degree marring their noble and faultless perfection. His complexion, which, in spite of its tinge of brown, might have seemed by daylight almost too clear and colourless, now, in the mingled reflection of lamp and firelight, glowed with a pale transparent crimson, which heightened his beauty into something ideal. It was a face which once seen could never afterwards be looked upon with indifference—a face to haunt a woman's waking fancies and nightly dreams, and which in its marvellous blending of fire and softness, passion and melancholy, remains, to our eyes, in the imperfect image which was all Lely's pencil could bequeath, the very mirror of a nature as chequered and incomprehensible as ever perplexed the student of history.

The bright wood fire crackled and blazed, the old Flemish clock ticked with its monotonous beat against the wainscot—no other sound was heard in the room—while Alice, with half-closed eyes and busy thoughts, sat vainly trying to identify Colonel Grahame; he, on his part, with his arm resting on the table, his lips lightly compressed, and his gaze fixed in vague but earnest intenseness on some far-off image of the past or future, had neither moved nor spoken. She ran over in her mind all the men of rank and fashion whom she had heard her mother and the neighbours mention, or met in her casual walks—Sir John Hay, the Earl of Drumlanrig, Fergusson of Craigdarroch, the young Laird of Dalmeny, the Master of Spynie, Captain Ogilvie of the Life Guards, and a few others—but some of these she knew by sight, others were too old or too young, and the rest bore a reputation for gallantry and reckless dissipation which her mind absolutely refused to associate with the delicate courtesy and exquisite reserve of her companion, and, strange as it may seem—universally known as he was—Alice had never seen Claverhouse. He had been absent from Edinburgh during the greater part of her short residence there, and such was the awe with which he was regarded—not merely by the superstitious peasantry, then as ever prone to every species of fanciful exaggeration—that the hardiest gossips even of the middle-classes were shy of making him the theme of their comments. His name never once, in the remotest distance, crossed her imagination.

She had been so deeply plunged in this reverie of mingled curiosity, interest, and admiration—in which the two latter sentiments were rapidly assuming an overwhelming preponderance—that she was startled by the clock striking the half-hour, and the simultaneous sound of Colonel Grahame's voice.

"Half-past eleven! Mistress Alice, if you are disposed——"

She started up hastily.

"Ready and willing, I see, and more than half-inclined to quarrel with me for not letting you away long before."

There was not much displeasure in her face, for all that.

"If you really feel quite restored, I shall be happy to wait on you home."

"Oh no, no, indeed!" exclaimed Alice—then, extremely confused, she could only murmur out something about its being quite needless.

"Pardon me, Mistress Alice, I cannot think so. I, on the contrary, am inclined to consider it indispensable. So, unless your repugnance to accept a stranger for your escort be really insurmountable, I must adhere to my previous intention of only quitting you at your own door."

"But, indeed, indeed, sir! what would people say? —what would be thought of me?—oh no! I can go alone," faltered poor Alice, haunted by all sorts of contradictory fears, which her protector's keen eye read at a glance.

"You are between two difficulties, I see; but, my poor child," he added very gently, "you need not fear evil tongues much. I am not one respecting whom that kind of slander has aught to say. You are as safe with me as in your own mother's chamber."

She believed him implicitly, and her discomfort half vanished, although her wonder increased tenfold. She had taken a desperate resolution to ask his name, when, suddenly recollecting that she was still enveloped in his cloak, she began timidly to throw it off. He stopped her movement.

"Keep it, keep it," he said, "it is the best thing you can have; your plaid seems to have been lost. It is rather cumbrous for you to manage—permit me to try——"

Folding the rich material lightly and carefully round her, he brought the corner dexterously over her head to serve as a hood, and thus completely screen her from the cold; while Alice, blushing, and with downcast eyes, trembled all over with a sensation of strange unaccustomed pleasure, and scarcely dared to breathe.

"But you, sir?" she ventured to inquire.

"Oh, I am provided, never fear. I am an old soldier," he replied smiling, as Lucky Jamieson, in obedience to a rather imperious summons from the small hand-bell, entered with a precipitation which seemed to indicate that her eye and ear had been in close acquaintance with the keyhole—an insinuation which we are, unfortunately, not prepared emphatically to deny. She handed him a Geneva cloak, which had, probably, been in its prime some forty years previously; its antiquated hue, and rigidly Calvinistic cut, contrasted so oddly with the gallant bearing and cavalier dress of its new wearer, that Alice could not repress a light laugh as he flung it over his shoulders.

The old woman's face grew disagreeably dark.

"Eh, ye may laugh, my bonnie quean," she said, "but yon cloak has hung over the shouthers of a better man than is like to ca' ye gudewife, I'm thinking."

There was a malice in her words and tone that startled poor Alice into a keen perception of her own equivocal situation, and drove the blood from her cheeks. She was so distressed that she did not even notice the look with which Colonel Grahame silenced the crone; she would have been a bold woman to have offended a second time after that. He took up his hat, and, bowing to Alice to indicate that he was at her orders, opened the door for her to pass out. They had reached the street, when he stopped.

"Excuse me one moment, Mistress Alice; I have left my gloves."

He sprang up the stone steps again, obsequiously followed by Lucky Jamieson. The gloves lay on the table; he had left them behind on purpose.

"Hark ye, Lucky!" said he, in a low voice, "I know as well as you do that you are perfectly acquainted with everything that has *really* passed this night—nay, you need not trouble yourself to tell any lies about it, because, on the whole, I, who have nothing to fear from them, am rather glad than otherwise of your corbie propensities."

Lucky Jamieson *would* have lied if she had dared; but she was a person of experience, and knew with whom she had to deal far too well to attempt any such folly.

"Now, my excellent hostess, I happen to know also that, like the rest of your craft, you have an infernal tongue; but, mark me, if ever it meddles with my concerns, or utters one word—one single syllable that might harm that innocent girl, you shall wish that it had been bored at the Tron with a red-hot bodkin sooner than that you had let it wag on such a subject. You know, I fancy, that I am not in the habit of speaking twice in any case, or of wasting threats any more than promises."

And, with a look which might have awed a much braver spirit than Mrs. Jamieson's, Claverhouse quitted the discomfited hostess, who had hardly self-possession left to light him to the door again.

CHAPTER VI.

CROSS PURPOSES.

> *Olivia.*—**Stay—I prithee tell me what thou think'st of me?**
> *Viola.*—**That you do think you are not what you are.**
>
> **TWELFTH NIGHT.**

IT was a splendid night—the rising of the moon, the brilliancy of the stars, together with the frosty clearness of the unsullied sky, made every object which they illuminated as visible as at noonday. Alice fancied, as they turned out of the narrow lane, that they were very near the spot on which she had been attacked.

"How strange it is!" she said, half aloud.

"What is strange?" inquired her companion.

"The horrible dream that I have been in, this night, sir. I was here, I think, or a very little way off, when I met *them*, and, although I remember being harled along a good distance, here I am again, like a rider bewitched by the ill women, that aye goes round and round, and canna win a step nearer to his journey's end."

Claverhouse laughed. "The spell, whatever it may have been, is broken now, I hope, Mistress Alice, and you are fairly on your road homewards. You must have been sorely frightened—you were quite insensible when, finding themselves on the wrong side of the hedge, they left me with you. Had they threatened you?"

"I only mind what I told you, sir," replied Alice, shivering at the recollection. "I know not even who and what they were, except one."

"Then I am better informed," replied Colonel Grahame. "I know at least that they belong to the Life Guard."

"To the Life Guard! ah, then, I wonder little at aught——"

She broke off, frightened at her own imprudence. There was a moment's silence, which was broken by Claverhouse.

"You have just paid me a poor compliment, Mistress Alice."

"How so?" she asked, in surprise.

"You stopped in the midst of what you intended to say, fearing lest I might accuse you of seditious speeches against His Majesty's faithful lieges, and that a slip of the tongue *might* chance to be repaid by a long sojourn in the Tolbooth, or an introduction to the Privy Council. What can I do to reassure you?"

"I had no intention of offending you, sir," answered Alice, astonished at seeing her own half-formed ideas put into such plain language, and held up before her.

"You have not offended me in the least, believe me—so far from it, that I am going to ask you to finish your sentence."

"But, since you know that such might be the end of my careless speeches, you can hardly expect me to continue them, sir," replied Alice, smiling. "You ken the old saying, 'Biggit wa's hae lugs;' *that* would not matter meikle if they had not tongues too."

"I give you my honour, as a gentleman and soldier, that of all the words you utter not one shall ever be repeated by me—save in so far as they may serve you—that they shall be forgotten as soon as said. Are you content?"

"You are too good, sir. I had nothing to say, except that I could not wonder at all I suffered when I heard who my enemies were. But, perhaps, as ye are a soldier yourself, sir, such matters may seem but a jest to you."

"Faith, no! Mistress Alice, you are wrong there; and sure am I that if Colonel Grahame could hear of this night's doings the doers would not come off free."

"Colonel Grahame!" repeated Alice, in a low voice; "oh, sir! he is not the man to punish wrong done to puir folk like us."

"Do you know him, then?" asked Claverhouse, with all the amusement natural under the circumstances, and more determined than ever to preserve his incognito.

"*I* know him!" exclaimed Alice—then in a moment she added, "You surely forget, sir, that I am but a poor country lassie, and not a great lady. I never even saw him."

"I fancied you might from the way you spoke. How do you know then that he is so unlikely to do justice?"

"In truth, sir, I ken little of him, and that little

is no good. But may be he is one of your friends, and I would be laith to hurt you."

"No friend of mine, Mistress Alice—I never spoke to him in my life, and most likely never shall—so you need have no fear of hurting me. I have been some time away from these parts; and, although I too have heard folk talk here and there of this Claver'se, I cannot say much good was spoken—none at all, indeed. Can all they tell of him be true?"

"I know not, sir, but the haill country has long rung with his name. Strange and fearful tales men tell of him—things to make your flesh grue and your blood run cold—strange and fearful things!" she repeated again, as all the wild legends, which filled the mouths of the peasantry, rose up in her mind, and she marvelled at her own temerity in mentioning them.

"Men say he is stern and cruel," said Claverhouse, looking intently into her face with his lustrous, penetrating eyes, as if to read there the whole extent of her dread and dislike of himself. "Has he ever injured you, that you seem to fear him so much?"

"No, sir; thanks be where they are due, we never lived in the West Country. My father was a minister of the Gospel in the eastern parts of Haddingtonshire. But oh, sir, he is a man of iron heart and ruthless hand, sparing neither hoar hairs nor brave youth—the very scourge of the country—he and others whom ye must surely have heard of too. And then men say, and long have said, that when he was only a stripling lad he made a league wi' the Enemy that bullet shouldna pierce nor steel touch him until his hour came, and that, in very truth, he cares nae mair for shot or sabre than I for the rain-drops in summer, or a prick of my 'broidering needle."

"This is exactly what I have heard myself; but is it much credited hereabouts?"

"Some folk say it is impossible, but I misdoubt it *must* be true," said Alice, in a rather nervous voice, somewhat astonished to find herself talking so freely about a man whose name was rarely spoken, yet irresistibly drawn on by the confidence with which her new friend inspired her. "I have heard my dear father—who was a discreet and learned man —say that he believed such things had been permitted, and that when he saw Claver'se at Bothwell Brigg"——

"Was your father in the battle?" asked Colonel Grahame.

"Oh no, sir. He was a douce and godly man, that would as sune ha' lifted his hand against himself as to harm a fellow-creature."

"But I have heard say that there were a great many godly preachers at Bothwell, Mistress Alice, and that had there been fewer the fight might not have turned quite as it did."

"May be so, sir; but they were not my father's sort, then. No, he saw the fight as it were by chance. He was in that part of the West just then, and, as my uncle Norman was in the tulzie, he could not return home in peace until he kenned how matters went; and it was there he saw him."

"Saw whom? your uncle?"

"No, sir, Claver'se," said Alice, hesitatingly.

"Why you seem as shy of uttering his name as if he were the old Enemy himself," answered Claverhouse gaily; "you would die of fright if you were to see him, I suppose? Don't walk so fast, Mistress Alice; you will certainly fall—you have already slipped twice on this horrible frozen pavement—and don't let go my arm, or I cannot answer for what may happen. Pardon me for interrupting you; you were speaking of your father, and his having seen Claver'se at Bothwell Brigg."

"True," said Alice; "and he said that as long as he lived he could never forget such a sight."

"Had he served in the Low Countries, like myself, he would have witnessed many such."

"I mind," she went on, "that often in the winter nights, round the ingle stane, my father would tell gruesome stories of the sair doings that bluidy day—how the wild Hielandmen came on shouting Lochsloy! how the cannon shot rushed through the crowds on the brigg, tearing the hill-folk down like grass, and their screams and groans as the soldiers trampled over the thick-fallen slain—then, at last, when the defences were broke down (I think he called them so), a sort of gate it seemed——"

"You are quite right—that is the word."

"When the defences were broke down, and the path was clear, Claver'se came on with his troopers like a levin-bolt. He looked, my father said, a very angel o' wrath, with his buff coat sae thick with silver lace that it glittered like a sun—with his black horse and his flashing sword and long white feathers—none could stand before him. Oh! it must have been a grand and terrible thing to behold, when the puir Covenanters, that could neither fight nor flee, fell before his sword as the ripe corn in harvest time, and in the hail of bullets none ever touched him, though it seemed as if no mortal could face it and live; for ye see, sir, all they that had sense and powder left fired at him to break the pursuit, for the Duke of Monmouth was a douce kind o' man, it's like, that never said nay to anything that was asked, and wouldna have pursued them at all."

"I see in all that nothing to prove that Colonel Grahame was more than a bold soldier, and that Fortune favoured him, as she ever does the brave. You allow yourself that he *is* so?"

"But," asked Alice, earnestly, "is it the part of a brave man and good soldier to drag innocent men from their homes to prison or to death, to injure women, and destroy the substance of the fatherless, to slay in cold blood, to spare neither for prayers nor tears, to put himself beyond all human feeling? Oh, sir, ye surely cannot have heard what we puir folk hear of him, and others like him, or I cannot think that one like you would defend his deeds to those that ne'er did him wrong!"

Her own excited feelings, and perhaps the quiet attention of her companion, prevented her from perceiving the dangerous nature of such remarks, and, with every emotion of indignant pity aroused by the subject, she went on.

"Ye surely must have heard, sir, of the many godly men that have died for the testimony here, in this very town, young and old—died with spotless hands and pure hearts, whose blood cries for vengeance on those who murdered them? And yet, God forbid that I should speak of vengeance!" she added sorrowfully; "their ain hearts must be a heavy curse to them."

An unaccountable sense of pain seized upon the mind of Claverhouse at the accusing words of this pathetic speech. He, the dauntless soldier, whose deep though mistaken sense of duty enabled him to crush down every pang of personal suffering and natural pity when they interfered with what he regarded as that duty, and would have made him confront with haughty daring the most formidable tribunal that could have been arrayed to judge his conduct—he, Grahame of Claverhouse, was irresistibly impelled to speak in his own defence, and show this simple girl that if there were cruelty on the one side there had been frightful provocation on the other—that there might, perchance, be that to urge for the oppressors which would diminish the lustre of the victim's martyrdom.

"Mistress Alice," said he, "you have shown me one side of the tapestry; perhaps I could show you the reverse, had I time and inclination. But one thing at least I will ask you: you, and those who hold your opinions, consider the Whigs, Rebels, Covenanters,—call them as you please,—as never having provoked the resentment of those who injure them. Do you call revolt a trifle? do you hold it of no weight, that the whole of the Lowlands are in a fever of civil war? that, not content with being allowed under reasonable restrictions the liberty of worship they demanded, these misguided men would establish themselves and their own fanatic belief supreme not only above the religion consecrated by law in the country, but above all other powers, human and divine? Is it a ground for merciful treatment that they have openly renounced the authority of their rightful monarch, insulted him with every outrage they could devise, and are ready at any moment to welcome a foreign usurper—nay, are intriguing desperately in every nook and corner to procure his success? Between such men and ourselves,—I speak as one who has long known what such struggles portend between authority and rebellion,—the question is simply one of life or death. One moment of weakness, one feeble grasp of the reins, and we are lost—utterly, irrevocably lost! Those very saints who are so loud in their reprobation of us, give them but a moment's power—such as they held in the days of Montrose and Argyle—and see which would be victim, which tyrant, then!"

He had spoken quite as much to himself as to her; and Alice, surprised beyond measure at the sudden vehemence of his manner, could only gaze at him in silence. The bright moonlight fell full on his face, and showed his quivering nostrils, his parted lips, and the flashing eyes that seemed to shine by their own inherent lustre beneath the shadow of his broad Spanish hat. He caught her wondering glance, and slowly the passionate light melted away into that thoughtful tenderness which until then had been their sole expression.

"You are astonished at my language, and are almost ready to fancy me one of the persecutors myself, I suppose? But, Mistress Alice, these pious men—these immaculate saints you revere—wot you the wrong they have done to me? I had a friend, an old and venerable man, my earliest protector, and he was *murdered*—murdered in cold blood, in open day, with numberless wounds, by these fanatic saints; with others standing by, deaf to his entreaties for aid, deaf to his helpless daughter's frenzied shrieks—nay, silencing them with coward blows. I had a relation whom I dearly loved, a young and noble boy, who died by their hands, treacherously shot in defiance of every law of civilized warfare, with words of peace upon his lips; and his body was found so horribly mangled by their barbarous rage, that it is shame to speak or think of. And this because they took him to be"——

He stopped abruptly, and again the fire gathered and crept in his large eyes as he slowly added—

"These things took place years ago; but the grief and bitterness stifled then have gnawed at my heart ever since. Oh, Mistress Alice! small cause have I to love these *godly* men, whose wild self-will and gloomy bigotry have made Scotland—what she is—and me—— But this is sad talk for you; perhaps you do not even half understand it. Forgive me!"

"I am very sorry for you, sir; ye seem to have had many troubles," said gentle Alice, her kind heart moved by the real though well-controlled emotion which her companion betrayed. "I never heard all this before, and doubtless there may be faults on our side as well as on yours. Truly, if hard thinking and harsh speaking of one another, and calling one's fellow Christians ill names when they dinna pray in the self-same words, or sing the self-same psalms, and such like matters, be folly, and much talking of faith, to the great disrespect o' charity, be sin, I think that the Lord's own people will have somewhat to answer for as well as their enemies."

"Sound sense and good theology, Mistress Alice!" said Claverhouse; "I have heard far worse from learned doctors and divines. Yet I fear that, in spite of all your gentleness, if Claver'se or Dalyel were to fall into your hands, a short shrift and a strong cord would be your best words for them."

"Now God forbid, sir!" exclaimed Alice earnestly; "I would rather pray that they might turn from their wickedness and live; and indeed I *have* heard some say that Claver'se has been known to show mercy when ye would have least expected it, and that puir creatures have found him a refuge, dour as he is, among the terrible Lords in Council, and that his own servants and folk would lie down and die for him. It seems hard to believe, though."

"Well, now I am again in Edinburgh, I shall perhaps be able to discover the truth for myself," replied Colonel Grahame, as gravely as he could. "I know many who are intimate with him, and shall be glad to find you mistaken."

"Ay, sir, it is a sair pity to think of," said Alice,

with a true woman's feeling; "for they say he is bonnie and winsome to gaze upon, and that many a fair lady would be blithe to win his love, but that he fancies none."

"I have heard that also."

During this remarkable conversation, they had passed the Netherbow Port, and were descending the Canongate towards the point where the church of that name was still being built; both silent, from different reasons. Alice was deeply struck by all she had heard and seen. No tinge of suspicion troubled her, but her whole mind was in a tumult of new ideas and sensations; and, while her naturally quick and correct understanding could not refuse to acknowledge the justice of much that her companion said, it is hardly to be wondered that the charm of person and manner, together with the evident sincerity of his whole tone, should have added to his words an influence almost irresistible, and a weight they might not otherwise have possessed, against the sectarian bias and violent prejudice which circumstances and education had rather added to, than grafted upon, a heart as warm and guileless as a child's. Too much confused to *think*, she only *felt* that some change was coming over her whole habits of thought: like one in an uneasy yet fascinating dream, she walked on, half wishful, half reluctant, to reach her home, and longing vaguely for the sound of that clear, soft, musical voice, (so different from the coarser tones to which she was accustomed amongst those to whose communications their poverty confined her,) which came to her ear like an echo of bygone days, when such tones were her familiar hearing. She did not notice that, as they crossed the street towards the entrance of the close where she lived, a patrol of soldiers met them, or that Colonel Grahame had drawn his hat down so as to conceal his face, and kept studiously in the strip of shadow under the houses.

But, as they neared the end of their walk, the old terror seized her, and compelled her to speak it aloud.

"Oh, sir!" she began, in an altered voice, "you have been generous and good to me, pardon me if the remembrance of my imprudence seems to make me mistrust you——"

"Mistress Alice," said Colonel Grahame, "I am of a race that for fifteen generations has never been sullied by treachery, or known to break a plighted word. Could I believe myself capable of betraying or injuring one who had so utterly trusted me, I would send a bullet through my own brain to save myself from such shame and wickedness."

"You are very kind to pardon my ill-advised plain speaking, sir," replied Alice humbly; "I forgot myself——"

"You forgot me, I suppose you mean," answered Colonel Grahame smiling; "but remember this, above all things I love honesty and courage, and never more than when I meet them in so gentle and fair a shape."

The grave simplicity which marked these words deprived them of all appearance of compliment; but Alice felt her cheeks burn and her heart throb so fiercely, that she was glad of the sheltering darkness.

They stopped before her door, and Alice glancing up saw the reflection of a light from a window in an upper story.

"Oh, my poor mother!" she said with a sigh, as she disengaged her arm from her friend's and turned to say farewell.

"Stay, take this," he said, hastily writing a few lines upon a leaf torn out of a memorandum book, and putting it into her hand. "Nay, you can read it another time, farewell for the present."

"Farewell, sir!" said Alice; then in a desperation of gratitude she went on, although the beating of her heart almost choked her voice: "I have no words to thank you for your goodness to an orphan girl. May God bless and keep you; and if ever your hour of need should come, as it may to all, I pray that He may help and save you, as you have done for poor Alice Scott this night."

In her innocent thankfulness she timidly put out her little hand. He took it in his own and held it for a moment. The gentleness of the action gave her courage to proceed a little further.

"I do not even know your name, that I may put it in my prayers; but if ever you should need any service that a poor girl like me can render a noble gentleman, any help not unbeseeming a modest and Christian maiden, I will never say you nay, believe me, sir!"

"I do believe and thank you," he replied, "and there is a kindness which you might do me even now; you will think it a hard request, I fear, but not unbeseeming any one to grant."

"Name it, sir," she said joyfully.

"It is this. Whenever in the course of your peaceful life you hear mentioned with bitter hatred and condemnation the name of a man who has been drifting along the open and stormy seas of this world while you lay safe at anchor; whenever you are tempted to believe too lightly the folly and calumny with which men are ever so ready to blacken those whom they have, or think they have, reason to fear—why then, in memory of this night's meeting, for the love of justice and truth, for the sake of one who would not willingly be hated by all the world, try, if you will and can, to think less hardly of John Grahame of Claverhouse."

He raised his hat gracefully and was gone.

Stunned by an amazement we need not attempt to depict, Alice staggered back against the large door, and leaned there like one bewildered. She heard his last words, saw his parting salutation — she mechanically followed him with her eyes; but it was not until his light quick step had entirely ceased to echo through the wynd that she recovered any degree of self-possession. Drawing the large key from her pocket, she tried to unfasten the door, but her trembling hands had scarcely strength to turn the heavy wards, and, when she had finally gained admittance and reclosed it behind her, she was obliged to sit down on the lowest step of the stairs before she could begin to climb the long steep flights that led to her mother's room.

CHAPTER VII.

MOTHER AND DAUGHTER.

> Be collected—
> No more amazement—tell your piteous heart
> There's no harm done. TEMPEST.

"ALICE, my puir bairn! back at last! whare hae ye been? Tell me, speak to me!"

Her mother's arms were round her neck, her mother's tears and kisses on her cheek. Alice felt like one newly snatched back from the fanciful illusions of Elf-land to the solid, sober realities of mortal existence. The old familiar room, every article of furniture, the dearly-loved inmate, were identically the same—nothing, down to the minutest article, had changed. Could so few hours indeed have passed since she left them! She stood immoveable, while her mother anxiously entreated to be told the cause of her long delay, with such expressions of fear and regret as may well be conceived.

"I hae been greetin' for ye, Alice. I thought ye lost and gane for aye; and bitterly I rued my folly in lettin' ye awa', my bonnie doo! Are ye indeed weel and safe?"

"Well and safe, mother, thank God! but I am so tired—*so* tired," she repeated faintly. "Let me rest a moment, and I will tell you all."

The excitement which had sustained her until now was gradually sinking—she could hardly force down her tears. Taking off the cloak she still wore, she folded it carefully together, laid it on one end of the oak settle near the fire, and placed herself at the other, leaning her aching head against the pillar of the chimney. The disorder of her dress, her pallor and depression, roused all the widow's fears afresh. She embraced her daughter again and again, and bound up her hair with the black snood which still clung amidst the entangled curls, begging to be told all that had passed, and describing pathetically her own hours of agonised waiting.

"Poor minnie!" said Alice, "it would have been far worse for ye if ye could have seen all; but it's over now. I've had a sair time of it; but in truth ye were right, and, although I was sorely bestead, yet no ill came. Don't look so scared, mother dear! sit down and I'll tell ye all."

She drew a little stool to her mother's feet and sat there, holding her hand, and striving to speak cheerfully, albeit she would have given much to be able to relieve her overwrought nerves by a hearty flood of tears. As she advanced in her narrative towards the point where she had met Claverhouse, the agitation of her invalid parent forced her to stop for awhile.

"Alice! I canna bear to hear it! Oh God forgie me for letten ye awa,' my bairn, my burdalane! If ony evil has chanced to ye, my grey hairs will just gang doun in sorrow to the grave."

"But listen, mother, listen," said Alice, caressing

the hand she clasped, "and ye will indeed see that God was with me—listen."

She felt her pulses quicken, and a warm glow flush her face, as she described her rescue, and the subsequent conduct of Colonel Grahame. All the respect and gratitude with which his delicate kindness had inspired her, coloured her language, and gave animation to her recital.

The widow listened in alternate fear and delight.

"Surely, surely the Lord hath been on yer side! He hath delivered ye frae the lion, and my darling frae the power of the dog," she exclaimed, in that Scripture phraseology which even now seems to rise intuitively to the lips of the Scottish peasantry on any remarkable occasion; and, taking Alice's head between her two hands, she laid it against her breast. "The blessings o' the widow and fatherless be on his head, whoe'er he may be! But, Alice, hinnie, didna ye speir after his name? how could ye forget that?"

"I did not *forget*, mother," said Alice, stooping forwards and leaning her face on her hand. A strong temptation possessed her to be silent upon the subject of her companion's name—she dreaded her mother's prejudices (how short a time before they had been so completely her own!)—almost her anger; and yet a desire as great impelled her to talk of him. After a short struggle the desire prevailed, and she added,

"But he told me, for all I dared not ask it."

"He tauld ye himsell!" exclaimed Madam Scott, with delighted curiosity; "eh, Alice, wha could it be?"

"You will not believe me, I know," said Alice, without looking up.

"And what for should I no? Tell me, my dearie; ye canna certes ha' forgotten already."

"It was Claverhouse."

The widow's breath was so completely taken away that for some seconds she literally could not speak.

"Alice, are ye daft?" she said, almost angrily. "Whatna gate is this for ye to jest wi' yer ain mother? or is yer heid just turned wi' yer tribulations? Claver'se indeed!"

"Did I not say you would not credit me, mother? And yet I speak truth, the very truth; as surely as I am your own little Alice, the man who saved me to-night was Claverhouse himself."

"But I winna believe it! I canna believe it!—he, the cruel, bloodthirsty tyrant, the ——"

"Mother," said Alice, "is this right? is it Christian? Be he what he may, he cannot be what we have thought him, or I should never have been here in safety and peace again."

"What mean ye, Alice?"

"I mean, mother, that, little suspecting with whom I spoke, I said words that—had he deserved the hatred we have ever felt for him—might have ruined us all. I said of him, to his very face, what you said just now, and more, far more besides."

"God keep us, Alice! were ye fey? oh, ye fule lassie, what garred ye loose your tongue on sic a man?"

"I know not—he spoke to me first—spoke of

Claver'se as if he had been a stranger to him, and asked me what I knew anent him. I spoke as I thought; but I'll never think so mair," she murmured, as a throb of memory brought back the last words she had heard from Colonel Grahame.

"Eh, but we're undone! we're just clean ruined!" ejaculated the widow, clasping her hands in dismay—"oh Alice, lassie, were ye dementit?"

"Fear not, mother," said the young girl, so calmly, that her mother looked at her in excusable astonishment: "*I* do not. Shall I tell you his own answer when I felt as you do now the folly of my sayings? 'If I thought myself capable of betraying or injuring one who had so trusted me, I would send a bullet through my own brain, to spare myself such shame and wickedness.'"

"Ou, ay! we a' ken that the deil can make himsell like an angel o' light to delude puir silly folk like us!"

"Mother, I cannot bear to hear you speak thus," exclaimed Alice, with great earnestness. "Is it at a time like this, when he has freshly saved me from—I know not what; but that I would rather have died than faced it—that *we* should treat him with harshness and reviling? Remember, that, while others who saw my need—men with wives and daughters of their own at home—stole by in craven fear, this man, enemy and oppressor as he is called,—this fierce pitiless soldier, sheltered, refreshed, and comforted me, an utter stranger—and that with such tender reverence and care as I can never forget! I too hated him, and believed him what he *is* not, cannot be; but now, come what may, he has a claim on our forbearance which we can never discharge. Oh, mother, we must have been sorely mistaken!"

"Hout, Alice!" answered the widow, really moved by her daughter's arguments, but unwilling to yield a single iota of her long-cherished belief; "hout, lassie! ye're ower zealous I'm thinking, for a minister's daughter, to defend the evil doer against them that's quiet in the land."

"Which of these, thinkest thou, was neighbour to him that fell among thieves?" said Alice, lifting her beautiful face with an expression of gentle reproach that was almost sublime.

The question was unanswerable, and the really kind heart of the widow smote her for her ungrateful speeches. "Ye are right, my love Alice, and I was wrong," she said, when the momentary vexation had passed off—"ye were right. Ye spake sae like yer ain blessed father, that ye seemed like his ghaist come back frae the grave to reprove me for my lack o' charity."

"I didna wish to reprove you, dear minnie," said Alice, "only to remind you that we may become Pharisees ourselves, if we will believe nae good of others."

"True, Elsie; I trust I may be forgi'en for ill speakin' o' ony creature; me that's a sinner mysell; and for being sae presumptuous as to think that His grace couldna melt even the hardest heart, and for sinning my mercies when I hae ye safe in my arms, whilk is mair than I dared to hope for an hour syne. But tell me my doo," she continued, passing her hand softly over Alice's hair, " were ye no just feared to death, whenever ye kenned wha he was?"

"Feared? oh no, mother," said Alice, smiling brightly as the image of her protector recurred to her —if indeed it had ever been absent—" no more could you ha' been, nor any one else. Besides, I didna even guess it until he told me with his ain lips, here at the door, and gave me this."

She unclasped the hand in which she had been holding the slip of paper Claverhouse had left with her, and read it for the first time.

" See here, mother,—what did I tell you?"

"Read it to me, Elsie; ye ken vera weel that I'm no that quick at readin' even the imprinted books—out taken the Word, and may be the Psawms. There werena sae mony in my airly days as the world is deluged wi' noo."

Alice slowly read out the hurried lines.

" After what I have heard to-night, I can hardly hope to obtain belief when I say, that, if my influence can procure justice for the violence you have suffered, it shall not fail to do so; and that if ever Mistress Alice Scott, or any one whom she loves, should need protection and advice, she may fearlessly command such assistance as I can give—if, indeed, she will accept it from one whom she has learnt to believe beyond human sympathy and human feeling."

No name signed this curious note, but the three initials of the writer " J. G. C.," entwined in an elegant and intricate cipher, stood below it.

"And ye think he wrote that, Alice?"

"I saw him do so: and look, here are the letters of his name, John Grahame of Claverhouse."

That name lingered softly on her lips, and she sat gazing at the paper she held.

"Aweel!" sighed the good widow, with an air of relief; "it's the Lord's doing, and marvellous in wer eyes! Little did Margaret Scott dream that ever she wad come to bless the name o' Claver'se; and yet, Gude kens, I *did* bless him maist abundantly when first ye spake o' him. Even now I canna find it in my heart to think sae ill of him as I was wont. So ye say he nappit ye in that braw cloak of his, Elsie, and tended ye discreetly?"

"If I had been his own and only bairn he couldna have done otherwise. But oh, mother, you should see him!"

"Wherefore, Elsie? What like is he?"

"What like? Indeed I canna tell. I never saw any like him," replied Alice, looking with wide dreamy eyes into the fire before her.

"Is he sae terrible, then? Eh, my puir darling if I had been in your place, I would just ha' deed wi' fear!"

"I didna say that; I didna mean it," said Alice in the same tone; "he is bonnier than any man I ever beheld."

"*Bonnie*, said ye, Alice?"

"Ay, mother; *more* than bonnie; with a face that is fair as a dream, and a voice that goes to your very heartstrings, and eyes that might make you weep, save when they flash and glance wi' pride, then, indeed, you might tremble! and a smile on his curling lip . . . I have seen fair faces, but never one like his," she broke off, with a hot cheek and beating heart, ashamed, in her delicate pride, of having even *thought* such passionate admiration.

"And a tongue like a serpent, I doubtna, to beguile silly women to their ain destruction," said the widow somewhat tartly.

"He said no beguiling words to me," answered Alice innocently, shaking her head.

"Did he no? then, indeed, I'm beginning to think he maun be vera unlike the rest o' his ain hellicate deevils of troopers, that's aye rampagin' aboot like roaring lions, seeking whom they may devour, as ye ken ower weel yoursell, Alice."

"He talked to me of many things, but with no word or look that you might not have given me yourself, dear mother, with all the respect and honour he would have paid to a queen. I would have gone without fear from one end of Scotland to the other with him."

Her mother looked fondly at the honest young face, all glowing with bashful earnestness, and kissed it again, tenderly.

"But oh, mother," exclaimed Alice, suddenly, "dinna tell Norman!"

"Not tell your ain brither, my Elsie?"

"No, no, pray do not; you know, mother, how fiercely he hates all these men, how he speaks of all dignities just like those gloomy dark-browed preachers who used to take refuge at our manse at Glencarrig, lang syne. I am well assured that, with his temper and ways of thinking, if he could but guess that any of them had been cause of evil to you or to me nothing could hold him. Judge for yourself, mother; is it likely that he would bear it patiently?"

"Nay, Elsie, I trow not; but what then?"

"You ken but too well, mother, how small a thing will bring a man to mischief in these troublous times, when not even the purest innocence can win through free, and Norman is so dreadful when roused that he would of a surety do some desperate act, and draw upon himself the eyes of the Council. You ken that he calls this religion, and says that he would joyfully bear his testimony wi' the martyrs of old (though to my mind it's an unco' sort of religion that bids ye provoke and slay your enemies). And, when to know all this miserable affair would but stir him up to bitterer words and deeds, why should we help to endanger him? I have scarcely a peaceful day or rest o' nights, lest he should commit some wild act, and die as my uncle Norman died, or in exile, or in the Grass Market."

"I canna just say but what ye're right, Elsie; if ye think it the discreetest plan to keep a calm sough anent the matter, I'm sure I am nae mair fond o' tale-bearin' than yoursell. And I'm free to confess that Norman's ways is a sair vex to me; not that I dinna think him vera sincere in the gude cause —— "

"But my dear father was sincere also, mother,

yet he loved his neighbour, and prayed for such as despitefully used us, instead of cursing and injuring them. God knows I dinna seek to deny their wickedness, but a' this fearful talk, this denouncing of vengeance, can only stir up the hot blood between us and them, and my mind misgives me that Norman is deeper in with all these unhappy turbulent men than we can yet conceive."

"What gars ye think that, Alice?"

"A thousand things, mother—the very way he speaks,—even my dear father's memory is not sacred in his eyes. Do ye not mind how he said, the very last time he was in this room, that he had been a lukewarm disciple, and that they who would follow the Lord must be zealous even to slaying? Oh, if he can think thus of our father, what would he do himself? Then, his looks are dark, and his voice stern, and, when he joins with us sometimes in the exercise, my blood runs cold at the prayers he makes for the uprooting and destruction of the ungodly, as if all men must needs be sinners because they think otherwise than he does."

"True, Alice; but it's wearing late, and ye maun be sore weary; gang awa' to yer bed like a wise bairn, and we'll speak mair anent this the morn."

Nothing, however, could persuade Alice to seek the rest she longed for, until she had extorted from her mother a formal promise not to tell her brother a single word of her romantic adventure, and particularly to refrain from all mention of Claverhouse.

CHAPTER VIII.

EXPLANATORY.

> **Yea, this man's brow, like to a tragic leaf,**
> **Foretells the nature of a tragic volume.**

BEFORE proceeding to the narration of any more interesting facts, we must now devote a few lines to the mention of those peculiarities of circumstance and character which induced Alice to insist upon a secrecy by no means congenial to her naturally candid disposition. And first let us note, by the way, that the widow's last unacknowledged doubts as to the possibility of any mistake in Alice's account of her rescuer's identity were quite dissipated by the discovery of the same cipher as that which signed the paper, beautifully embroidered in gold thread, inside the collar of the splendid cloak which Alice had worn. She spent a long time in examining and admiring it, in appraising the rich velvet of which it was composed, the gold lace which covered the seams, and the fine sables with which it was lined—all with a sort of nervous, fearful enjoyment in her knowledge of the possessor, that would have amused Alice excessively, had her mind been less preoccupied with important thoughts, and which was perhaps increased by Madam Scott's alarm at the possession of such a "corpus delicti,"—lest her son, arriving on one of his unfrequent and always sudden visits, should discover its existence, and draw his own conclusions therefrom. But this latter perplexity was disposed of in the easiest and simplest way imaginable a day or two later, by the appearance of a staid and handsomely-dressed serving man, who, without mentioning any name, said that he had been commissioned by his master to fetch it. Unluckily, Alice's difficulties were neither so insignificant nor so speedily terminated.

She had but too good reason to dread her brother's gloomy zeal and revengeful temper, although even her knowledge of him did not compass the real state of his mind and tenor of his conduct. The master to whom he was apprenticed was Andrew Kerr, a well-known printer and bookseller of that day, a zealous and bitter Cameronian; but who, being endowed with a much larger portion of worldly wisdom than generally distinguished the more *exalté* members of his sect, had contrived, with some risk indeed, but successfully, to weather the various storms which had swept away in their passage all the most prominent apostles and testifiers. The fact is, that Maister Andrew Kerr, although perfectly sincere in his religious enthusiasm, and quite willing, if no better might be, to have gone to the gallows or scaffold for the sake of Covenant and Kirk, had never been able to see the dignity or merit of throwing himself headlong into the lion's mouth, and affording thereby a "triumph to the adversary,"—any more than the good sense "o' lootin' him bite aff yer head when ye might sae easily sting his heel." Which odd version of Scripture he put in practice with all the shrewdness and dexterity of a canny Scot—contriving, by means of the facilities afforded by his way of business, to sustain the under-current of disaffection and intrigue which was fermenting in the country; and especially assisting to carry on that secret correspondence with Holland which spread its ramifications over the whole of the Scottish Lowlands. During the course of these adventurous undertakings he had more than once found himself in imminent danger,—but his own sharp wits, aided by the protection of some Whig noblemen, whose rank and influence enabled them to brave even the redoubtable Privy Council—backed too by that singular power which, for want of a better name, we are forced to denominate good luck, had as yet brought him off entirely unscathed. It may be easily imagined how congenial to the restless, vindictive, and sullen nature of a youth like Norman Scott, must have been such opportunity of aiding in the overthrow of a Government deservedly detested, and the hope of re-establishing the final and—we must write it—tyrannical supremacy of the tenets held by his own sect. He had thrown himself heart and soul into all the complicated designs of which his master was an agent, thus adding to the native intolerance of his spirit all the rancorous animosity of party hatred. The gentle doctrines of his wise and amiable father were in his eyes a halting between two opinions—the truly Catholic benevolence with which that father had in turn benefited all parties, whatever their form of worship might be, he stigmatised as a sinful sparing of the heathen, and compared it to the offence of the Israelites, who slew not the Gibeonites, but took compassion upon them —the charity that loveth, hopeth, and believeth all things, had no existence for him. He thirsted for an opportunity of proving that, like the early martyrs of the Kirk, he could be faithful, even to the shedding of blood—and nourished in the meanwhile, with a bitterness of which we can have no adequate conception, a deadly and unsparing abhorrence of the "enemy, persecutor and blasphemer;" under which comprehensive denomination he included all who opposed the spread of his cherished doctrines, whether they had deserved that hatred by wanton cruelty, or had simply incurred it by the discharge of lawful service, unaccompanied by any unnecessary severity in the execution of orders they were bound to obey. In short, it would have been hard to find throughout the length and breadth of Scotland a more desperate, uncompromising, and gloomy young bigot than this brother of the gentle Alice Scott.

The innate and acquired fanaticism of his temper had been much heightened since his arrival in Edinburgh, where, in the discharge both of his avowed duties and of the secret employments entrusted to him by his master, (who fully appreciated all his qualifications for such trust,) he had had considerable intercourse with two or three of the ultra-Independent preachers—and those the most thorough and unscrupulous of their class. No man, unless he have attentively perused the annals of that time, would credit that these religionists—whose first and foremost principle was utter detestation of Popery, and of everything which perverted ingenuity could distort into the faintest shadow of resemblance to "the accursed thing" —who carried that detestation to a pitch repugnant not merely to Christian charity, but to the most ordinary common sense and decency—whose intolerance equalled that of their opponents—that these men, I say, practised and inculcated one of the worst doctrines of the Romish church, and, like those they condemned, justified the means by the end. Bloodshedding, even in the form most repugnant to human feelings—that of deliberate assassination—was, in the apprehension of these fanatics, a laudable zeal for God's glory, a smiting of the Philistines, a slaying of Agag by the hand of Samuel, of Eglon by the dagger of Ehud—and they brought, to justify these views, dozens of texts from the Old Testament, wrested from their natural situations and proper meaning, interpreted literally, and applied as best suited the purpose of the speaker. The extent to which this perversion of Scripture was carried on by the very men who clamoured for its integrity and supremacy, and denounced so furiously all whose understanding of its precepts differed in the slightest degree from their own, is a peculiarity attested by every record of the period—by none more plainly than their own productions—and, although neither unexampled nor unnatural, affords a striking proof of the terrible power of self-deception lurking in the human heart, above all when blinded by spiritual pride as ferocious in its way as the worldly tyranny it braved.

The communion of such spirits as these, the wild enthusiasm and reckless violence of their doctrines—the reports they brought in of the state of the country—painful enough, but still further coloured and inflamed by the exaggeration of their feelings—their descriptions of their own sufferings—often self-provoked, but all the more meritorious in their eyes—the very circumstances of secrecy and danger which attended their movements and meetings, had worked upon the young man's imagination to such a degree, that the alteration even in his usual austerity struck his mother and sister, as we have seen, with dismay. Not so his new friends, who began to regard him as a "chosen vessel," adding thereby all the excitement of vanity (by no means so distinct a thing from such sanctity as his as some would fain believe) to the fire which only awaited a favourable chance to burst forth into open flame.

The reader will now perceive, with tolerable clearness, the necessity for precaution on his sister's part, and her natural aversion to any disclosure that might render the governing class still more obnoxious to him.

But, in spite of all her discretion, she could not entirely succeed in concealing the fact that something unusual had occurred on the night of the 16th of March. By what means she never could comprehend, he certainly became aware of the fact that she had been seen at nearly midnight alone in the streets of Edinburgh with a stranger, who appeared by his dress and bearing to be a gentleman, a member, to wit, of the very caste on which the great burden of his hatred directly weighed. She was alone when he charged her with the circumstance, and insisted upon knowing whether the statement were correct or not.

Alice was incapable of an equivocation, even to avoid the disagreeableness of such a scene as she foresaw, she therefore replied—unwillingly indeed, but distinctly—that it was.

We could hardly undertake to describe, without appearing to exaggerate, the tempest of reproach which she drew down upon herself by this admission, but his violence only convinced her the more of the necessity for adhering to her resolution of silence. She bore with patient sweetness all the anger of her brother, merely telling him that his indignation was entirely misplaced, and that instead of falling upon her companion, whose name she studiously concealed, it were far better bestowed on those whose brutality had rendered his succour so welcome and so necessary; and slight as was the information, she soon had reason to repent affording it, when he insisted, in a manner which almost overthrew her forbearance, upon being made acquainted with every detail of the adventure. Her refusal became the origin of suspicions so degrading in themselves, and expressed in language so unguarded, that Alice's womanly pride was stung to the quick. She rose hastily from her seat, and coming close to him where he stood, eyeing her in gloomy indignation, cut short the interview at once—

"Brother Norman, my own conscience and our mother's approbation are better cautions to me for right and wrong than these passionate, shameful words of yours. Had ye spoken as a brother should, had your speech been sober and your life discreet, I would not have scrupled to tell you all I prudently could, but now, be assured that ye have sealed my lips more closely than ever. The babe unborn is not more innocent than I in this matter, and perhaps, when this frantic fit is over, ye will blush to think that the first thought of such evil that ever crossed your sister's heart was placed there by yourself. Shame on ye!"

"Ay, shame on me!" retorted the young man, "because I dare to call darkness darkness, and not light. I have said what I came to say, and, behold, my words have returned into mine own bosom. Still, careless and hardened as thou art, I will strive to drag thee from the broad and flowery path where thou art beginning to walk so young,—but if thou becomest indeed one of those who work folly in Israel, *beware.* I only say beware!"

He left her without one word of affection, for nothing could have persuaded him of her complete innocence. True she had confessed to having been thrown into imminent danger, from which nothing but the courage and generosity of her companion had saved her, but had she not positively refused to reveal the nature of that danger, the name and quality of her protector? And was he not—so Norman knew—a man of apparent rank and distinction—a son of Belial—an oppressor—a sinner—one of the heathen? Was it likely that any good could proceed from such a source? Was not all this supposed adventure a subterfuge—a fable cunningly devised to conceal some disgraceful intrigue?

To do Norman as much justice as he deserves, the conduct and habits of the younger nobility and gentry were such as to warrant any suspicion in regard to one of their number; but the perfect truthfulness and purity of his sister's character, their mother's piety, and the anxious care with which she had instilled into her daughter's mind the highest principles of religion, might have re-assured a very sceptic. Re-assured however he was not—his domineering temper was irritated by his sister's spirited defence of herself—his evil opinion confirmed by her silence—his detestation of the upper classes still further inflamed by the assumed injury received from one of their members; and, with the usual absence of common sense and moderation displayed by men of his stamp, he brooded over the affair in sullen silence, from which he only roused himself to renew his angry attacks upon his sister, in the vain hope of discovering the name of one on whom he so ardently desired to wreak his displeasure.

Poor little Alice! between her brother's anger and the necessity for keeping him aloof from her mother, between the fear of distressing her and the craving for sympathy in her vexation and shame, she had a hard part to play. But she knew how to let patience have its perfect work, and bore unmurmuringly not only these minor troubles, but others which, in strange and untried semblance, were springing up, unseen to human eye, in the innermost recesses of her young heart.

CHAPTER IX.

THE GUARD-ROOM.

> He is knight, dubbed with unhacked rapier . . . . but he is a devil in private brawl; souls and bodies hath he divorced three, and his incensement at this moment is so implacable, that satisfaction can be none but by pangs of death and sepulchre.
>
> TWELFTH NIGHT.

THE town residence of Colonel Grahame of Claverhouse was situated in the High Street, near its junction with the Canongate, and close to Leith Wynd. It consisted of the ground floor and first story of a large and very handsome house, which he occupied whenever military or political business detained him in Edinburgh. This house, which has probably been destroyed or greatly altered since the period of which we are writing, was then one of the most fashionable residences in that fashionable part of the capital, and generally presented all the animated appearance of business which might be supposed to mark the head-quarters of so distinguished an officer; who, besides his colonelcy of the most brilliant and patrician regiment in Scotland, held the rank of major-general, and was also a member of the Privy Council. From eight o'clock in the morning until long past noon, the coming and going to and fro was continuous—messengers from the Parliament house—visitors on public or private affairs—officers on duty—

orderlies on horseback and on foot—couriers and servants, formed an almost constant stream; and this concourse, which sometimes rivalled the levees of the commander-in-chief, was naturally very much increased after Claverhouse had been absent for any length of time.

On the morning following the adventure related above, we must beg the reader to imagine himself in a spacious stone paved hall, on the ground story,—which, being immediately contiguous to the entry, and communicating by a private staircase with Colonel Grahame's apartments, served as a sort of antechamber and guard-room. Its central position had rendered it quite a favourite resort with all the officers and gentlemen troopers of the Guards, who looked upon it as a capital lounge, made appointments there with their comrades, friends, and fashionable acquaintance—discussed social scandal, military gossip, and political news—criticised the female passers-by from the very convenient windows, and spent the greater portion of their mornings there, either when summoned thither by business or duty, or when merely attracted by the hope of hearing and seeing some new thing.

About eleven o'clock on the morning to which we refer, the room contained but few of the visitors who had filled it during the earlier hours of the day; but near the tall, deep chimney, beneath which blazed a splendid fire, stood apart from the rest a group of five gentlemen—three belonging to the Life Guard, the other two officers of Dunbarton's Foot—a regiment almost as exclusive and aristocratic as that of Claverhouse himself, and quite as much detested by the Covenanters, Whigs, and other disaffected sects or individuals.

"It is no earthly use, Lindsay, asking me again and again a question which I can't answer. I could not enlighten you any more on *that* point, if you were to put on the thumbikins."

The speaker was an officer of about fifty years of age, with grey hair, a black moustache, and a bright shrewd grey eye, a thorough soldier in manner and bearing. The person whom he addressed as Lindsay was a nephew and ward of his, a mere lad, about eighteen or nineteen, who had only just joined the Guards.

"Is Drummond with the Colonel now?" asked Lindsay.

"Has been for the last half-hour, as I told you. Wait a bit until those loiterers have cleared out, and then I'll let you into my own opinion on the subject. There—now we are more private——"

"Hallo! there's Craigdarroch!" exclaimed one of Dunbarton's gentlemen: "perhaps he knows something."

Fergusson of Craigdarroch, a tall, stalwart, handsome young fellow of six or seven and twenty, with a dashing air and open pleasing face, came gaily up to them; all hands were extended to him, for he was a great favourite, not only with his own corps, but with all who knew him—including, and this especially, the ladies.

"Good morrow, gentlemen; your servant, Captain

Crawford. Lindsay, I'm delighted to see you amongst us. How goes the world with you all?"

"The world's going rather hardly with a dear friend of ours just now—at least I hope so," answered the third guardsman, laughing.

"Who's that? What's the matter?"

"To the first question I answer, Drummond," replied the elder officer, whom he had called Crawford; "to the second, that I haven't an idea, beyond that there is the devil to pay, and plenty of pitch hot."

"Drummond, eh? Got into one of his cursed scrapes with the Colonel? Well, never mind—if he were Old Hornie himself, I'd back Claver'se to give him his crowdy!"

A general laugh greeted this speech, and an exclamation of, "So you don't know anything about it, after all?"

"*I!* Faith now, gentlemen, this is a bad jest. You know very well that I only came up from Lanark with the Colonel late yesterday afternoon, and you ask me for Edinburgh gossip, when I came hither in the happy confidence of getting my fill of that same from you."

"Tush, man!" ejaculated Crawford; "we only hoped you might have some inkling of the matter, as you have been pretty nearly *tête-à-tête* with Claver'se for the last ten days."

"A bonnie piece of news! as if I did not remember it! I never spent a harder ten days in my life—and I've seen some campaigning, too. By all the devils!

I have not had an hour's peace or a decent night's rest since I left town."

"What have you been about?" asked Lindsay.

"Everything under the sun, moon, and stars; fighting, riding, hunting up conspirators, getting in prisoners, preparing reports, examining spies, harrying Whigs——"

"What! cannot Claverhouse let those poor devils alone for a while?" said Maxwell, one of the Royal Scots.

"Devils as much as you please," answered Fergusson, readily, "but I rather demur to the pathetic adjective. If you had been in my place for the last ten days, you would pity them considerably less than those who have to keep them in order. There's one comfort though, Claverhouse treats himself as badly, or perhaps worse, than us his poor followers. But, as I am not made of cast iron and gunpowder, a time comes at last when I give in. I *must* have five hours' rest out of the four-and-twenty, and hard work always gives me an intense appreciation of food, drink, and sleep, which it was pretty nearly impossible to come by. Now it's my solemn belief that our Colonel could go without either for six-and-thirty hours, and never a whit the worse."

"I have seen him do so,—a good example for you youngsters," replied Crawford.

"Well," said Craigdarroch, shrugging his shoulders and twisting his chestnut moustache, "all I know is, *I* cannot. I'm willing to stand anything in reason—but one night I was so confoundedly hard up, that I fell asleep in the saddle, and rode a matter of two miles thus. When I awoke, who should I behold but the Colonel himself riding beside me, and holding my beast's rein. 'I'm really sorry to drive you to such extremities, Mr. Fergusson,' quoth he, 'but duty before everything.' 'Under your favour, Colonel,' said I, 'I'd rather take it *after* a good night's rest. *Do* you ever sleep?' 'Sometimes,' said he, 'when I've nothing better to do.'"

The indefatigable activity and singular endurance of Claverhouse were too well known to all present not to give them a full appreciation of the value of the reply.

"Well," continued Fergusson, "that very night the Colonel had one of the narrowest escapes I ever saw. A Whig fellow, whose life he had spared, for some reason as incomprehensible as himself—(*I* expected every moment to hear the order for him to be shot, and 'pon my soul he deserved it)—this fellow's life, I say, had been spared for a time—and he was brought along with us, trussed up behind young Kincaid. On the road he contrived to make his escape, and the next thing we heard of him was the report of a pistol, some two hours afterwards, from behind a fauld-dyke. Of course there was a tremendous halloo after him, but he gave us the slip, reached some water, dived like an otter, and disappeared, Heaven knows where. All the bullets missed him—and no wonder—for it was a pitchy night. I should know the rascal again, though, if I saw him."

"Was the Colonel hurt?" asked Lindsay.

"No; the very devil's own luck he has! I don't wonder at the whigamore blackguards believing him invulnerable. The ball struck the hilt of his sword, glanced off, and dropped into the folds of his cloak. He just took it up in his hand, and said, as coolly as I say it now, 'This is the usual reward of clemency; I shall know better next time.' Faith! but he looked grim though!"

"A set of blackhearted, ungrateful scoundrels, that know not what honour means, save perchance the sort that is said to dwell among thieves," said Captain Crawford, scornfully; "I should have fancied Claver'se knew them far too well to commit such a woman's trick as letting one of them off beyond the space needful to get a tough halter ready. Did he whine and snuffle for mercy?"

"Nay, good brother, that did he not," returned Craigdarroch, in a sanctimonious tone; "he did testify valiantly—he did take up his parable, with a mighty voice and an outstretched arm, against the ungodly and the oppressor, and the Edomite, and the Amorite, the Philistines, and them that dwell at Tyre——"

A shout of laughter interrupted him.

"Capital! capital! but that will do, Fergusson," cried the two Royal Scots; "it is pity of your life you were not born a Cameronian preacher, you look the character so admirably when you turn up the whites of your eyes."

"He has learnt the genuine nasal snuffle, and thorough-bred cant, amongst his Whig friends from Nithsdale! I would be a pupil myself if the fair

Mistress Annie were teacher there," added Maxwell maliciously.

The young Guardsman's face flushed scarlet.

"What do you mean to insinuate, gentlemen?" he asked, with a slight motion of the hand to his rapier hilt.

"Why, Craigdarroch, man! hast lost thy temper for so poor a jest?" said Ogilvie, the other Guardsman, laughing; "for shame! thou wert wont to be fonder of a joke, even against thyself. Art thou sleepy still?"

Young Fergusson, who was a good-natured fellow, although rather touchy, laughed in his turn.

"What about Kincaid?" asked Crawford; "I suppose he wished himself at the bottom of the Clyde."

"I confess to having felt anxious for the lad," answered Craigdarroch; "but there appears to have been very little fault of his in the matter. The Whig fellow—a perfect Hercules—had escaped whilst we were passing a small moss, and had hard work enough to keep ourselves high and dry, let alone looking after a third party; besides which, Kincaid's horse, a young animal, had grown completely unmanageable under the double load. But I can't tell you much about it, for as soon as I perceived that matters were going pretty straight, and that Kincaid was likely to come off easy, I fell asleep in the midst of the examination. The Colonel's as hard as steel, but as just, and Kincaid as gallant a lad as ever wore buff, that has done good service once and again; so between this and that he got safe through, only I can't say exactly how it was."

"What, when the Colonel's life had been compromised by his fault?" asked Lindsay, surprised.

"If I judge Claverhouse rightly," replied Fergusson, "I should say that his contempt of danger is so supreme that he would scorn to let it be thought that any consideration for his personal safety could influence him one way or another. If my life or yours had been imperilled, I should have feared more for the offender, I promise you. The poor lad was wild to discover the rascally Whig's hiding-hole, but, although he and three others scoured the country, no trace of him could they find. So the whole matter remains a mystery, as well as how he got possession of a weapon, for he had been thoroughly searched by myself. We found out, afterwards, that he was the very individual we had been hunting for high and low,—Heatherfield the preacher."

"I am delighted, at any rate, that Kincaid escaped scot free," said Ogilvie; "I like the young fellow. I am afraid, nevertheless, that this *malheur* may interfere very much with his promised promotion."

"He may thank his patron saint that it is no worse," replied Crawford, gruffly. "I have seen many a pretty fellow brought to court martial for a less matter, and I must say such leniency is not a whit like Claver'se's usual good discipline. However, I suppose he knows best, and I have no call to interfere, so there's an end on't."

"Amen! with all my heart," said Craigdarroch; "and now that I have emptied my scanty budget of news, let us hear somewhat of this business of Drummond's. I have not made out a syllable of it yet."

"All I know is this," said Crawford: "when I came hither this morning I found Drummond in deep conference with Hay. Both stopped short when they saw me, and Hay left immediately. I spoke to him as he went out, but he gave no answer, and I saw that he looked as surly as a bear. This surprised me, for we had spent the evening together very jovially until about nine o'clock, and I parted from him and Dalmeny excellent friends. I next tried Mr. Drummond, but he was still worse, and as I didn't feel greatly inclined to get into a quarrel, for which recreation he appeared to have considerable appetite, I left him to enjoy his own reflections, which were doubtless of an enlivening tendency. Presently, in came Claverhouse from his morning ride, and, after speaking to me as civilly as he does to every one, asked if I had any reports to make, and what regimental business was on hand. Drummond upon this makes a step forward, 'I wish to speak to you, Colonel Grahame,' says he. You ought to have seen the look the Colonel gave him! 'I intend to speak with *you*, Mr. Drummond, but at my own time. Crawford, I am ready.' So I followed him, gave in the reports, transacted the business, and had some half an hour's conversation with him. Unluckily, I had a good many complaints to make against Drummond for neglect of duty—you remember, Ogilvie—which I dare say did not tend to improve the Colonel's humour or his prospects; but I was just as far as ever from any idea of the immediate offence. It must have been out of the common, I fancy, for the Colonel's face was something tremendous."

"I did not notice anything unusual about him," said young Lindsay; "he always looks grave, but his voice was not altered, and he spoke quite kindly to me."

"Pshaw!" answered his uncle, "when you have known Claverhouse for twenty years, boy and man, as I have, you will be better able to judge. I know every trick of his face, '*comme le fond de ma poche*,' and I never yet saw his eyes drop fire and his lips turn pale as they did this morning without experiencing something as like fear as I can conceive one man capable of feeling towards another."

"I never yet experienced it at all," replied the lad haughtily.

"Then I advise you to take the first chance of mortally offending Claverhouse, and you will come to a knowledge of that sensation pretty speedily," retorted his uncle laughing. "Tut, boy! you know not of whom you speak. I never came across the man who cared to defy his wrath—and, when an old soldier like Ludovic Crawford makes such a confession, you need not fear to dishonour your smooth cheek by a similar avowal."

Lindsay made no reply, but threw up his head with boyish petulance, which brought a smile on the lips of Ogilvie and his friend Craigdarroch.

"Lindsay!" said the former, laying his hand on the youth's shoulder, "you need not be so hurt at the imputation on your manliness; had you been longer with us you would have known that we have a saying in the regiment—'Better face the devil and fifty wild Whigs than the Colonel in a passion.'"

"He has no notion of anger showing itself in any other form than Drummond's thundering oaths, or a little easy blood-letting; he'll be wiser in time," replied Crawford.

"Meanwhile, Captain, we are waiting for the remainder of your information," said Maxwell. "What has become of Mr. Drummond? He was not here when I came in."

"He had just been summoned to the presence, and I do not intend to stir a foot hence until I see something of the results. It could have been no trifle that caused Claverhouse to look and speak as he did just now."

"And I for one should not be loath to see him depart, once for all," continued Craigdarroch. "The fellow's insolence and presumption are quite too much for my stomach; and just because he calls himself my Lord of Perth's cousin, forsooth! I wonder how that relationship could be made out, or whether he thinks himself a better gentleman and better officer for being kinsman to an Earl!"

"Ay; or fancies that the reflected lustre of a coronet can make his coarse features and tavern talk more acceptable to a certain fair dame, whose blue eyes have done more mischief amongst our gallant sparks than a thousand Whig bullets," concluded Maxwell.

"Impossible!" exclaimed Craigdarroch—"ten times impossible! I thought I had chastised *that* out of his drunken head long since. What makes you say so,

Maxwell? have you heard or seen since my absence—By Heaven!" he muttered, sinking his voice, for all turned to look at him, "I'll slit his nose and ears if he has dared—"

"Get your dagger ready then, for here he comes!" said Crawford drily, as a heavy foot descended the private stair, and Drummond entered the guard-room. He was so closely covered with the skirt of his cloak drawn over one shoulder and his hat pulled down, that his face was not distinguishable, but beneath the folds of the roquelaure his hand griped the hilt of his sword, and his very tread had something menacing in it. He crossed the room towards the outer door, without taking any notice of his comrades. But their curiosity was too highly excited to be baulked thus—and, at a sign from Crawford, Ogilvie called to him.

"Drummond, do you intend to go down to the Leith races to-day? there is a splendid match coming off, you know, between my bonnie Grey-steil and Melfort's Prince Rupert." He had not finished before Drummond was in the midst of the group.

"Hark ye, gentlemen!" said he, in a voice husky with rage, and scarcely able to articulate; "I am in no humour for trifling, and a match with ground rapiers and case of pistols would be more to my taste than any other style of diversion." He paused a moment. "I have this morning been exposed to what no gentleman can endure without everlasting dishonour. I defied my insulter to his face, and the coward shelters himself behind his rank to refuse me what alone can atone for the disgrace he has inflicted.

But blood can wash out every stain, and his blood *shall!*"

The frightful oath, spoken through his ground teeth, which sealed this threat, made even their accustomed ears tingle. The powerless hatred and baffled fury that raged within him were fearful to see, as he raised his clenched hand and struck the heel of his boot upon the stone floor, repeating his imprecation with a cold malignity, more fiendish than words can convey.

A murmur of disgust ran through the group; two or three other gentlemen joined it; voices arose in confused exclamations, and young Lindsay, stepping boldly forward before all his comrades, exclaimed—

"Whoever dares to couple the name of *coward* in the same breath with that of Colonel Grahame of Claverhouse, utters a dastardly and shameless falsehood; and here am I, David Lindsay of Burnielaw, ready to avouch it as a gentleman may!"

His frank young face was flushed with indignation, his eyes sparkled, and, plucking off his long military glove, he flung it at the feet of Drummond.

This fiery and romantic speech fell like a spark on tinder. Two or three rapiers were half unsheathed, the whole conclave fell into noisy confusion, and some scene of disorder must inevitably have ensued had it not been for the cool presence of mind of Crawford, who, in virtue of his age and experience, seemed to possess a tacit influence over all his younger comrades.

"Lindsay," he exclaimed, drawing back his excited

nephew, "this cannot be. You are a brave boy, and I honour your spirit, but such a challenge is the merest waste of valour."

"'S death!" grumbled one of the Royal Scots, "if any man, were he King James himself, had ventured to say before me that Dunbarton was a coward, I'd have crammed the lie down his rascally throat ere it had well left his lips!"

"Hush!" whispered Maxwell, "Crawford knows what he is about; no fear of his forfeiting the dignity of his corps."

"Take up your glove, Lindsay," said his uncle coldly, "and remember another time that a gentleman only fights with his *equals*."

"Nay, that I will not do," replied the headstrong youth, "I never will stoop to retract a defiance once given."

"Then I must do it myself, I suppose," said the veteran, with perfect composure, and suiting the action to the word.

"Who dares to say that I am not his equal?" asked Drummond, looking round with a defiant stare. "It is well that the Laird of Burnielaw has allowed his pledge to be withdrawn, or it might have chanced that I had used it to clean my rapier, as I have done with many a better man's before."

The sneer which accompanied this speech was even more odious than its coarse insolence, but contempt had by this time almost drowned anger in the hearers. Crawford motioned to Lindsay to put up his rapier, and, coming closer to Drummond, said, "I do not know whether you are aware, Mr. Drummond, that your expressions concerning Colonel Grahame bore a strong resemblance to a threat of assassination, at least I know not what other construction to put on them. If you still call yourself a gentleman, I beg you, for the credit of your class, to afford some explanation of such unseemly language."

"I will give none beyond this—that Claverhouse is from this day forth my mortal enemy—that I *hate* him! I *hate* him!—do you hear that, one and all of you? that from this hour I cease to be his hireling, to come and go at his bidding, and that, as he has dared to refuse me the meeting I demanded, I will proclaim him a liar and poltroon in every town in Scotland."

The veteran captain laughed aloud in disdain, but the young men's blood was hotter, and this was more than they could bear.

"Confusion seize you, Crawford!" exclaimed Ogilvie passionately, "are we to stand by all day and hear him blackguard the colonel this way! Look ye here Mr. Drummond, all Edinburgh knows you for a ruined gamester, a bully, and a rake. *I* have good reason to hold you for something worse—ay, you may scowl! what care I, do you think? I am not a woman to be terrified at your brutality. The whole town knows you to be what I say, and all Scotland reveres Colonel Grahame as a gentleman of purest integrity and stainless honour. Appeal to the world, if you dare, and let it judge between him and such as you!"

A few words in Ogilvie's speech had struck Drummond with dismay, as they seemed to indicate a knowledge of several circumstances which he had fancied buried within his own breast. Not that he was ashamed of his course of life—he was far past any weakness of that sort, but a public disclosure of facts must place him so hopelessly in the wrong as to prevent his ever attempting any open retaliation for his dismissal, and throw him absolutely on the mercy of Claverhouse. He looked round him like a baited bull, which, assailed on all sides, knows not where first to vent its fury.

"I have but one life to risk," he said, his face white, and his whole frame trembling with smothered passion, "and revenge is too deliciously sweet to be thrown away for the sake of gratifying a moment's anger. But, if I survive *that*, you will find that a heavy account lies against you for this morning's insults. Worthy followers of your renowned leader! worthy soldiers of your noble chief! I always hated him, but now I hate him tenfold, with a bitterness which nothing but his death or mine can quench—and in that detestation you have your ample share. Grind your blades, gentlemen! keep them sharp, in the devil's name, for in an hour when you least expect it you may need them!"

He took up his hat, which he had dashed upon the floor, and with one last muttered curse moved away. "One moment, Mr. Drummond, if you please," said Crawford; "there are two words to that bargain. We all know Colonel Grahame too well to attach any importance to such accusations as in your insane passion you have degraded yourself—not him—by uttering; and, credit me, any gentleman would be slow to grant an honourable meeting on equal terms to the man upon whom his noble lips had pronounced the word *disgrace*."

"Doubtless! what slave dare even lift his hand when his tyrant threatens?" retorted Drummond. "But I shall easily find means to evade that difficulty."

"Slaves! threaten!" repeated Lindsay—as Drummond, with a hoarse laugh, strode from the guard-room. And even the more experienced Ogilvie echoed the words.

"'Fore George! I doubt whether we have done right in letting that fellow away!" exclaimed young Fergusson; "he said enough to warrant putting him under arrest. I wonder how I kept my hands off his throat! Slaves, forsooth! If Claver'se were like any other man, I'd have taken up the word on his behalf as gladly as ever I danced a couranto; but we *might* have got small thanks for our pains, as we know nothing of the matter."

"Colonel Grahame is quite competent to manage his own affairs," answered Crawford, gravely, "and he can have nothing to fear from the bluster of a *roué* and cut-throat like yonder: it is the old fable of the serpent biting a file; but I don't feel quite as easy upon all other points. The spirit of mischief incarnate seems to possess Drummond—he will stick at nothing—and if, as is very proper, Claverhouse has refused to meet him, there's a flavour of poison or dagger about his discourse that don't suit me. I shall take an early opportunity of mentioning the matter to the Colonel."

"You may spare yourself the trouble," said Maxwell; "he will thank you politely for your zeal—and not do anything."

"Possibly; in which case *I* shall. Come, David, come along with me. I'll not lecture you publicly for your chivalrous folly, but, if it came to Claver'se's ears, he would give you more sharp words than thanks, I'm thinking. Confound the boy! what were you dreaming of, to fling a firebrand into a powder magazine that gate? You're not fit to be trusted with a rapier, upon my soul!"

"I could not bear to hear Drummond insult our gallant Colonel without saying a word," answered Lindsay. "I should be unworthy to serve under him if I could hear such calumny unmoved."

"Oh, I've nothing to say against the *words;* they were perfect of their kind; only they came some two centuries out of date," replied his uncle, laughing good-naturedly. "Nay—never blush and frown, my lad! thou art a fine fellow—a worthy grandson of old Alick Lindsay of Edzell—but there's a season for all things, says Solomon, and thy unlucky piece of knight-errantry had nearly drawn blood in Colonel Grahame's antechamber. He would have owed thee small gratitude for *that*, I trow. Here's thy glove, rescued from an inglorious fate; though, i'faith, had I to choose, I would rather see it employed to clean the good steel his brave uncle used so well at Kilsyth, than touched as a gage of combat by a hand so unworthy.

I wonder, did he fancy our hides so thin as to smart at his blunt thrusts!"

The uncle and nephew left the room together; and Fergusson, turning to Ogilvie, said with a peculiar smile—"I can't help thinking that Crawford knows more of this business than he chooses to tell. I cannot understand why he should seem so anxious to prevent any discussion respecting Drummond's disgrace—for disgrace it clearly is. Perhaps Colonel Grahame has reasons we cannot fathom for getting rid of him,—perhaps the sweet youth knows something that would have made it inconvenient for our punctilious commander to bring him to court-martial, else I'd swear that Claverhouse would never have had such language flung in his face for nothing."

"Now, out upon thee, Fergusson!" exclaimed the chivalrous Ogilvie; "how can'st thou, like yonder ruffianly braggart, dare to suspect a man of Colonel Grahame's stamp of aught that could shun the light of day? Did any one that ever knew him as we do breathe a syllable against his fair and unsullied repute? I would lay my life, my fortune, my honour, on his word, with less scruple than thou hast shown in trusting the lies of that reproach to his ancient and noble race."

"Doubtless, doubtless," answered Craigdarroch, laughing; "faith is an excellent virtue, and removes mountains—so say the preachers—but it would take more than I possess to convince me that here is not *anguis in herba.* Claverhouse is not a man to be braved with impunity; and if Drummond's offence called for ignominious dismissal from the regiment—which seems to be the case—why it must surely have deserved a court-martial. I must probe this matter to the very bottom, if I can."

"Thou art a most incorrigible gossip, Craigdarroch," said the graver Ogilvie, with a look almost of displeasure; "and thy curiosity seems to me in the present instance somewhat unbecoming. I never doubt until I have been betrayed; never suspect where I can see no better motive for suspicion than a most wanton love of scandal, which might better suit a tattling old carline than the tongue of a brave gentleman."

"Tush, man!" laughed Fergusson; "dost thou take me for a blind believer in our good Colonel's utter indifference to such things as please all other men? Dost thou think that at his age, and with his looks, beauty has no charm, and the wine-flask no flavour, to him? I say nay. I love him none the worse that I believe him less stony than he would fain have us and all the world take him to be; but I should love him the better if he were more frank in confessing himself not above the ordinary weakness of dust and ashes. How many a fair face have I seen bestow such smiles on him as might have moved the soul of a reasonable being to fling himself over the Campsie Linn to merit them—and he as calm!—I swear, that, had I no more human infirmity left about me, I would hang myself on the first tree I came near, for a lamentable fool, that knew not the good things provided for him in this pleasant world of ours! My life on't! I believe the very spirit of all the Whig preachers Claverhouse ever hanged is concentrated in his single self: he is enough to freeze the marrow in one's bones, when he looks so coolly on at feast and revel."

"Nay," said Ogilvie, "this is beside the question. The point now is, not whether Colonel Grahame shows much judgment in his contempt for pleasure—I am no Puritan myself, God wot—but, whether we have any right to believe him otherwise than sincere in his assumption of an austerity, by which, as we all know, little enough is to be gained now-a-days."

"And therefore the more likely to tempt one who never does anything like his fellow worms. I admit thy position is most fairly put; Lockhart or Rosehaugh could not have spoken more pithily; only, as Fate will have it, I am inconvertible. But let it pass. Art thou for Leith Sands this clear morning?"

"You forget the race which is to decide between the merits of the two best horses in the Lothians," said Ogilvie.

"True,—then it is time we were off; for St. Giles is crying aloud to warn us of the approach of noon."

They departed arm-in-arm, for in spite of great difference of character, and almost constant disparity of opinion, the two young officers were fast friends—and their departure was followed by that of all the other loungers, who dispersed, ready and willing to spread over the military circles of the capital the singular and by no means unwelcome tale of Drummond's evil case.

"I shall fasten on to Dalmeny next time I can

find an opportunity," said Fergusson, as he rode with his gossip on the Leith Sands; "he is Hay's bosom friend; and, from what our sage old Mentor Crawford said, Hay seems to have had a finger in this pie. I am morally convinced there is a woman in the case—and faith! it would be too exquisite a joke to ferret out the hidden mysteries of this most mysterious affair. How Annie will laugh to hear that the proud, cold Claverhouse has been more than half suspected of the "*doux délit;*" perhaps convicted upon circumstantial evidence!"

Ogilvie, rather nettled by his friend's ridiculous pertinacity, had it on the tip of his tongue to answer, that the young lady of Maxwelton had been more than half suspected herself, on her first appearance in society, of a desire to attract the admiration of the elegant and courtly soldier, whose rare personal beauty made him a very cynosure for ladies' eyes—but, remembering that Craigdarroch was really attached to her, with equal wisdom and kindness refrained from annoying him, and contented himself with forcibly turning the conversation into another channel.

CHAPTER X.

CLAVERHOUSE.

> **A duty to a certain sign,—a vice**
> **When overstrained; and this I fear in him:**
> **And then he has been rash from his youth upwards,**
> **Yet tempered by redeeming nobleness.**
>
> **MARINO FALIERO.**

THE preceding account of the morning's occurrences may serve to show partially the light in which Colonel Grahame was regarded by those immediately about his person; but, in order to form anything like a correct idea of the real character of this singular and unfortunate man, some slight detail becomes necessary.

On no point, perhaps, of our Scottish annals, would a chapter of "Historic Doubts" be better bestowed than in elucidating the real nature of those circumstances which have hitherto given such sad celebrity to the name of Claverhouse; and few men, perhaps, in the range of modern history, would afford a more interesting subject for research, if directed by a spirit of common impartiality. The nature of our present tale forbids any attempt to investigate minutely his chequered career, but we may be excused for suggesting a few considerations which tend to throw important doubts, not only upon the motives and circumstances of many of his alleged actions, but upon the very actions themselves.

We would not have it supposed, that in any thing we may advance upon this subject we intend to deny the existence of tyrannical cruelty which no nation could have borne tamely, and which, for being inflicted in the name of the law, was scarcely less culpable in the tyrants, and even more exasperating to the victims. Any attempt to defend a cause so essentially indefensible, could only result in merited failure. But it is, nevertheless, worth while to consider how far the persecuting spirit of the age was shared by those who have been generally regarded as harmless and inoffensive objects of gratuitous injury, and to examine whether, after so much has been said and written in honour of the oppressed, there may not be something left to say or write on behalf of the oppressors—a portion of equity very much neglected in general, but none the less indispensable to justice. It can surely be no violation of historical probability, to separate by a broad line those whose tyranny was joined to a selfish venality and treachery which deprived their errors of the very semblance of respectability, from the few who seem to have been actuated throughout by some perverted sense of duty, and by an exaggerated loyalty as fatal to the cause they upheld, as the religious bigotry of their opponents was injurious to the best interests of Christianity. Difficult as it must be in our peaceful times to conceive the existence of any such misguided sense of right and wrong, impossible as we may find it to understand how any men, gifted with a moderate share of sense and humanity, could devote themselves to the unscrupulous support of a system so utterly vicious, yet the fact is incontrovertible—and that some such principle must have actuated at least the better portion of the "persecutors," is sufficiently proved by the unselfish, unhesitating generosity with which they flung away everything that can make life sweet, in order to preserve unstained their loyalty to their prince. Worthless as his cause appears to us, who behold from afar off the *real* nature of the struggle which then convulsed Scotland, yet to them that cause was the path of duty and honour—and, if we give a just and deserved tribute of admiration to the constancy of those who died as martyrs to a rightful cause, is it too much to concede some portion of charitable indulgence to the motives of those who honestly believed in the justice of what we, more enlightened now, perceive to have been a wrongful and tyrannical one? That such sincere, though mistaken—nay, let us say *criminal*—men, did exist, cannot be denied; and it is equally undeniable that, on the other side, there too often prevailed a degree of intolerance, self-will, and obstinate folly, which drove matters to extremities that might otherwise have been happily avoided.

It would be difficult to explain how—surrounded by men whose actions equalled his in rigour, and whose private life and political conduct will not bear a comparison with his — Claverhouse should have ever attained such a pre-eminence of odium as that which attaches to his memory. Stern and relentless as he was, many traits have been handed down to us which show that nothing less than the exasperation of civil warfare, the evil influence of the age, and the misguided zeal of a nature passionate and extreme in its cruel fanaticism of duty (alas! that that noble word should ever be so debased!), could have sufficed to create such a character,—while, on the other hand, many men, as fierce and terrible, even more hated then, have been remembered with comparative indifference, although in them cowardice and meanness enhanced all the darkness of oppression. This may, perhaps, arise from the singular accident by which, in spite of the prominent position he occupied for so many years, in spite of the talents, influence, and reputation he so indisputably possessed, the little we know concerning him has been handed down almost exclusively through his enemies; by the writings of persons who, politically or religiously, regarded him as their worst foe. When we add to this some consideration of the inveterate rancour of the sectaries of that age, the gross credulity and abject superstition which prevailed, the extreme improbability of many of the stories so positively related of him, and the absolute physical impossibility of some others, it will be allowed that much corroborative testimony would be needed, before any impartial judge would pronounce a verdict of cold-blooded wickedness on evidence so one-sided. Without wishing for one moment to palliate crimes and severities which really were committed, we think it desirable, for the sake of historical accuracy, that some reliable evidence should be obtained, and some more candid (not to say charitable) mode of inquiry adopted, than indiscriminate reprobation, ere we condemn as a heartless murderer and tyrant one of the most remarkable personages of Scottish history.

For our own part, we confess that one of the chief emotions aroused by the name of Claverhouse is deep regret, similar to that with which we contemplate certain portions of Turenne's career, at seeing a noble nature warped by prejudice and bigotry, a proud heart and generous temper degraded by the pernicious atmosphere of those miserable times—talents of the first order thrown away in the service of a Prince equally unworthy and ungrateful, and a name which might have adorned the annals of any country remembered with dislike by most, and with mingled admiration and sorrow by a few less obstinately credulous judges. Yet even those most adverse to him agree with writers of the opposite faction in giving certain outlines of his character, which in some measure account for the respect and personal awe, independent of his deeds, in which he was held, even by the members of his own party.

He possessed to a remarkable degree all the qualities of a consummate soldier—for in him a fiery headlong valour, so wild and chivalrous as almost to justify the popular superstition of his invulnerability, was united to a prudence so far-sighted, a *coup d'œil* so keen, and a calmness so imperturbable, that danger and difficulty seemed not only as familar to him as the very air he breathed, but the atmosphere in which that breath was most naturally and freely drawn. A rigid disciplinarian, yet easy of access, and perfectly familiar with the wants and habits of every man under his command; hardy, enduring, patient of fatigue, the first in every charge, the last in a retreat; cool, resolute, and indomitable,—his own soldiers might well be excused for half believing in his supernatural endowments, when they saw him face with unruffled *insouciance* dangers and privations at which the hardiest veterans looked grave. And these qualities were rendered still more striking by the contrast they formed with the personal appearance we have already described, and with manners and habits so refined, that, as an elegant courtier and finished gentleman, he could scarcely have found his match in the broad realm of Scotland.

His ancient descent and considerable fortune, joined to the brilliancy of his civil and military career, and his rare advantages of person and demeanour, had long since procured for him the highest rank in society. The noblest houses were proud to claim him as an honoured guest; all admired, many courted, some few loved him. Yet, strangely enough, he never seems to have attained extensive popularity even amongst those of his own class. The best and purest points of his character were precisely those with which they had least sympathy. The men were often disposed to look coldly on one whose moderation, amounting at times to abstemiousness, was a tacit reproach to the intemperance then so fatally prevalent that its indulgence was not considered to militate against the reputation of a gentleman—the women were inclined to think him haughty and heartless, when, in the prime of life, surrounded by all the seductions of a gay—nay, dissipated—state of society, he remained to all outward appearance unmoved. Many gay and coquettish dames, to whom gallantry was as the breath of their nostrils, were by no means disposed to let so noble a prize pass by without exacting tribute to their charms, and one or two of the most enterprising had resolutely set themselves to the task of subduing the unconquerable rebel, and bringing him fairly to their feet. But report said, that, although these spirited beauties, deceived by the exquisite grace and habitual gentleness of Colonel Grahame's demeanour, had early plumed themselves on a supposed victory, yet this exultation had only been the prelude to signal discomfiture, which the remembrance of a premature triumph served to aggravate.

Ogilvie had spoken the truth when he asserted that there was small credit to be had by any assumption of austerity in that age of universal licence, and Claverhouse was far too experienced not to be perfectly aware of this. But with him it was no assumption. His extreme pride and self-command, joined to a keen sense of self-respect—perhaps to some still nobler principle—had preserved him in early youth from the vulgar excesses of what is called pleasure, and in maturer years the absorbing interest of public life left him little time, even had he possessed any taste, for dissipation. He had flung himself with all the force of his ardent and aspiring temper into the whirlpool of events which were gathering to overwhelm the dynasty of the Stuarts—and amidst the almost insurmountable difficulties of that crisis, day after day, and year after year, saw him grow a sterner, more thoughtful, and melancholy man. Some few dear and long-tried friends had indeed penetrated this outward armour of reserve, and knew well what passionate enthusiasm lay hidden beneath it; they looked up to him with a confidence, affection, and respect as earnest as it was unbounded; but these formed rather a small minority—by the greater number he was far more feared and admired than beloved.

In his intercourse with most of his colleagues of the Council the same state of feeling prevailed. True he shared in their opinions, he had generally acted with them, he was responsible in equal measure for the harsh and despotic acts which had rendered the very name of that body hateful to the Scottish nation; but they felt his superiority, they knew that he was by nature of nobler mould than they—and that, although he might be capable of crimes, selfish, mean, or false he never could be. The noble lords and honourable councillors who in those troublous years sold their religion to their king, and their king to their interest and safety, felt his unflinching loyalty weigh inconveniently upon them, the false dreaded his uncompromising integrity, the obsequious and fawning shrunk from the infliction of a sarcasm so keen as to preclude retort, so perfectly polished as to render anger or offence-taking ridiculous. Except to one or two men as honest as himself, Colonel Grahame's empty seat at the council-board was a welcome sight, although one which was not frequently presented to them.

The Lord Chancellor Perth and his brother Lord Melfort shared to an especial degree in this general though secret dislike of Claverhouse. For their lordships had but very lately, along with some other statesmen equally generous and disinterested, forsworn the faith of their ancestors to enter the pale of infallible Rome, and they could neither forget nor forgive the profound contempt and cutting sarcasm with which Colonel Grahame had received the news of this *conversion.* Besides, it so happened that he had once or twice interfered in favour of some unhappy prisoner whom the Council had thought fit to treat with unusual severity, or to check my Lord of Perth's too great fondness for boot and thumbscrew—all which trifles had engendered a state of hostility, latent indeed, but none the less decided. The two gentlemen were on terms of the most perfect good understanding outwardly, for the simple reason that it was by no means easy to quarrel with Claverhouse unless he chose it; but the Earl desired nothing better than an opportunity of humiliating and mortifying his constant antagonist, a man whom he feared, and by whom he knew himself to be despised. This opportunity presented itself quite unexpectedly in no very agreeable shape, in consequence of the recent adventures of his cousin and *protégé*, Drummond; and the mention thereof brings us back to the main thread of our story, from which a digression of no importance, save from a certain historical interest, has already detained us too long.

CHAPTER XI.

"GANG WARILY."

Grace me no grace—I am no felon, Sir—
Give it to such as crave it—I'll have law.

It requires no great stretch of imagination to conceive that, ere night-fall of the same day, the whole history of Drummond's disgrace, garnished with all the arabesques of conjecture, exaggeration, and comment with which the simplest matter is sure to be heightened in the course of transmission through a hundred mouths, had gone the round of the military circles and gossiping *réunions* of Edinburgh, and been conveyed in a highly embellished state to the Earl of Perth. Now, his lordship had for many years been in the habit of upholding and patronizing his cousin, with a pertinacity quite remarkable, considering that gentleman's demerits; and invariably gratified his pecuniary demands with a readiness which seemed to betoken very unusual forbearance towards a relation from whom neither profit nor pleasure was to be derived. On the present occasion, this habit of sustaining and defending the young profligate, even when he least deserved such support, was brought into still greater play by his personal grudge against Claverhouse, and the anticipated satisfaction of bringing that officer to account for his dismissal—his *unjustifiable* dismissal, said the irritated peer—of a scion of so noble a house, merely for a freak of venial gallantry in which no gentleman had the right to molest another—such being the view of the case which Drummond had sedulously instilled into his kinsman's mind, when interrogated by him upon the delicate subject. He was by no means prepared, however, for the inconvenient zeal with which his lordship declared his intention of proceeding the next day at an early hour, to demand satisfaction for what he resented as an affront offered to himself. Drummond had his own reasons—exceptional and weighty reasons—to dread anything like an "*éclaircissement*," and did all in his power to avert so undesirable a consummation; but the earl was obstinately bent upon his design, and Drummond was at last forced to accede to it; declaring at the same time, with insolent haughtiness, veiling real alarm, that *he* would never have stooped to beg redress from any living man, least of all from Claverhouse. His only secret hope—a very feeble one—was that his protector, with whose officious self-importance and utter want of tact he was well acquainted, might so mismanage the whole affair, as to provoke the fiery temper of Colonel Grahame into an absolute refusal of all explanation whatever.

In this unenviable frame of mind, at war with himself and everyone else, he left his quarters the following morning and wandered about the city, desiring nothing better than the chance of a hearty quarrel, to give vent to the virulent passions that were raging within him. Every hour increased, if that were possible, the hatred which he had sworn against Colonel

Grahame. He hated him for the strong discipline with which during five years Claverhouse had quelled his intractable and sullen nature,—for the inflexible justice which, irrespective of political relationship and powerful protection, had ever visited his repeated breaches of duty—he hated him for having rescued Alice from his libertine pursuit,—for the short decisive words in which Colonel Grahame had intimated to him, that any further injury to the young girl would be at his own peril—most vehemently of all he hated him because he felt himself thoroughly known, and dared not kick against the pricks lest a word from Claverhouse should plunge him into still more irretrievable ruin. Beggared as he had been before in morals and in fortune, he was beggared now in reputation, insulted by his former comrades, without one chance of regaining that poor share of worldly consideration he had until now possessed;—and all this was one man's work—the man at whose command the proofs of his baseness had risen as it were from the dead to confound him. The very clemency which had spared him the last shame of public exposure only exasperated his animosity: the spirit of Cain held mastery over him.

In this amiable mood he crossed the Lawn Market, then a very fashionable promenade, and the first persons who met his eyes were Ogilvie and Craigdarroch, accompanied by the Laird of Dalmeny. This young gentleman had unfortunately, on his first entrance into the world, fallen into the society of Drummond, who, with the perversity of a thoroughly corrupt nature, had taken pleasure in initiating him into all the follies and vices of a great capital. His easy goodnature, inexperience, and large fortune, had rendered him a rich prize to the unscrupulous and ruined gamester. He had long regarded Dalmeny as a piece of property of his own, and, if anything could have aggravated the irritation under which he laboured, it was to meet the youth in company with the two gentlemen who had most openly resented his outrageous conduct the previous day. They all passed him with a stiff salutation, but an irresistible impulse moved him to try what effect the news of his disaster had produced upon his pupil,—for so Dalmeny might be termed. He followed them, and touched him on the shoulder.

"One word with you, Dalmeny."

"Wait for me, gentlemen—I will be back instantly. At your service, Mr. Drummond."

"I see you are informed of what has passed," said Drummond, haughtily. "Pray spare yourself the trouble of announcing that you intend for the future to dispense with my society: your manner speaks for you."

"Drummond," said the young laird, in whom not all the dissipation into which he had so deeply plunged could drown natural generosity and good feeling, "I must speak the truth. I would not have poured water on a drowned rat, but I assure you, since you *will* hear it, that I have little more taste for your society after the dilemma into which your folly last night led me—and I confess to being heartily ashamed of having had art or part in illtreating that poor girl, as if there were not wild limmers enough and to spare!

But I am *not* in the least ashamed of owning when I have been wrong; and, finally, I have no fancy for risking another night quarrel with Claverhouse, or a morning reprimand from him. I only wonder, when I remember how I handled him last night, that I have escaped with whole skin. I told you at the time you would ruin yourself."

"The dominie has been whipping the naughty little boy, who has promised never to do it again —or be caught at it," retorted Drummond with a sneer. "Faith, Laird of Dalmeny, you are an apt scholar, and recite your lesson fairly enough. Ruin, forsooth! and who is Colonel Grahame, that his fiat should ruin as good gentlemen as himself? Ruined I may be, but not by him. However, he has done enough to make me his bitter enemy, and, for all his insufferable arrogance, he may find me an inconvenient one, as also those false friends who turn their backs on an unlucky comrade, and who will perhaps feel, when it is too late, that dead men *can* sometimes bite. You understand me, I presume?"

They parted. Dalmeny, very much staggered by this sudden outbreak, returned to communicate to his friends a suspicion that Drummond's dismissal must have arisen from something more important than the cause to which it was assigned, to wit, insubordination and violence towards his commanding officer. Leaving them to discuss the pros and cons of the matter, by the aid of such lights as conjecture or memory could throw upon it, we will accompany the Earl of Perth, who, in pursuance of his previous intention, had betaken himself at an early hour to the residence of Colonel Grahame. The tall grey-haired servant, who was always in immediate attendance upon Claverhouse, received him with the deference due to so distinguished a personage, and introduced him into what would now be termed a study, or morning-room, where his master was.

It was a very handsome room, of moderate size, wainscotted with bright brown walnut, and panelled with leather stamped and embossed in gold, after a fashion which was already beginning to be somewhat out of date, but was still adopted by those who consulted their own taste in preference to the reigning mode. The furniture was all of the same wood, beautifully carved, the chairs and couches fitted with cushions of crimson damask to match the ample hangings of the doors and windows; the ceiling was painted, and the polished floor nearly covered by a thick foreign carpet, a luxury by no means so common then as now. The chimney-place was of marble, with large brass dogs, and round the walls hung five or six portraits in gilded frames, amongst which the dark armour and bold chivalrous countenance of the fated Montrose, were the first to strike a visitor's eye. The sober elegance which pervaded the apartment was very remarkable, and quite in keeping with the appearance and habits of the inmate.

Claverhouse, dressed with military precision and almost Puritanic plainness, in dark velvet, relieved only by the falling collar and large loose ruffles of exquisite lawn, without peruke or sword, was seated at a table placed before one of the tall windows through which the winter sun streamed cheerfully in. He had been writing, for the table was strewed with papers, but when the servant announced the Chancellor's visit he started as from a brown study, and rose with the ghost of a smile flitting round his lips.

"I thought so," he murmured to himself; "and yet I fancied my Lord of Perth too old a hand to cross steel with me!"

The graceful nonchalance with which he saluted his colleague, and the courteous inquiry as to what could have procured him the honour of so early a visit, rather disconcerted his Lordship, who hardly knew how to enter upon the disagreeable business which he had undertaken—somewhat precipitately, as he now began to think. It was too late, however, to draw back, so, seating himself with great gravity, he proceeded after a careful preamble to open his subject.

The two men formed a curious contrast to one another; neither mentally nor physically was there the slightest point of contact. The Earl of Perth was a tall imposing looking man, somewhat beyond the prime of life, but retaining a certain portion of good looks, in spite of rather harsh features, a very sallow complexion, and a strong attachment to good claret, the results of which were plainly visible in his countenance. He possessed a full share of that sapience of aspect which is so often joined to an almost complete absence of the quality suggested; his language and deportment corresponded, by a species of elevated condescension, to the stateliness we describe; so that it would have been almost as difficult for a casual observer to detect beneath this dignified senatorial aspect the shallow weakness and unmanly vacillation which characterised this distinguished personage, as to recognise in the slight elastic figure, with its delicate hands, its shadowy eyes, and rich curled tresses, the stern soldier, whose name was a watchword of terror to his foes, a tower of strength to his friends.

During the long and confused harangue in which the Earl gradually unfolded the object of his visit, Claverhouse sat perfectly still, one hand drawing imaginary fortifications on a sheet of paper which lay before him, the nervous slender fingers of the other clasped over his chin, with such immovability that the Chancellor stopped more than once, under the impression that his auditor was not listening, until a quick glance as often intimated the reverse, and requested him to proceed. But such extreme silence and profound attention annoyed Lord Perth so much, that, after setting forth at great length his own view of Drummond's case, he began to grow rather embarrassed, lost his temper a little, missed the thread of his discourse, and ended abruptly by a rather angry request for an answer.

"Which," he said with great dignity, "I have an undoubted right to demand, and which I am certain Colonel Grahame will admit that he has no right to refuse."

A quick observer might have seen Colonel Grahame's dark eyes dilate with a strange, almost threatening expression, beneath their fringe of black lashes, but the Earl of Perth, not being a quick observer in any way, was not surprised at the perfect composure of his tone, whatever he may have thought of the words.

"In the first place, my Lord, in order perfectly to comprehend on what footing we stand, you will do me the pleasure to remember that the word *demand* is one which I am totally unaccustomed to hear, and to which therefore I shall pay no attention. In the second place, I do not regard myself as responsible to any one but his Majesty, in whose name I hold my commission, for whatever use I may choose to make of the unlimited authority it confers upon me."

"You will admit my right to interfere in an affair where the honour of my family is so nearly concerned?" said the Earl, with much *hauteur.*

"Pardon me—I admit nothing of the kind."

"Every gentleman has the right to claim common justice at the hands of another, and, that justice not having been granted to my cousin, I come to request it on his behalf, however preposterous the request may appear to Colonel Grahame of Claverhouse."

"Your lordship is perfectly correct on one point, at least," said Claverhouse coolly; "justice has not been done to Mr. Drummond, and, were I in the habit—which I am not—of indulging in second thoughts, I should say that I regret the course which I pursued towards him."

A smile of triumph crossed the earl's countenance at this admission, which of course he accepted as the first-fruits of his own eloquence; but a moment's consideration of its equivocal nature, and a glance at the expression of Colonel Grahame's face, materially abated this self-gratulation. There was an indescribable touch of irony in the soldier's composed voice, an easy self-possession in his look and attitude, as distinct as possible from the bearing of a man conscious of having committed a wrong, and desirous to repair it. His lordship hardly knew what to make of the whole speech, and could not decide whether to take it in the most obvious meaning or resent it as sarcasm. The first alternative was however so much more flattering to his vanity, that he chose it, in spite of misgivings which *would* intrude that he was on a wrong tack.

"I am happy that you will allow even so much, Colonel Grahame," he said, "although I am utterly at a loss to understand how a gentleman of your birth and station can have been so regardless of the credit of a noble house as to inflict an irreparable and degrading injury upon one of its members, on grounds so slight. For I certainly need not tell Colonel Grahame that abrupt and unexplained dismissal from his regiment is equivalent to a public declaration that the culprit has rendered himself unworthy any longer to serve his Majesty, or to remain the comrade of men of honour."

"Precisely so," said Claverhouse, bending his head with an air of polite acquiescence in an incontrovertible proposition.

The earl reddened angrily at the failure of this second attack. He had hoped by the asperity of his language to provoke Claverhouse into some manifestation of displeasure or self-defence; but he found, and by no means for the first time, that he was a poor match for such an antagonist.

"Then I am to conclude, I suppose," he exclaimed indignantly, "that these are the accusations you are pleased to bring against my cousin's honour?"

"Oh, content you, my lord," replied Claverhouse, with a smile which made his lordship feel rather nervous, "your cousin's honour is of a robust constitution, or it could barely have survived the repeated shocks it has received ere now."

"Colonel Grahame! this language ——"

"Is such as befits the occasion. I had hoped to convince you without the necessity for harsh speaking that this affair is entirely undeserving of your interest or that of any gentleman, but you now force me to state in plain terms that such is the case. Credit me, your best and wisest plan is to leave things as they stand, without pushing your inquiries any farther; and that is friendly advice—take it, my lord. It's ill stirring foul waters."

"Impossible, sir!" exclaimed Lord Perth, who had by this time quite lost his temper. "Whatever secret motives you may have for wishing to hush up an affair in which you acknowledge yourself to have acted with injustice, you cannot expect me to be influenced by them, and I, on my cousin's part, must persist in desiring some more satisfactory conclusion."

"In sooth, my lord earl, you forget yourself strangely!" said Claverhouse, raising himself with a look of supreme haughtiness from the careless attitude which he had hitherto maintained. "This is not the Council Chamber, nor am I a refractory Whig prisoner, I imagine; although the tone you are pleased to adopt would lead any one to conclude that you laboured under such a delusion."

"Your pardon, Colonel Grahame, I labour under no delusions, but again repeat my steadfast determination, in the event of your maintaining this extraordinary silence, to lay the whole matter before those whose authority is superior even to yours."

"Before his Majesty, doubtless? or the Commander-in-Chief?" asked Colonel Grahame. "Do so, my lord, by all means; but, if you have any real regard for that family honour which seems so weighty a charge, do not summon *me* as a witness."

There was something so threatening in the words, that the earl was quite staggered both in his opinions and his resolution; but, being as obstinate as most weak men, he instantly resumed his interrupted sentence.

"And I shall make it a point of conscience, a religious duty, to obtain for my kinsman some reparation for the injury done to his prospects by such unexampled severity."

"Your lordship's zeal on all such points is too well known for me to doubt the statement one instant," replied Claverhouse, with exasperating politeness.

More irritated than ever, the earl bit his lip furiously; the arrow had flown straight to the mark, and rankled all the more venomously that it was double-barbed; for not only had he forsworn with servile alacrity the religion of his ancestors to adopt the faith which alone found grace in his sovereign's eyes, but had made himself remarkable ever since his *conversion* for the exaggerated punctiliousness which he displayed in following the minutest rites of his new creed—a scrupulosity which contrasted rather ridiculously with certain points of his general morality. He sought in vain some retaliatory answer; the double-edged blade could not be so easily grasped; assailed by a galling fire in front and flank, to which he had no means of replying, he became aware that he had advanced too far, without any correct idea of his opponent's position, while his own lay thoroughly open. To drop metaphor, my lord of Perth, who was quite aware that he was in the wrong as to manner, began to be disagreeably impressed by a suspicion that he had been quite as mistaken as to matter, and to find, as he had often found before, that he had the worst of the argument. The extreme gravity with which Claverhouse had spoken respecting the advisability of keeping quiet rather alarmed him with the idea that, if his family dignity *had* been sullied, his *roué* kinsman was rather the offender than the victim. The first skirmish was over, and he paused in some uncertainty as to how the combat was to be renewed. At last he said,

"I am, I confess, so completely bewildered by the inconsistency of your statements, Colonel Grahame, that it only remains for me to abandon all attempt at fathoming your reasons for such arbitrary interference with a gentleman's actions in the first instance, and such a wanton abuse of irresponsible authority in the second. You have chosen your course,—I shall take mine, as I have had the honour to inform you. I never yet heard that in an affair of gallantry mere military rank gave any right to control even the poorest private gentleman."

"My lord," said Claverhouse, his beautiful dark eyes glowing with liquid fire, and his clear cheek crimsoning to the very temples as the suppressed indignation at last found vent in words—"my lord, I have borne this long enough—too long. Were it not that I believe you to have been, in part at least, deceived by another, I would not have endured for five minutes the tone and manner with which it has been your good pleasure to insult me for the last half-hour, and the sophistry by which you would extenuate the profligate brutality of your cousin. An affair of gallantry! and when did you know me fool enough to interpose between my wild troopers and the excesses they may choose to commit when they injure none but themselves or the enemies of the State? and, as to their private doings, if they *will* waste health and fortune and good repute in dicing and drinking, on sharpers, gamblers, and worthless women, let them look to it! I am no John Knox to take up my parable against vices which I despise but cannot amend, against evil which has existed since the world began, and will exist as long as there are men to betray and injure, and women to be deceived and fooled. But is that a reason that three drunken brawlers, and your cousin the chief, should cruelly assault a modest, helpless girl, a mere child, whose age and innocence should have protected her from the veriest ruffian, and that I, a Scottish gentleman, should hear her agonised shrieks for help and pass by on the other side? You gaze at me like one stupified, my lord; did your chivalrous kinsman tell you anything like this?"

"I certainly heard—I understood—" began Lord Perth, quite dismayed at the unexpected eloquence of his, until now, taciturn antagonist; "that there was great excuse, the excitement of wine——"

"The old song! using one vice to defend another! Noble logic, and quite in the taste of such morality as Mr. Drummond's. He probably also related how, when I presumed to rescue his victim from a danger which had already deprived her of her senses, he assailed me with the coarsest abuse, threatened my life, and was not afraid to offer to me, to *me* his commander, the grossest insult one man can inflict on another, a blow on the face! By heaven!" continued Claverhouse with such haughty passion that the earl almost shrunk from him, "you must deem the hot blood of the Grahames turned to ice in my veins if you expect me to brook any longer the daily sight of the man who had uttered such a threat and not paid the penalty with his life!"

The intense energy with which he spoke was all the more startling from its contrast with the repose and quietude of his usual tone. The Chancellor, whose whole existence was a tissue of weak passions, mean interests, and petty oppressions, had never been able to accustom himself to this volcanic nature, so cold at the surface, so burning beneath, or even to enter into the sentiments which Claverhouse sometimes expressed when urged beyond his habitual serenity. *He* only understood clearly one point, and that he answered.

"You have the remedy in your own hands, Colonel Grahame; there is a reparation for insult which every gentleman may claim, and which my cousin would be but too happy to afford, especially as he considers himself the insulted party, and has, if I mistake not, already demanded a meeting."

"Ay, he challenged me," answered Claverhouse smiling; "and I did myself the pleasure of refusing to soil my good rapier by using it upon him."

"And may I presume to ask *why?*" inquired the earl with portentously knitted brow.

"For two excellent reasons. First, because it would be a source of everlasting delight to the open-mouthed gossips, high and low, to hear and tell how Claver'se had fought hand to hand with one of his own drunken troopers, and I have no intention of providing them with so delightful a pastime; and secondly, because I never would cross steel in private combat with a man whose hand I should blush to touch in public friendship."

"There may be a vast difference in rank and fortune, but birth and descent make the gentleman, and on these points Mr. Drummond is the equal of any one in Edinburgh, even of Colonel Grahame himself," said Lord Perth almost insolently.

"Under favour, my lord earl," replied Claverhouse,

"there is a third essential to the character, failing which, your cousin sinks lower in my eyes than the meanest horse-boy who follows my regiment."

"What do you mean, sir?"

"That your cousin is a dishonoured man, and that he is not publicly so is the effect of a clemency which you chose just now to attribute to some secret motives, the offspring of your own imagination. And the regret I expressed for my conduct towards him only referred to the momentary weakness which allowed him to escape the punishment due to his crimes. Is *that* sufficiently clear, my lord?"

"The *assertion* is a very distinct one," said the earl, who could hardly conceal his agitation, "but such an assertion requires support."

A contemptuous smile played over Colonel Grahame's lips as he answered,

"Most assuredly. The proofs are entirely at your service, in so far as I possess them; for the rest you will do me, I suppose, the honour to accept my word. The facts are these."

The earl, excessively disturbed, shifted his position, had recourse to his snuff-box, and tried in vain to present an undisturbed countenance, conscious as he was that Colonel Grahame could read through any veil of affected indifference the irritation which devoured him, not more at the discovery of his cousin's course of life, than at his own discomfiture. He would gladly have rejected the explanation he had so imperiously demanded, but his pride rebelled; he could not hit upon any feasible means of breaking off the interview without compromising too much his own dignity, and, after a few moments silence, moved his head as a sort of sullen indication that he intended to listen. Colonel Grahame began, looking steadily at his companion.

CHAPTER XII.

A GENTLEMAN OF THE OLD SCHOOL.

A very worthy knave, a proper fellow,
Prompt with his hands, at backsword, broadsword, dagger—
Loving all these, but specially the last.

"It would of course be quite superfluous to make any comment upon Mr. Drummond's habits and conduct, with which I have neither the wish nor the power to interfere. Neither would it be much to the purpose to enlarge upon certain singular reports current about two years ago, respecting the poisoning of a horse belonging to Captain Ogilvie, by whose failure Mr. Drummond is known to have won heavy bets at the Leith races. Such matters are only trifles."

The earl winced visibly.

"But your lordship may remember, about three months ago, the mysterious death of the young laird of Burniclaw, elder brother of my new cornet, Lindsay, who thereby succeeded to the estates."

"Perfectly. I chanced to be near the spot when the body was discovered; it was pierced with seven dagger wounds in the back and neck. But what has that to do——"

"One moment,—you will learn soon enough. About ten days back, in the course of a raid against some troublesome Whigs who had kept us on the alert for a week or more midst dargle and glen, we chanced to fall in with what, under the disguise of a conventicle, was simply a political meeting for carrying on treasonable correspondence with Holland. The rebels were all well armed, and a sharp skirmish followed. We dispersed them, leaving half a dozen or so on the spot, but took only two prisoners, on account of the darkness which favoured their escape. One of these contrived to give us the slip on our road towards Rutherglen; the other was desperately wounded; but some papers found on him induced me to spare his life, in order to have him regularly examined in Council. We passed the night in the village; and, after seeing everything made secure, I was preparing to retire to my own quarters, when one of our men came to say that the prisoner earnestly requested to see me. I refused at first; but, upon the messenger representing the dying state and extreme urgency of the prisoner, I went to him. The Whig fellow begged some private speech; and, when the room was cleared, asked me if I did not recognise him. I rarely forget a face I have once seen; and, after a moment's reflection, remembered him as having been in your kinsman's service, and dismissed by him about the period of Burnielaw's murder, on an ostensible charge of robbery."

"Gideon Armstrong!" exclaimed Lord Perth.

"That was the name," said Claverhouse.

"And I remember," added the earl, "feeling much surprised at the time at such an accusation being laid on him, for he had always seemed a very attached servant, and had been with my cousin for fifteen years. He was born on my estate."

"Armstrong was dreadfully wounded; two pistol-shots had passed through his lungs, and it was evident that he had but a short time to live. He wished to make a confession before he died; and that not so much to ease his own conscience as to revenge himself on his former master. It was he who struck the blows by which Henry Lindsay died; but he had done so at Drummond's command, and under promise of a large sum of money."

The earl turned paler than ever, and softly dried the large drops of moisture that stood on his brow. Like an experienced surgeon watching a patient under the knife, Claverhouse never for one instant released his hearer from the scrutiny his deep eyes kept over him.

"You may easily conceive that, at the first blush of such a disclosure, I took steps to assure myself of its correctness by every means in my power. I wrote down with my own hand the man's deposition, taken upon oath; and, after reading it over to him to be certain of its accuracy, insisted upon his signing it. He could not write, but affixed his mark in presence of two witnesses whom I summoned."

"Witnesses? Merciful heaven!" exclaimed the earl.

"They knew nothing of what the paper contained, reassure yourself, my lord," interrupted Claverhouse. "The document—I have it by me—was long and confused, but its gist was this: Drummond had for some time past been passionately attached—if such a term can be used for such a purpose—to a girl named Marion Craigie, who lived in the very street where young Burnielaw's corpse was found. She had been Drummond's acknowledged mistress, and had, I believe, by her extravagance and propensity for gambling, assisted in the ruin of his dilapidated property. He was, even at that period, overwhelmed with debt, and had had recourse to the most desperate expedients to procure money. Amongst others, I could instance a forgery, which I have every reason to suspect was committed in my name; but of this I have no legal proof."

"I knew of his embarrassments, but extravagance is too common a fault amongst our young men for me to have attached any importance to the circumstance," replied the earl. "For heaven's sake, if there is worse behind, let me know it at once!"

"*Worse*, in a legal sense, there is not, my lord; but the details of the crime surround it with a halo of such meanness, falsehood, and base selfishness, as to enhance in my eyes even such guilt as his. Drummond had long suspected his mistress of having transferred her favour to the laird of Burnielaw, whose wealth and inexperience tempted her cupidity. She was very handsome too, they say; and the hairbrained youth fell into her snares as easily as others had done before. Suspicion once awakened soon became certainty, certainty begot revenge—and that revenge Drummond resolved to have, not by the uncertain chances of an open rencontre, but secret, swift, and deadly. By the threat of betraying to the Council some near relations of Armstrong's who were bitter Presbyterians, and by the influence of a valuable bribe, he succeeded in inducing his servant to track Lindsay on his visit to Marion Craigie. Armstrong, to make the attack as secure as possible, armed himself with a Spanish dagger of his master's, of marvellous temper and keenness. That dagger Armstrong kept, and I have it now."

The earl made no reply, borne down by the distinct, consistent narrative, which many trifling occurrences within his own knowledge tended to confirm. The tables were so completely turned upon him now, that he hardly dared to open his lips, lest each word should bring forth some blacker tale of shame.

"I will not inquire whether the fact had anything to do with your cousin's preference of private assassination to open redress for the injury he conceived himself to have sustained; but young Lindsay, as you know, was a very powerful man, and reckoned the best swordsman in the Guards, which is equivalent to saying the best in Scotland."

"My cousin's *courage* at least has never been impugned until now," said Lord Perth, whose miserable vanity asserted itself even upon such an occasion.

"With that I have no concern—I merely suggest the question. The prisoner's confession proceeds to say that, after the murder (which took place on the night of December 18th), he had been alarmed by the vigorous search which was prosecuted, and demanded of his master the reward of his guilt, in order to place himself in safety, in case the doer of the deed should be discovered. But this Drummond, who had lost largely at play on the very evening when his accomplice was executing his detestable orders, refused to pay, well knowing that Armstrong dare not accuse him of prompting the crime without by the same act betraying his own share in it. Enraged at this perfidy, and dreading every hour to be discovered, Armstrong took the resolution of flying to the West, which he put in practice successfully, taking with him the dagger marked with Drummond's name, as the only witness he possessed against him. This man, who had not scrupled to sell himself for gold to commit a foul murder, and who could perhaps scarcely have been induced, even after what had passed, to betray his master, was driven to revenge by the same means that master took to account for his disappearance. I cannot say how the report reached his ears that Drummond had accused him of dishonesty, but from that moment, as he told me, he had sworn to repay him if ever he could compass it without sacrificing himself. Dying as he was, he had nothing to fear from the law, and therefore chose me as the depository of his confession, in the hope of thereby ruining the man who had seduced him into crime and then basely abandoned and slandered him. There is said to be honour among thieves, but there seems little between assassins, methinks!" added Claverhouse, with a contemptuous laugh.

"Is that all?" asked Lord Perth, who, writhing

under the sense of his family disgrace, and still more at being, so to speak, at the mercy of the man he feared, and whose contempt galled him more cruelly than that of any other human creature, hardly dared to raise his eyes. "Is that all, or am I to sit here much longer and listen to the history of my own blood relation's crimes?"

"My lord, it was your own choice," replied Colonel Grahame, severely. "Had you taken the advice I offered, and believed in the justice of a man against whom his worst enemies never proffered a dishonourable charge, in preference to the tales of one from whose vices I know you to have already suffered, you would have spared yourself the pain of hearing all this, and me the necessity of confessing that I have deeply erred in not bringing Mr. Drummond to public justice. What untimely consideration for private feelings, unpardonable under any circumstances, but most of all on such an occasion, could have moved me to spare him, I know not, and my mind misgives me that I, and perhaps not I alone, shall have reason to repent it. Nay, my lord!" he continued, as the earl by an instinctive movement drew his rapier hilt closer to his hand, "not in that fashion, or in broad daylight,—but beware the dagger which drank the life-blood of Henry Lindsay, and the poison which destroyed Marion Craigie within a week of her hapless lover!"

The earl's sallow complexion grew a livid white—he started up, and resting with both hands upon the table for support, exclaimed—

"Good God! Can these things be true?"

Claverhouse said nothing, but rising deliberately, unlocked a small drawer in a cabinet close behind him. He drew from its recesses a long three-sided stiletto, which bore manifest traces of having been stained with blood and carelessly dried, together with a large folded paper. These he laid before the Chancellor. Lord Perth stretched out his hand mechanically to take the dagger, then drew it back, as if the dark stains had scorched him.

"Read that paper, my lord," said Claverhouse sternly, "it contains the evidence of my assertions."

"I never doubted the integrity of your word, Colonel Grahame."

"You did, Lord Perth, and in a manner which nothing can justify. Read it, or I will do so myself."

A momentary flush of anger changed the ashy hue of the Chancellor's face, as he unfolded the paper and tried to peruse it.

"I cannot!" he said, throwing it from him, "the letters burn my eyes."

"Look, at least, at the signatures, my lord," said Claverhouse, almost moved by his distress, which confirmed him every moment more strongly in a long-cherished suspicion—"they are those of men of irreproachable repute."

"They are, they are!" replied the earl, turning to the end, where stood the irregular ill-formed mark of the assassin, followed by the names of Kincaid and Charteris, two of Claverhouse's gentlemen privates. "But, Colonel Grahame, is it generous in you thus to add proof to proof, heap charge upon charge, to overwhelm a friend?"

"You treated me in no friendly fashion, my lord; and, when my word is doubted, the doubters must submit to have it supported as *I* choose, not as they may desire. But I will spare you the rest, which is not necessary to my own vindication, I having already, I hope, succeeded in convincing you that in this miserable affair my only fault has been one not often laid to my charge,—that of unseasonable leniency."

"The *rest!* What more?" exclaimed Lord Perth. "Speak at once and plainly, Laird of Claverhouse!"

Claverhouse hesitated, then resuming his seat opposite the earl, said, in a milder tone than he had yet used, "You have nothing worse to hear of than loaded dice, and one may well let that pass; the shame of treachery and murder can scarcely be deepened by dishonesty. Sorry am I, that I should have been forced in self-defence to reveal to you the villainy of your son."

"My *son!* He is no son of mine," said Lord Perth, hardly able to articulate the falsehood beneath the fixed gaze which seemed to lay his soul bare.

"You will excuse my believing the contrary, and, as I *know* the facts to stand thus, any further denial will neither honour you nor convince me. Tush, my lord!" he continued, with an ironical smile, as his companion broke in, "what boots it denying a fact that a hundred people suspect, and of which I am certain? We must cut this matter short, I see, or words might arise between us, more easily spoken than recalled.

Therefore, to the point. I, whom you accused of ruining the reputation of a noble family, have saved it at the expense of my own self-respect; but this I swear, that were Drummond fifty times your son—were he my own—if ever he venture to present himself before me again, I will order my dragoons to shoot him down like a wild beast; nay, I would do it myself, as remorselessly as ever I slew armed rebel or renegade Whig. He knows me, and you know me, my lord—I have given him fair warning of what he may expect if he remains in Scotland, and I tell you, that you may decide between that one hope of saving him, and the chances of a legal trial. See now which of these two paths you will take, for, by mine honourable word, you have no other choice!"

Crushed by the inflexible firmness of Colonel Grahame, weak in adversity as insolent in prosperity, unable to look his position honestly in the face, the earl sat abject and trembling. He had not even the poor courage to resent the authoritative tone of his colleague; natural alarm at the imminent danger of his worthless son, indescribable vexation at beholding Claverhouse in possession of a secret hitherto concealed, and which his recent marriage and his wife's jealous temper rendered it more desirable than ever to maintain, horror at crimes from which even his unscrupulous but feeble nature revolted, chased each other through his mind in such wild confusion as to render him for some minutes incapable of forming a decision of any kind. But uppermost of all, in that selfish and worldly heart, rose the dread of personal exposure; the shrinking from public scorn which would fall on all connected with the murderer, the liar, and cheat, and a determination to free himself by any means, however servile, of the remotest danger to his own influence and interest. That must be done first and foremost: Colonel Grahame's silence secured on terms as advantageous as possible: then, perhaps, he might have leisure to express a little virtuous detestation of crimes which had this particular and crowning baseness, that they drew down such alarm and trouble upon himself. But how to open the request,—how to put the humiliating fact that his family credit depended upon a word from Colonel Grahame's lips?

He rested his head upon his hand, and strove to find words of entreaty not too intolerably humble, but none would come; he was hedged in on every side, and there was no time for delay or negociation. A trial would have been death to his son, and have brought to light such a mass of infamy as must overwhelm the name and house of Drummond with odium. The risk was not even to be thought of. He passed his hand over his brow, wet with the cold drops of irrepressible terror, and looked anxiously at Claverhouse; but his countenance expressed only passionless expectation—neither information nor hope could be gathered from it.

"Colonel Grahame," said the earl, after vainly waiting for his companion to speak, "you have acted hitherto with such noble generosity, that I can have no hesitation in throwing myself absolutely into your hands, so sure am I of finding sympathy and assistance. You perceive the unhappy position into which, without any fault of mine, I have been forced; as the head of my house I am bound to use every means to protect its reputation, and the circumstances which surround us forbid me to risk the slightest portion of whatever political or social influence I may possess. If this tale were to fall into the hands of my enemies, I should be ruined; insecure as every thing now is, I never could weather the storm which intriguers and slanderers are only waiting an opportunity to raise. You well know, Colonel Grahame, all that I have been obliged to sacrifice to defend myself against the insidious attacks of those who envy me my poor share of our Sovereign's favour, and how gladly they would avail themselves of any handle against me or mine: to you I appeal, trusting that you will continue to exercise the same delicate discretion, which must command my eternal gratitude; and I cannot think that any one would appeal to Colonel Grahame in vain, still less a friend and colleague of such old standing."

"You do me too much honour, my lord," said Colonel Grahame, with cold civility, for he could scarcely repress his disgust at the heartless egotism which saw in such infamy no darker shade than danger to a political power already precarious, and the fear of sharing, in however remote a degree, the reprobation of society. The contempt with which he listened to this abject request for pity, from the man who an hour before had treated him with such supercilious arrogance, spoke in his face.

"Let me entreat you for an answer, Claverhouse," said Lord Perth, with a look of intense anxiety: "you are not wont to be so tardy in giving a decision. For the sake of our old friendship, have some regard for the cruel suspense under which you *must* be aware that I labour."

"My lord," answered Claverhouse, firmly, "I am a plain soldier, and no lawyer to make black appear white, or white black. I have told you freely my opinion of your son; and I shall tell you as distinctly my irrevocable determination concerning him—too merciful a one, when I reflect upon the fate he richly merits. As to the friendship on which you so confidently lean, I might observe that it has rarely served me in difficulties; but, as I have compromised my duty for the first time in my life, I am not unwilling that you should profit by the error." He paused awhile, with a look of scorn on his handsome, disdainful face, which seemed to light quite as much upon himself as upon the servile courtier he addressed—then resumed, marking his words with decisive clearness: "Your son must leave Edinburgh within a week—Scotland within a month—never to return to it during my lifetime—any infraction of this condition leaving me entirely free to act as I choose, under whatever circumstances may present themselves. *You*, my lord, can judge of the probable issue."

"And," said Lord Perth, "is Colonel Grahame not afraid that such a condition may be commented upon, as inferring a dread of scandal for his regiment, or an avoidance of personal danger to himself?"

"I believe I have already given some proofs of my ability to maintain and extend the reputation of my regiment, without the assistance of Lord Perth's advice: as to myself, those who are pleased to imagine that I pay Mr. Drummond the compliment of being afraid of him, must be responsible for the absurdity of the opinion. I have never been in the habit of wearing a cuirass in private life," continued Claverhouse, passing his hand beneath his velvet doublet and fine lawn shirt, "nor do I wish to begin now—although some folks might think the precaution justifiable, if your son remained in Edinburgh. Waste no care on me, my lord—your own affairs are sufficiently pressing. Shall he go, or stay?"

"He shall go!" said the earl, with gloomy irritation: "he shall go! and rid me of the intolerable burden of supporting and feeding his vices. As for yourself, Colonel Grahame, by whatever means you became master of a secret, which I trusted was hidden from every one but myself and—and—one other person, I implore you to forget that ever such knowledge was yours—to bury it in oblivion, as deep as that which I venture to hope will cover all that has passed to-day. Your simple word will suffice to me—may I count upon it?"

"As regards your relationship to Mr. Drummond, certainly—the part of tale-bearer and scandal-monger is not one for me to play. And now, my lord, any other request that you may have to make, I will endeavour, in reason, to comply with, in order to prove to you that I am incapable of personal rancour on the subject."

"Then I should wish," said the earl, "that until I can make some arrangements for sending my—Drummond abroad, you would, to prevent all idle comments on the subject, replace him in his former station, and allow him, for a short time, to resume his accustomed duties. It may, perhaps, be an additional inducement for you to comply with my wishes, to learn that the peerage which his Majesty intends to confer——"

With flashing eyes, Colonel Grahame started from his seat, and struck his hand fiercely on the table.

"'Sdeath! my lord of Perth!" he exclaimed, "either you are become idiotic, or think me so! but, if you are trying to exhaust my patience, I warn you it is at an end! Is it not enough that I have rescued your villanous son's neck from the gallows, when for a tithe of his offences better men have swung there—and am I to be insulted by a demand to lick the dust before *him*, whom all honest men must abhor as the most loathsome insect that crawls in the dust? to take shame to myself, by receiving him back, even for an hour, while my blood is yet boiling with indignation at the outrageous accusations which he dared, no later than yesterday morning, to proffer to my face, until I could have slain him where he stood, had he not been too foul a thing to fall by a gentleman's sword? Our conference is ended—you have my promise, for which I shall never cease to despise myself—but the conditions it is now my *will* to alter—if within a week I have not *authentic* assurance that your son has left Scotland, I shall lay the whole case before the competent authorities, and transfer every proof in my possession to that of my friend Lord Balcarras, who I doubt not will be as prompt in obtaining justice for *his* kinsman as you in seeking it for *yours*. That is my final word—and I will listen to no other proposition. Your servant!"

The earl had risen also; dismayed at the signal failure of this last effort to obtain easier terms—he now hastily tried to smooth away, protest, explain, extenuate—but Claverhouse was utterly intractable, and the chancellor was forced to take his departure, in a state of mind little more tranquil than that in which Drummond awaited his return.

"The paltry hound!" said Claverhouse to himself, as the door closed on his retreating visitor. "I thought I knew him, but never could I have guessed the existence of such unredeemed egotism! Not one blush of genuine shame! not one sentence of noble indignation! not a thought beyond his own miserable griping interests—Public opinion—men's chattering tongues—the love of place and pension—the fear of forfeiting his—ha! ha!—*his* fair name! and these were the first, the only thoughts of the man whose son had just been branded before his eyes and ears as coward and liar—assassin and thief! God! I should have died!"

He strode up and down for a moment, with curled lip and sparkling eye—then muttered to himself, as solitary men are often wont to do,

"So, for that vain, selfish man, I have done what many a more deserving one has sued in vain to win. I have borne with threats and bribes, both more endurable than his fawning pretence of friendship.

Has he not for ten years crept before me as he did just now, till my soul sickened, only to lie, intrigue, and backbite, where his end was won and there was nothing more to be gained? But I have him fairly bitted now, I fancy—let him kick if he dares. Aha, my lord of Perth! you thought to ride roughshod over Claverhouse! The steed is not foaled that shall bear you on that errand!"

"Lie there, mute witness!" he said, replacing in the drawer the bloodstained dagger; "lie there. I have been grinding with my own hands thy fellow, destined, perchance, to taste my heart's blood. Was ever folly greater than ill-timed clemency? did I ever give way to such false pity that I did not dearly abye it? And yet, knowing that in these two men I had two mortal enemies, like a silly woman I listened to the pleadings of secret pity for the agonies of an unhappy father, and sought to spare him a knowledge which would have blasted my own heart, instead of walking in the straight line of duty. Like father, like son! the father sells his conscience, the son his friend; the representative of the knightly Drummonds of old thinks shame no shame discreetly hidden, and a villain no villain unless he be found out. But it is all of a piece—a child of dishonour, he has lived in vice, to die, perhaps, a felon's death—the reward he has laboured for."

He rested his chin on his hand, with an expression of stern melancholy on every feature, then sought amongst the papers scattered before him until he found that containing the confession of Armstrong's guilt.

"And this may sooner or later be my end! Strange how every fibre shrinks from the thought! I ask no nobler fate than a soldier's gallant death—I ask no sweeter rest than a soldier's bloody bed—but to perish like a dog by the hand of some vile bravo!—poisoned, perhaps —— Pshaw! what folly!"

With a short bitter laugh he threw the paper into the drawer, locked it, and, calling his servant, prepared to set out for the Council. There was no trace on his countenance of the morning's agitation—no shade of passion marred its calm beauty; but there was, perhaps, an additional inflexibility in his always uncompromising line of argument and conduct; and when, once or twice, the chancellor met his eye, that nobleman was observed to yield an opinion or a project more easily than seemed quite natural to those who knew him best. That was all.

CHAPTER XIII.

AN OLD TALE AND OFTEN TOLD.

Love at first sight, first born and heir to all!
Made this night thus.

TENNYSON.

WHILST all these events were transpiring in regions too high for such modest folk as the widow Scott and her daughter to suspect that they had aught in common with the noble inhabitants thereof, circumstances as interesting, perhaps more so, to the reader, were slowly but surely establishing a powerful link of sympathy between the heroine of our tale and the very man whom, up to that moment, she had so honestly feared and abhorred.

During many days following her dangerous night's adventures, the changes and chances of that curious episode in their retired life had afforded an unceasing source of wonder, terror, delight, and comment to good Madam Scott—as she was always called by her neighbours and gossips. ("For," said old Janet, the porteress, "wasna she sister's bairn to the auld laird o' Raeburn —a daft cankered auld body he was, sure enough, but of as gude bluid as ony in Eskdale—and hadna she been a minister's wife, and wasna the bairn Alice as douce and weel educate a lassie as ye would meet in a lang simmer day—that could write and read English as brawly as Maister Knockslie the dominic, forby doing white seam and fine sewing, and broidery baith in gowd and siller?") The necessity for observing complete discretion with all but her daughter increased tenfold the ardour with which she discussed the subject in its minutest points; and we do not think it a very serious imputation upon the good lady's character to conjecture that, no evil effects of any kind having ensued, she would have felt a sort of void in not having it to talk about. I appeal to all who are acquainted with her excellent countrywomen as to the correctness of this supposition.

Alice, on her side, took at first no inconsiderable share in the animated conversations which beguiled weary hours of the invalid with something of the interest of a drama; but when, after a time, every accident of the night had been passed in full review, she began to experience a certain reluctance to renew the recital of some portions of her story; and it was only with an effort that she could bring herself to speak of Claverhouse. Her mother soon perceived this, and attributed it to the disagreeable remembrances which must naturally be connected with him. She therefore gave up questioning and commenting which appeared unwelcome, and, save for two or three daily references to her providential escape, and emphatic cautions to prudence every time the girl was forced to set her foot out of doors, the subject gradually dropped between them.

Alice rejoiced at this—not that she feared to recal it, not that she disliked speaking of Colonel Grahame, but because, on the contrary, she had begun to perceive that his name itself was assuming too delightful and dangerous a fascination. So she tried, by interdicting to herself, and, as far as possible, to her mother, all mention of everything connected with him, to shun the importunate image which, long ere she knew it, had settled irrevocably in every fibre of her young brain.

From the hour in which she met Claverhouse his memory had haunted her, and in truth this was little to be wondered at. Alice was a girl of very peculiar temperament, not easily elevated or depressed by trifles of everyday occurrence; the very strength and tenacity of her feelings deprived them of that elasticity which is so valuable a defence against the trials of life; she was one of those women who can live and die devoted to a single idea, but who often pass through the world in apparent insensibility to love, from the constancy with which they seek an ideal object, never to be attained. Gifted from her infancy with a passionate admiration of beauty, whether in nature or art, the craving for refinement, for something beyond the coarse cold realities of her daily walk of labour and quiet endurance, had grown almost insupportable since she exchanged the free fresh air and sweet scenery of her country home for the close dull lanes of a crowded city. She fought with this longing, she forced it down and trampled upon it as a rebellion to God's will, she prayed that it might not be counted to her as a sin—but the sixth sense would not be stifled, the young and imaginative spirit *would* soar; and, whilst those around her praised her tender patience with a sickly and often fretful mother, her steady industry and modest piety, her whole inner life was one continuous struggle with the unquenchable poetry of a nature sensitive and romantic in proportion, not to its weakness, but to its strength—a rare and beautiful, but dangerous gift. At length, on the darkest night of her life, in the midst of the most terrible distress she had ever experienced, she had been thrown, as it were, into the arms of one who was the very embodiment of her wildest fancies; and in that moment the smouldering embers shot into flame, the misty images of her brain took shape and soul; she loved, though as yet she knew it not, with all a pure-hearted woman's intense and spiritual fervour. Too late to save her came the knowledge of who he was;—gratitude, admiration, and that mysterious alchemy of nature which no human eye can analyse, no human pen define, had already transmuted hatred into love, and her fate was fixed.

It was with a bewildering mixture of self-condemnation and exceeding wonder that the poor girl first awoke to a consciousness of the extraordinary change which one short hour had wrought in her whole being, when the grateful remembrance which she had at first cherished as so natural and right, instead of fading into placid indifference, gradually deepened into an ineffable yearning to see him again; when the mere sound of his name from another's lips would bring a burning colour to her cheek—of joy, if a kindly voice added to it one charitable word—but more often of intolerable pain when it was coupled with some epithet of dislike—when, amidst her daily occupations, her nightly fancies, one image was ever uppermost—the vision of those lustrous, melancholy, passionate eyes, whose strange charm had thrilled her very heartstrings—when all this became so clear to her that no ignorance could escape, no self-delusion shun the conviction, who shall describe what Alice suffered?

Those who only know love as the happy and authorised interchange of mutual affection, or even as darkened by sorrow for separation from an object by whom our tenderness is reciprocated, and in whose faith and fidelity we calmly repose, can never conceive the long feverish struggles of a passion like this, resistless in its fervour, unselfish and immaterial, yet opposed to every acquired habit of mind, and bringing with it the subversion of every idea inculcated by education and prejudice. And here we would be fully understood. The only knowledge which could yet have crushed in the bud the new upspringing love—that of his marriage—was, by one of those singular chances woven round the destiny of some beings, withheld from Alice; had it ever reached her, her love must have died out at once, though life had perished with it; never, for one instant, in that pure heart, could it have survived the shock; but, ignorant as she still continued of this all-important fact, the sting was not there. *That* lay in the dread which filled her mind, lest, by loving unsought, she might be degrading herself below a woman's modesty,—lest, by loving the enemy of her sect, her class,—report said of everything good and holy,—she might be committing a sin of the deepest dye. These were the fears which wrung her tender conscience with such exquisite pain; these the sufferings which made her cry in the heaviness of her spirit—

"Oh, what folly is this? what possesses me? Oh that I could wake to find it all a dream, and be my happy blithesome self once more!" And clasping her little hands, weary with their ceaseless toil, over her aching temples, she would try, in her innocent grief, to *think* herself back into the same Alice as before; to view Colonel Grahame not as her helper and defender, the chivalrous gentleman, the generous friend of the orphan girl, the realisation of every romantic dream she had ever formed, but as the ruthless soldier, at whose presence even bearded men grew pale. In vain! memory, gratitude, every awakened instinct of her new existence, rebelled; the die had long been cast, and she might as well have hoped by prayers and tears to raise her lost father from his mossy grave in the green kirkyard, as to conjure back by any effort of will a phase of her life gone by for ever—to wipe out the past and make it as though it never had been.

And yet, strange to say, amidst this constantly recurring strife between the overpowering might of love, and the equally unconquerable voice of conscientious resistance, Alice was not wholly unhappy. In the fiercest moments of her inward pain, she was often visited by gleams of joy so bright and delicious as to repay her for all she endured. Never of hope—

for surely a love more remote from the indulgence of any such extravagant fancy could not exist—but of enchanting reverie, in which she lived over again every second of that time so swiftly passed, so poorly valued then,—which she would gladly have brought back at the price of all the wretchedness which preceded it. At such hours she would not have exchanged *her* right to love him, the memory of his delicate generosity, the possession of that rich mine of delight, for any other treasure this world could have bestowed—and round that once dreaded image came clustering now every trait of lenient mercy, of chivalrous honour, of unselfish devotion, which had found their way even on to the lips of his enemies, to enhance the halo with which her adoring imagination had invested it. What mattered it that others should fear him? *she* could not;—what mattered it that he was called cruel, intolerant, revengeful, by others? she only thought of what he had proved to her. If the whole world had been leagued to hate and revile him, by one humble friend he was fervently loved, one heart, at least, was bound to him for ever. His last words, so earnest—almost touching—rang in her ear; she could never weary of recalling with a thrill of timid joy that her good will had seemed worth seeking—nay, had been asked by him.

"For the love of justice and truth, for the memory of this night's meeting, for the sake of one who would not willingly be hated by all the world—try, if you will and can, to think less hardly of John Grahame of Claverhouse."

"If he only knew, if he could only have guessed, how too, *too* easy the task would be!" she would murmur to herself; "if he only dreamed that poor little Alice would die to requite him; must live to love him —to pity him for the evil he has done to others; to pray for him and bless him for what he did for her——"

And this was the conclusion of all her doubts and fears and self-denying stoicism! Alas, when was it ever otherwise in such a nature as hers? "Successful love may sate itself away," but love such as hers, born in sorrow, watered by tears—that knows neither hope nor desire, that is content to feed upon the shadow of the past, to merge all thoughts of self in single-hearted adoration of the one idol—such love is by its very essence imperishable. The heart that is capable of conceiving and sustaining it may break, but cannot change; the impress once given cannot be effaced until the material itself be destroyed.

The affectionate and devoted spirit which Alice inherited from her father was mingled, in no slight proportion, with her brother Norman's iron tenacity of disposition. Both stood her in good stead now, nerving her to exertion, and giving her courage to act and bear, where a feebler nature would perhaps have failed. She was her mother's sole support, the stay of her declining years and precarious health; Alice would have worked her fingers to the bone—would have undergone martyrdom—rather than have allowed her mother to want any comfort, or even luxury, her labour could procure; or grieved her by betraying a sorrow no human hand could heal. With the angelic patience of true womanly heroism—that silent heroism which has, since the world began, endured more to soothe pain than man's so-called valour ever braved to inflict it—she went on her quiet way, busy, cheerful, and self-subdued—smiling to hide a heavy heart, and never by word or look adding one touch of bitterness to her mother's afflictions. She was one to "die and make no sign."

Madam Scott, who loved her daughter as much as she deserved—*more* she could not—saw with much regret how pale and slender she grew, as day after day she arose unrefreshed, and lay down to rest sweet and uncomplaining, but restless and unable to sleep. Her penetration, however, never compassed any approach to the real cause of this change; she naturally conceived it to arise solely from the unwholesome atmosphere of the city, from want of exercise and amusement, as well as from the constant work necessary for their support, and in which she could, unfortunately, be of little assistance. She was therefore delighted when an incident occurred which promised to be a source of interest and pleasure to Alice—little suspecting that this particular circumstance would, in the end, only contribute to aggravate the evil. To understand what will follow we must go back a little way.

When Alice was a child, her father had been the minister of a parish in the Mearns, near which stood the ancestral seat of the noble family of Glencarrig. The last earl, a very young man, had been unfortunately killed in one of the first skirmishes with the Covenanting party; and his widow, with her infant son and newborn daughter, had retired thither from society, to nurse her uncontrollable grief in solitude. She was a lady of the house of Grahame, and belonged in consequence to the Episcopalian Church; but, having become acquainted with Mr. Scott, she could not refuse to acknowledge the worth and piety of the Presbyterian minister; and their acquaintance gradually ripened into solid friendship. When the first excess of her mourning had subsided, she began to take pleasure in his society; and, although on many subjects they differed—and agreed to differ, the young countess was at once soothed and strengthened by his pious, affectionate exhortations, especially when supported by an example of resignation in the midst of calamities almost as great as her own—for he had lost three of his children at one fell swoop. Mrs. Scott, although a more common-place and uninteresting character than her husband, shared the countess's regard; and little Alice, the youngest of their stricken flock, who was born a few months after Lady Glencarrig's arrival, naturally became the playmate and friend of the little earl and his sister Flora—both rather older than herself. Nor was her father at all displeased at the intimacy. He was, as we have said, a very tolerant and liberal-minded man for his age; he had no fears, as many a one of his sect might have had, that his young daughter would be contaminated by intercourse with those whose form of worship differed from his own. He was fully sensible of the advantages likely to accrue to Alice from the companionship of a woman so amiable, so refined, and in every way superior, as Lady Glencarrig, and appreciated all the value of the instruction which the child was in the habit of receiving along with Lady Flora. He had few prejudices to overcome; so, after exacting and receiving from the countess a promise that she should not be taught to dance, or allowed to read romances, he felt satisfied to leave her in a great measure under the care of her noble friends, attending scrupulously himself to her religious education, but trusting the rest to them, and thankful for having been thus enabled to provide for a necessity which his own heavy duties and his wife's delicate health rendered it likely would have been very imperfectly supplied at home.

Alice and Flora grew up together until the age of fourteen, spending the greater part of their time at the castle. Sometimes the countess would allow her daughter, as a reward for good behaviour, to pass a day or two at the pretty manse; but in general Alice was domesticated at Glencarrig House, and enjoyed the benefit of the instructions administered by Madam Rachel, the countess's *dame de compagnie*, who acted also as governess to Lady Flora. That young damsel, full of the spirits natural to her age, in the pride of rank and budding beauty, was not always amenable to discipline; and poor Madam Rachel had often a hard struggle to enforce obedience to her mild authority. Flora's generous and affectionate, but hot and volatile, disposition manifested itself in a defiance half playful, half resolute, of any authority but her mother's, and any influence but Alice's. To either of these she would yield readily; while the good duenna's admonitions and reproofs were terribly thrown away. In consequence, it almost always happened that Alice, although the younger of the two, surpassed Flora in everything they undertook; for she worked hard, and studied with a downright goodwill that often amused and sometimes provoked her less diligent friend, but which made her a great pet with Madam Rachel, and a favourite with the countess, who saw in her the elements of a superior character. She learned in this way to read and write as perfectly as the state of education at that period permitted, to cipher accurately, to speak a little French, to sing with taste and simplicity, and to work with exquisite skill the various kinds of embroidery then in vogue, and in which she showed from the first a fanciful inventive delight. However meagre at the present day may seem such a catalogue of accomplishments, it was very extensive then; many ladies of high rank could not have shown one so complete. But Alice had been richly repaid for the toilsome hours spent in acquiring knowledge, to which there was then no royal road, by the ecstatic delight with which she had pored over the contents of a very small library at the castle, and the books in her father's still smaller collection, until Lady Flora and her brother surnamed her "The Dominie," and swore (at least, we mean his lordship did so; Heaven forbid we should cast such an imputation on a young lady of quality!) that Elsie Scott was qualifying to succeed her father at the manse, and would be to the full as learned a preacher. But Alice laughed pleasantly at their jests, and studied on to the best of her abilities, caring only for her father's approving smile and her mother's look of innocent pride in her daughter's talents. She had that reward, and was satisfied.

So time passed on, and Alice began to grow up into a beautiful and discreet lassie—rather too quiet and sedate perhaps for her years, but cheerful and lovable, with a ready spring of kindly sympathy and a charm of modest sweetness that won every heart. Her affection for her parents and constant desire to please them repaid them for the sacrifice they had made in parting with her for so long a time; and half consoled them for the moody waywardness of Norman, who was already beginning to tread in the steps of his uncle and namesake—one of the stern enthusiasts who had been most prominent in the insurrections of the Pentland Hills and Bothwell. The lad had early manifested a decided leaning towards the ascetic pride and morbid gloom which characterised the rigid Cameronians, and it was in the hope of checking this tendency that his father had sent him, when about seventeen years of age, to Edinburgh, to follow a mercantile pursuit. This change was soon followed by a second. Mr. Scott removed from his parish, and accepted the charge of another, situated in Haddingtonshire.

It was no small sacrifice to him to leave the spot where the happiest and saddest hours of his life had been spent—to which he had brought home his newly-wedded wife—where his children had been born and died—where every nook and corner spoke to him of a well-spent Christian life: but, in addition to several reasons unimportant to us, he had one which may well seem cogent. He had observed, with much uneasiness, the attentions which the young earl bestowed upon his pretty Alice; and, although he was but a boy of sixteen and Alice a mere child, yet it was not easy to foresee the amount of unhappiness which might ensue, if this boyish affection were to ripen in the course of three or four years into a serious attachment. At present, Alice only regarded him as a favourite companion, whose old acquaintance, youth, gaiety, and good humour prevented her from feeling their disparity of station: but this could not last for ever, and, like a wise man, Mr. Scott applied the remedy as a preventive, instead of waiting until a cure was required. Lady Glencarrig parted from the family with sincere regret; and Flora was, for a time, perfectly inconsolable. The young earl was absent, pursuing his studies at Aberdeen, when the "flitting" took place; but when he returned, and found his companion, gossip, and foster-sister, pretty Elsie Scott, gone for ever, he displayed quite as much sorrow as his sister, and perhaps felt even more.

In those days correspondence was by no means so easy a process as it has since become—the width of three or four counties was an immense distance, and the two girls had few opportunities of communication during the space of nearly three years which elapsed between the removal and death of Mr. Scott. We have already related the motives which induced the widow and her child to establish themselves in the capital, as well as the circumstances in which they stood; and it had been, up to the moment of which we write, a real trouble to Alice, that the friend she loved so dearly should have completely forgotten to afford her any news of herself for so long a period. That regret had been somewhat deadened by the keener pain of her new trial; but, like all Alice's feelings, once rooted, it remained unchanged.

CHAPTER XIV.

AN OLD FRIEND WITH A NEW FACE.

> Who art thou? . . . . . .
> Thy face is of a stranger, but thy voice
> Disturbs me like a dream.
>
> RODERICK.

AMONGST the numerous ladies of rank and fortune who patronised Alice, the Countess of Dunbarton was one of the most benevolent. This amiable, and for the time accomplished, woman had early perceived the girl's superiority of mind and manner; and, whilst employing her liberally, treated her with the most kindly consideration. Alice's perfect skill in the making of those innumerable articles which were then requisite to complete the costume of a fine gentleman or lady—gloves embroidered in gold or silver thread, fringes, purses, cravats, ruffles, and handkerchiefs, of the most elaborate work—became a source of profitable employment, and the countess did all in her power to assist her young *protégée*.

One beautiful morning towards the end of April, Alice set out to execute some commissions in the town necessary for the completion of various pieces of work on which she was engaged. She had settled her mother comfortably near the window, opened to admit as much air as the high walls opposite would permit—had given her her Bible, and placed two pet jars of violet and rosemary so that their scent might refresh the invalid—then, glad of a little solitude, had departed. Solitude it was to her, even in the midst of the busy throng, for there none knew her—none cared to watch the shadows on her brow—there no one would grow uneasy if she did not speak—or

"Look in her face till her heart was like to break:"

in the crowd she was really alone, and felt at liberty to relax a little the steady guard she kept over herself by day and night.

The narrow lane was cold and dull; Alice, feverish and tired, shivered as she left the house, but a few steps brought her into the broad, sunny Canongate. There all was alive with light and motion, and she felt almost cheered at the gay sight.

No one who thinks of the Canongate as it now is, inhabited only by the poorest classes—in many cases by worse than poverty—can quite conceive the appearance it presented when thronged with the *beau monde* of Edinburgh, a resort for the ultra fashionables of both sexes. The reader must remember that no part of the New Town was in existence at that period; the city was enclosed within its walls and fortifications, its extreme limits being the Castle to the west and Holyrood to the south-east; while on the south it was shut in by its massive ramparts; and on the north, bounded by the bare, rugged Calton and the Nor-loch. This sheet of water covered the whole space, now drained and occupied partly by buildings and partly by gardens, crossed by that unsightly mound for which the denizens of the modern Athens have little reason to thank the improvers of their noble city. The loch extended to the very base of the Castle Rock, adding greatly to the natural strength of that position; and its opposite banks, now the site of the handsomest portion of Edinburgh, were little more than heath and field, rock and wood, thinly dotted by a few old baronial mansions and scattered hamlets. The town, thus cooped up, had not spread, but risen, until every available morsel of ground had been covered with gigantic edifices, within which a population of 50,000 souls was crowded, in a space barely sufficient, according to modern notions, for one-half that number. The only open squares or places yet left were the Grass Market and the Parliament Square; and the only thoroughfare really worthy of the name was the long, irregular street extending in almost a direct line from the Castle to Holyrood House, dividing the Old Town into two portions, of which by far the larger lay to the south. This street, from its great length and breadth, as well as from the above-mentioned causes, had become the promenade of that part of the population whom no necessity kept within doors; and, when we consider the close darkness of the narrow alleys and wynds where even the wealthiest dwelt, we shall not be surprised that it was crowded during the greater part of the day. There were all the best shops, attracting notice, not by the ostentatious display familiar to the nineteenth century, but by exhortations to purchase, and recommendations of wares addressed (somewhat clamorously, it must be owned) to the ears of expected customers; and, albeit these shops were little more than booths or cellars, they possessed quite sufficient attractions to call forth the fair inhabitants of Auld Reekie, who flocked on every possible opportunity to inspect the stores of the drapers, the jewellers, the milliners, the goldsmiths, and dealers in perfumes and fancy articles, who occupied the ground stories of the buildings in the Lawn Market and the Craimes—to display the rich stuffs which composed their dresses, the elaborate work of their ruffs, the curious fancy of sleeves and stomacher, the new cut of a Paris hood—to gossip, to flirt, to see and be seen. Hither came merchants to meet their correspondents and brother traders; fine gentlemen, who, like the fine ladies, had little to do—or did little else than dress, walk, and talk; gay young sparks, fresh from college or home, ambitious of attaining the fashionable characteristics of costume and gait; grave lawyers and senators fiercely discussing public affairs; and last, but in many respects not least, military men, officers, soldiers, and gentleman privates—always the gayest of the gay. Here might be seen a knot of the Scots Musketeers, loud in talk over the merits of the New Army Regulations, just published by authority; from which laudable occupation they were greatly distracted by the constant passing to and fro of curious, bright-eyed damsels of all ranks, who had always a favourable glance to spare for such gallant gentlemen, renowned for equal success in love and war. There, more admired still, Claverhouse's splendid Guards, in all the consciousness of rank and reputation in the field, and of being the observed of all observers, lounged and chatted, ogled and flirted to their heart's content; betted on Lord Melfort's hounds and Captain Ogilvie's racers, on the chances of the next Leith Plate, or the coming trial of skill between two great fencers from Paris against two picked swordsmen of their own body; kissed their hands to the Lady Maxwelton as she passed with her lovely daughters, or watched for the arrival of the beautiful Lady Melfort, and other well-known cavalier dames. There were few horsemen to be seen, and fewer carriages, save perchance some hackney coach—then newly introduced—or lumbering family equipage; sedans, followed by one or more livery servants, and escorted by husband, brother, or admirer, were the usual conveyance, and this mode of showing public attention to some chosen fair one was a very favourite and fashionable practice with the beaux of the seventeenth century, and indeed for long afterwards. We must admit that, amidst all this gaiety, the pavement was such as would not now be tolerated in an English country town; drains, lamps, and walks for foot-passengers, were things unthought of; but, in spite of these and various other drawbacks unnecessary to record, the scene had about it a brilliancy and picturesque animation, which arose chiefly from the unlimited variety of colour and material allowed in the male attire of the upper classes, and which the dull uniformity of modern dress prevents our most splendid assemblies from rivalling. And over all this ever-changing scene fell the warm rays of the spring sun, throwing more than half the street into dazzling light, and flecking the shadowed part with streaks and gleams of reflected brightness which resembled the sparkling tints of a kaleidoscope.

Through the thick of this bustling multitude Alice slowly wended her way, occupied with the two sole thoughts that filled her mind when in the open streets —the fear of meeting Drummond, and the hope of seeing Claverhouse. To be sure, at that time of day, and in such a spot, she had little absolute injury to apprehend, and this reflection rather re-assured her; but the feeling was so strong that the sight of every uniform alarmed her; and, great as was her desire to lose no chance of perceiving Colonel Grahame, she scarcely dared to look around, lest she should meet the insulting stare of her persecutor. Thus, divided between hope and fear, she passed on, not observing that many a gay gentleman turned to look after her, and bestow a sincere, though perhaps not very respectful, commendation on her beauty; and unconscious that in her plain black dress and close hood she was far lovelier than many of the high-born ladies, who, while resenting the admiration bestowed on her by their susceptible escorts, would have purchased at any price the delicate regularity of her features, the soft length of her brown eyelashes, the clusters of golden chestnut curls that fell from under her black snood, and the pure rosy tinge of colour which warmth and exercise had called up into her usually pale cheeks. A few months before, Alice might have experienced a touch of innocent pleasure in the admiration she excited; but she thought far too much of another now to care what others thought of her.

She had just reached the head of the Canongate, and was glancing towards the mansion which she knew Claverhouse inhabited, when her eye was caught by the appearance of two gentlemen advancing directly towards her, deep in conversation. One of them was a stranger to her, the other——

Her heart sprang to her lips, and throbbed at her throat, her temples, and wrists, as if the arteries would give way. What *should* she do? She had wished, longed to meet him—now the time was come, and she felt tempted to fly from before him. If he should see her and not know her, or, knowing, show no sign of recognition—poor little Alice thought she must die of grief on the spot. She had no choice but to go on and pass them, or deliberately avoid them; and before her perturbed ideas could decide which was the best way to spare herself a cruel disappointment they were close upon her.

"A fair day to you, Mistress Alice," said Claverhouse, saluting her with all his habitual courtesy and grace; "I hope I see you in health."

"I thank you, sir," murmured Alice, and, bending her face, which had flushed scarlet to the roots of her hair with surprise and emotion, went by without venturing to look at him. But she had not gone three steps when a hand touched her shoulder, and a frank, gay voice exclaimed, "Why, Alice Scott, dear Alice!"

Frightened and angry, the girl started round, and

found herself again face to face with Colonel Grahame and his companion. It was the latter who had stopped her.

He was a very young man, rather tall, and exceedingly dark—not handsome, but with an open, intelligent expression on his boyish features, which, with his bright dark-brown eyes and good-humoured smile, might have made a far plainer face agreeable. He wore no periwig, its place being well supplied by a quantity of crisply curling raven hair; but in every other respect the most fastidious critic could have found no fault with his dress—could not have suggested an improvement in his peach-blossom velvet coat overlaid with gold lace, in his immense cravat and ruffles of Brussels point, or altered by one-eighth of an inch the cock of his beaver, of which the crimson feather, instead of drooping over the shoulder in the graceful Cavalier fashion, was fastened up round the crown—a new mode from Paris—very ugly, very unbecoming, and very fashionable; which last recommendation sufficed in the eyes of all the younger generation to convert the two former drawbacks into positive advantages. His hatband was clasped with a superb diamond buckle, his cane was tasselled with gold, his hand—one being hidden by a long white embroidered glove—sparkled with rings; in short, it was clear that no expense or pains had been spared to render his whole person a mirror of taste and elegance, and his looks showed that he was by no means unaware of the splendid appearance he presented.

It must not be supposed that Alice saw all this

during the few instants that elapsed ere a word was exchanged; she was too nervous and excited to do more than wonder what this new annoyance meant, and to hope that it could not be anything very serious, while her new friend stood by her side.

"Why, Alice! did you not know we were in town? And how came you here? Have you not seen Flora yet? What does it all mean? By all the holy martyrs, the dear lassie has forgotten me!"

"I ask your pardon, sir," began Alice, in unfeigned wonder.

"I am your old friend, playmate, gossip, Glencarrig, your sister Flora's brother, since you must be told in so many words. Why, you turn as pale as my ruffles, dear Alice; I frightened you dreadfully, I am afraid."

"No, no, my lord; I am delighted to see you," replied Alice warmly, and with real satisfaction.

"The pleasure is mutual, I assure you. How the devil did you come to be in Edinburgh? How long have you been here?"

"Six months," replied Alice, with a sensation that she never could be surprised again at anything that might befall her. "Is Lady Flora here, may I ask, my lord?"

"*May* you ask! of course you may. What new-fangled speech is this? One would think you were a stranger. Oh, yes, Flora is here, in all the joys of shopping, dancing, flirting, and heaven knows what more. I left her just now at a jeweller's in the Lawn Market yonder, ruining herself after the most approved fashion. She and my mother have been here some time, but I only arrived this week from Paris; we have been living there and in London these two years past."

"I will try and find her," said Alice eagerly; "is she with the countess?"

"Stay, stay, Alice!" exclaimed Lord Glencarrig, "don't fly away in such a deuce of a hurry; if you don't care for an old friend's company, I do. No, Flora is not with my lady-mother; *she*'s grown rather *dévote*, as the French say; (she always had a call that way, you know;) so she generally turns over Flora to the guardianship of my Lady Dunbarton. I would I were a young damsel myself, to be put in such sweet ward," added the young earl, laughing.

Alice coloured brightly, but laughed too; while Claverhouse said—

"You have asked a dozen questions of Mistress Scott, my lord, and not given her time to answer a single one."

"True, true; but I was always 'gleg wi' my tongue,' as poor Madam Rachel used to observe, when I had outraged her propriety by any unusually brilliant remark. But, now, in sober earnest, dear girl, do tell me why you are here; and, first of all, how is your father? the only minister I ever liked. Can he be dead? Confound my heedless tongue!" muttered the goodnatured youth, as for the first time he noticed her mourning dress, and saw her face contract and her eyes fill with tears at his careless tone.

"I did not mean to grieve you, upon my soul, Alice. I am heartily sorry, so prithee forgive me." Then, unable to find more suitable terms of apology, he hastened to quit the disagreeable subject by saying, "I never was more astonished in my life than when I saw you. I really think I never should have believed in the possibility of its being yourself if Colonel Grahame had not called you by name. But I never knew you had friends in Edinburgh; how on earth did you —— Lady Leven, Lady Murray — your most humble servant. I shall do myself the honour of waiting on you this evening."

This sudden interruption was addressed parenthetically to two elegantly attired women, who had that moment addressed him. He turned to look after them as they acknowledged his bow with coquettish grace, and the short respite gave Alice time to exchange a supplicating glance with Colonel Grahame. It was impossible to speak a word apart, but her timid, imploring look, and the instinctive pressure of her two hands together, said as plainly as language, "For pity's sake keep him in the dark—leave *that* secret hidden between us—trust it not to the keeping of a hot-brained boy!" If there were in those soft, pure eyes any deeper meaning, any tale of how indescribably precious that secret was to her, any vague shadowing forth of the great love which was become her second life, she surely knew it not. He saw, indeed, something beyond—something which sank down into his mind and was understood long after, but his eyes only answered her request as simply as it was made; they said, "Trust me, and fear nothing." And again she trusted, feeling that for that look and smile she could gladly have died.

"If you cannot find Flora there, come straight to our house in Peebles Wynd," said the volatile young earl, who had for the moment left off wondering at the singular acquaintance between Alice and Claverhouse. "Don't fail. I shall not say a syllable about you at home, to leave them all the delight of surprise."

Holding out his jewelled hand, which Alice timidly clasped, Lord Glencarrig bid her a cordial, affectionate farewell, and continued his walk. Neither of the gentlemen spoke for some minutes, but at last the younger broke out into a fit of hearty and apparently unprovoked laughter. Claverhouse looked at him.

"By St. George!—though that's not a leal Scottish oath either," exclaimed Glencarrig, "I should as soon have expected to see the great black deil himsel'—horns, hoofs, tail, and all complete—walking up the High Street as Elsie Scott, and may be a shade sooner! Not but what she is a pleasanter sight. By Jove! she's grown even prettier than I expected. What a hand and foot, and what melting eyes! But then she has gentle blood in her veins, has my little Alice."

"Indeed!" said Claverhouse, carelessly.

"Ay, that has she. Her father was a border man of the old stock of Harden, who loved better a black cassock than a buff coat, and preferred the spiritual weapon to the carnal, thus robbing his country of a sturdy soldier, to guess by the spirit he has handed down to his son and daughter. But, in Fortune's name, Claverhouse, how came you acquainted with Alice?"

"I was so fortunate as to render Mistress Scott some trifling service not long ago," replied Claverhouse, with perfect composure. "But you spoke of a son?"

"To be sure—her brother Norman—a sour-faced, canting, crop-eared, spawn of the Covenant," replied the young earl, who seemed to find great relief in these opprobrious epithets, "as tough and bitter a young Whigamore as ever swung from the gallows-tree. Even for his sweet sister's sake I never could endure him. Certes, if ever I liked and respected a Whig, it was good Maister Scott, her father. I couldn't despise him even in my wild young days (Claverhouse tried hard not to smile—the earl was nineteen!); but Norman was antipathetic to every nerve I possessed. Just fancy the fellow's cursed impudence: he had the audacity to tell me one day, when he was about fourteen, that I and my sister were Babel's brats, and that my soul was devoted to destruction. I replied that I should have the greatest pleasure in devoting his body to that same unless he went down on his knees and apologised instanter, which he, being as obstinate as ten thousand —— Whigs," said the earl, after hesitating for a fit simile "refused to do, and I proceeded to maul him pretty severely; for, although three years older than myself, he was a puny slip of a lad."

Colonel Grahame laughed outright this time.

"And what came of it?" he asked.

"Oh! there was such an awful collie-shangie that Flora and Alice (she was our darling from her birth, you must know,) came rushing to the place. My wise sister stood crying and wringing her hands; but Alice, who was only ten years old then, and a slender little creature, dashed gallantly in between us, fought me off like a dragon, put Norman to flight, and got for her pains such a blow in the *mêlée* as it makes me quite sick to think of. But she was a mettled lassie, faith! I fancy I see her now—how white she went, and half-swooned with pain, but made never a moan; and when my lady-mother, who hates even a fair stand-up fight as the devil does holy water—she can't be much of a Grahame surely—heard of the fray and held me to bail for good behaviour, Alice would not betray a word that might harm me; and when they asked how she came by the hurt said, 'it was only an accident.' They could not have got more from her if they had racked her."

"A brave girl!" said Colonel Grahame, calling to mind the little champion's slight form and delicate features.

"Ay, truly. But, bail or no bail, it was lucky for Master Norman that his father took care to keep us apart, else I certainly *must* have sent him to the devil before his proper season, or at least have settled him that completely as to put him out of mischief until his sable Majesty came to fetch him, which will undoubtedly happen one of these fine days, unless he fall into your hands first, my noble kinsman, which some folk say would be pretty much the same thing."

Colonel Grahame did not appear in the least moved by this elegant compliment, but walked on, softly stroking his silky, dark moustache, as he often did when thinking deeply. Glencarrig was occupied for some minutes in trying to impart to his very youthful features and figure something of the self-possessed graceful dignity which so peculiarly distinguished his military kinsman; then, failing in that—and the failure was very complete—with observing the effect produced by his own brilliant appearance upon the female passengers. This recreation proving much more satisfactory than the preceding one, he was beginning to feel quite restored to the sunny, self-satisfied good humour which the mention of Norman Scott had slightly ruffled, when Claverhouse asked abruptly—

"How old is he?"

"How old? Well, 'pon my life I hardly know exactly; too young any way to be such a confounded hypocrite."

"I did not know that hypocrisy was peculiar to any age," said Claverhouse drily. "I have known it belong, like folly, to young and old alike; but you are right, if you mean that it is even more unnaturally hateful in the young than in the old."

"*I* detest it anywhere," said Lord Glencarrig with great fervour; "and I hated him most cordially. About his age—let me see—he can't be above two-and-twenty," continued the young earl with a careless air, intended doubtless to convince himself, and, more desirable still, impress upon his hearer, that *he* had long ago attained that patriarchal age; "no, certainly not more than that. But in treason, cant, and double-facedness, he's as old as Methuselah."

"Where is he now?"

"Heaven knows, I don't. I only hope he may not be with his own folk, or I shall have no pleasure in meeting my sweet little gossip. If ever a fellow were destined by nature for the hangman's profit, that man is Norman Scott. I confidently count upon seeing him one day brought along the West Bow with his feet tied under his nag's belly, and his face to the tail thereof, and hearing him testify lustily in the Grass Market. No human power could keep him out of sedition, privy conspiracy, and rebellion; what's bred in the bone comes forth in the flesh; though how, with such parentage, it got into *his* bones, passes my poor skill to discover. If ever you chance to fall in with him, Claverhouse, remember my words."

"I am obliged to you for the caution, my lord. Do you really believe him dangerous?"

"Dangerous! by the Lord, I believe I do. Shall I tell you who he swears by? Balfour of Burley—no other; and I've heard him, with these ears, vow that if ever the bloody Claver'se came within reach of his arm, it should not be shortened to spare him. That's their cant, you know."

"It is fortunate that words are but empty air, else I should have long been sped," answered Colonel Grahame coolly. "But I am really sorry for your sister's friend."

"My own, too! Zounds! I am by no means inclined to abandon my old share of pretty Elsie's good graces. I must try and find out how you and she came to know each other so well. I shall be growing quite jealous. Ha! ha!"

The face of his companion betrayed no signs of having heard this speech, except a slight frown upon the broad white brow, and that curious dilation of the dark hazel eyes which in him was an invariable indication of gathering displeasure. The boy, for he was little more, neither noticed, nor cared to notice, this, and was only instigated by his impenetrability to hazard a downright question.

"Will you not vouchsafe any information upon the subject? I am dying of curiosity, and, if that curiosity make me seem indiscreet, you must pardon me."

"Consider yourself as pardoned then, I pray you, my lord," replied Claverhouse with a smile of quiet amusement.

The rebuff was so delicately administered that Lord Glencarrig did not even seize its meaning, but urged the question again.

"I am sorry to refuse you such a trifle," said Claverhouse; "but, although at liberty to speak of my own affairs if I please, I do not consider myself free to dispose of other people's secrets, if they wish them kept, whatever their motives for privacy may be."

The tone was conclusive, and Lord Glencarrig, comforting himself with the hope of soon learning all he wished to know, through the medium of his sister, gave up the ungrateful task of wringing information from his cousin, and did not renew the conversation until they reached the gate of Holyrood Palace, the place of their destination.

CHAPTER XV.

FLORA.

Her very smile was haughty, though so sweet;
  Her very nod was not an inclination;
There was a self-will even in her small feet,
  As though they were quite conscious of her station.

ALICE, after quitting her new-found friend, hastened on towards the Lawn Market in a state of mind more nearly resembling happiness than she had for some time experienced. She was overjoyed to hear that her foster-sister Flora was again so near her, and this may have had some share in the short-lived exhilaration which raised her spirits; but that sisterly affection was not the only, nor indeed the chief, cause of it, she knew perfectly well. A few words of ordinary courtesy, a glance, a smile—these were the cordials of gladness which made her heart leap lightly, and her step grow elastic, and brought ever and anon a glow to her cheek, as she recalled them one by one. Alice was still very young, and youth *will* seek and find its happiness, where the wasted heart of age can see nought but emptiness, vanity, and vexation of spirit.

She looked about her eagerly as she passed the low dark shops of the Craimes to catch a glimpse of Lady Dunbarton's livery-servant awaiting her orders, or her chair in attendance before some fashionable merchant's. She had occasion to enter several of these stores herself to make purchases, but in none did she meet the object of her search. After going some distance beyond her original destination, she was about to turn homewards in despair of finding Lady Flora that day, when in one of the remotest shops she caught a glimpse of the countess, accompanied by another person. She stepped in, and, seizing the opportunity while Lady Dunbarton was examining some splendid stuffs, touched the younger lady on the arm, saying timidly, "Flora."

Flora Bethune started as Alice had done; then crying out, "My little Alice! my own Gowan!" flung her arms round the young girl's neck, and kissed her repeatedly—the impetuous, warm-hearted, affectionate Flora of old.

Not altered even in person—developed and improved, but the same still—a very handsome likeness of her brother the earl, with magnificent black hair, and a skin of mingled crimson and brown, with eyes as full of mischief and laughter, save that hers were of the deepest blue—a figure tall, rounded, and graceful, that would have been stately but for the perpetual motion which animated it—and a voice ringing and fresh as a silver bell, no trace or sorrow, or even of discipline, in face, or tone, or gesture. The similarity between Flora and her brother was still further increased by the style of her dress of dark rose-coloured brocade, with its silver embroidery and fringes, which seemed chosen for the purpose of setting off to the best advantage every charm of figure and complexion, besides being put on and worn with true French coquetry and grace. In all the glittering *éclat* of her showy beauty she quite eclipsed Alice, who at first sight would hardly have been noticed beside her. What might have been the result of longer acquaintance, and closer inspection, is quite another thing.

Such was the friend who now seized Alice, and held her fast by both hands, as if afraid that she might disappear as unaccountably as she had come, and vanish into thin air; while Alice, quite as glad, and almost as excited, looked and smiled, but did not venture to speak. It was morally impossible to answer the flood of questions which Flora showered upon her, to the intense astonishment of Lucky Fleming, the mercer's wife, who could not understand the sudden intimacy between her aristocratic customer and the modest young embroidress, whom she had herself sometimes employed, or the pleased face with which the Countess of Dunbarton looked on at this little scene.

"I'll never be tired seeing you, Elsie!" exclaimed Lady Flora, as soon as she recovered her breath; "you are the bonniest wee thing my eyes have lighted on since I left old Scotland. Oh, Lady Dunbarton! have you not done looking at that tiresome brocade yet? I want to get Alice all to myself."

The countess good-naturedly hurried over her purchases, and the two ladies left the shop, accompanied by Alice, and followed by the countess's servant.

The first inquiries were, of course, as to how Alice had become acquainted with her friend's residence in the capital.

"So Glencarrig told you? Well, I am going to carry you off and let my mother see you before he gets home, or his long tongue will never be able to stint itself, eh Elsie?"

"Indeed, madam, you are very good, but I cannot go just now."

"*Madam!*" retorted Flora, laughing; "and when was Flora Bethune ever *madam* to Alice Scott, I would crave to know? Am I not the same as I was, or do you love me no more?"

"You are, indeed, the same Flora, kind, dear, and true," replied Alice, sadly, "but I am *not* the same Alice that played so gaily on the sunny braes of dear Glencarrig. I have passed under the cloud—I have seen death face to face. My father is gone from us."

Flora's bright blue eyes sparkled with sudden tears.

"I did not see your black dress—or no, I *did* see it, but thought not of its cause, in my joy at meeting you again. Oh, Alice, love! I am grieved!"

She was—honestly grieved; but as soon as the first shock had passed off she began to talk again, although at first in a more subdued and sedate manner.

"And your mother, my Elsie?"

"She is here, madam, but indifferently well—and the physicians can do little for her."

"Oh, I must see her—dear Madam Scott!" exclaimed Flora, "think ye, Elsie, that she will know me for the little ranting lassie that so sorely tried her patience whenever she set foot in the manse; that tangled her wool, and unwound her pirns, and let drop her knitting stitches, and overturned her spinning wheel so many weary times?"

"Ay, indeed, she will," answered Alice, smiling at the many laughable memories of Flora's childhood which these words called up; "but," she hesitated, and blushed deeply, "we live very poorly, Madam Flora, and I fear ——"

"That Flora will disown her friends for lack of this world's gear and goods; fie, Alice! But are you indeed so poor, my little gossip?"

"Yes, madam—we live by the labour of our hands, and most times my mother is too sick and weak to work."

"That must not, shall not, be!" exclaimed Flora, impetuously. "You shall come and live with me again, Elsie; my mother will be only too glad to have you and dear Madam Scott—we will all be so happy together. Nay, Alice! why dost thou shake that wise little head of thine? What hast thou to urge against so notable a device?"

"This, dear Flora," said Alice, turning rather paler, and speaking in a low, firm voice, "that my father's wife, my own mother, shall never be a burden to any one whilst her child has health and strength to support her."

"Health there *may* be, though I doubt it meikle," replied Flora, looking sharply at her, "but there is little strength, I trow. To live by the labour of these wee hands of thine can be no easy task, my Gowan."

She took up smiling one of the girl's slender hands, almost wan in its delicacy, and compared it with her own plump, rosy, creamy fingers, ungloved for the purpose of better handling her large fan, then an important part of a fine lady's paraphernalia. "My hand is well nigh twice as large as thine, yet, were I condemned to live only on what it earned, I must certainly starve. Oh, Lady Dunbarton! is it not terribly sad to think of?"

"It is, indeed," replied the countess, gravely; then whispered to Flora, "You are a silly lassie to stir up sorrow that wants no waking, unless that poor girl's face belies her heart."

"Alice," said the young lady, "one other question, and I will not say a single word more anent all your troubles to-day."

"You do not pain me, madam," said Alice, sweetly, "I have learnt to look at sorrow without dread."

"Where then is your brother Norman? How is it that he does not help to support you, instead of leaving you to do more than your strength will allow?"

"Oh indeed!" said Alice, who, little reason as she had to love her brother, could not hear him blamed without defending him; "indeed, Flora, it is not his fault. I think, I hope—I am sure that he would assist us if he could, but he is not yet out of his term, you ken, madam, and the master who teaches him his trade, the bookselling and imprinting, gives him his food and lodging, and even his clothes, which is all we can hope for yet. Maister Kerr speaks very well of him, and has great trust in him; so I suppose he will do excellently some day. Norman is very little here; he travels on his master's business, he says, and has been much in the Lowlands o' Holland, from which many of the books come, I have heard."

"Is he at all changed?"

"No, madam, not in the least," replied Alice, with a short quick breath that sounded very like a sigh.

Flora, who probably shared the earl's aversion to Norman Scott, did not pursue the subject, but began to talk of her brother.

"Is not Glencarrig grown a shocking coxcomb, Elsie?" she said, laughing; "he thinks himself perfectly irresistible in that Paris beaver, and lays siege to all the ladies he comes near with as much confidence as if his smooth, beardless face were that of some gallant soldier or *preux chevalier* of old. He hath not been here a week, and hath already declared himself sworn knight of one of our gayest belles—not to mention that he is at the feet of my Lady Dunbarton here, who drives us poor damsels to despair. We must all wear the willow when she appears, for she carries off our lovers by the score; witness my Lord Spynie, and young ——"

"Thy tongue is longer than thy wit, my pretty Flora," said the countess, half displeased, rather perhaps at the time and place chosen for the speech than at the compliment itself, for she was very beautiful and quite aware of the fact. Her diminutive figure, lovely complexion, blue eyes, and blonde tresses, derived additional charms from Flora's brunette beauty, which the contrast served in turn to heighten. But she probably thought the most crowded part of the High Street not quite the spot for indulging in *viva voce* observations, which, however flattering, might be overheard and misconstrued by a dozen unscrupulous pairs of ears; and the countess, in spite of a dash of coquetry innate and not unbecoming to one still so young and handsome, was a prudent and discreet lady.

The reproof only amused Flora.

"Glencarrig was always a great squire of dames," she said; "do you mind, Elsie, how he always stood by you, right or wrong, when you were both little things, and vowed that if you were a Whig preacher he would like nothing better than to go to conventicles every day? He would do for the lifting of your little finger what mother and sister and Madam Rachel and good old Dominie Todd might sue for hours to obtain. Oh, Elsie dearest! there was such an awful scene when you had left us! Glencarrig stormed like one demented, and swore so dreadfully! and, when the chaplain rebuked him for evil speaking, David threatened to twist his craig! But all our young gallants do just the same—fie! they are a sad set of wild ne'er-do-weels!"

Flora's virtuous reprobation of the evil tendencies manifested by the younger generation did not, however, appear to diminish in any way the satisfaction with which she received the salutes and glances of the numerous gentlemen who claimed the honour of her acquaintance. She was radiant with smiles, good humour, and coquettish glee, and looked a picture of health and loveliness. Alice could not help admiring her heartily, and marvelling at the extraordinary difference which three years had made in the tall and handsome but unformed girl she remembered so distinctly.

At the entrance of Peebles Wynd they were met by two gentlemen, who accosted them. One of these was Lord Gilbert Hay, second son of the Marquis of Tweedale, a handsome aristocratic-looking young man of seven or eight and twenty; the other Walter Charteris, one of the gentleman privates of Claverhouse's Lifeguards. Lady Dunbarton inquired after his sister, the Lady Mary, while Hay addressed Flora; and Alice, an unprejudiced spectator, saw that her friend seemed by no means indifferent to the gallant speeches and insinuating address of the young nobleman.

"Good bye, dear Alice; come to-morrow, or I shall come and fetch you," were Flora's last words, and Alice, grateful for the affection she showed, and still exhilarated by her unexpected good fortune, went home to shed upon her mother's heart a portion of the sunshine which, transient as it was, still enveloped hers.

"What's wi' ye, Alice?" inquired old Janet, the portress, who was standing at the door of her own little room on the ground story as the girl passed in; "What's wi' ye? yer face is brighter than I hae seen it mony a day past."

"I've met a friend, Janet," said Alice, as she went up stairs, smiling to herself at the double signification the answer bore to her, and the perilous sweetness of one of its meanings.

But sunshine, alas! cannot last for ever, and slowly as the day went down, and the early twilight came on, something of its shadow began to creep over the young girl's spirits again. A passing word—she hardly knew what—had stirred up in her mind the long-forgotten prophecy of Lucky Wilson. It had a sound of real and dangerous meaning to her ears now. "For the love o' him that can ne'er love you;" *that* had come so quickly true, who could tell but what the rest of the weird warning might prove as fatally ominous. A loss to be borne, a crime to weep for, and both to come from her own flesh and blood! How could she connect such fears with any but her mother and Norman? It grew dark, and Alice sat for a short space of rest by the wood fire which the necessities of the invalid forced them to kindle in the chilly spring evenings — on a low stool by her mother's side, wrestling in silence at that quiet hour with the sorrows which surrounded her, like phantoms in their vague, formless terror, but only too real in their power and keenness. It was such a fight as few men wage —fought with a courage such as women show in many a sacred battle-field of the heart—the old, old struggle between the weakness of Nature and the strength of Faith, wherein those who endure to the end shall surely triumph. So Alice fought, and prayed, and strove, and, if joy could not return, peace at least was not so hopelessly far off as in the first days of her trial.

CHAPTER XVI.

NORMAN.

> Vainly in his face
> Of gentle feeling Hope would seek a trace,
> And pleading Mercy in the sternness there
> May read at once her sentence to despair!
>
> CONRADIN.

GOOD Madam Scott, in happy ignorance of her daughter's feelings, was kept for some time in a state of pleasureable excitement by the arrival of Lady Flora and her family. She was considerably better about this time, by one of those sudden variations in her deceitful malady, then so little understood or studied; and insisted upon Alice's accepting the constant invitations of Flora and the countess to visit them at their house. Alice often wished to refuse, from a nervous dread lest some mishap—she did not precisely know what—might occur during her few hours' absence: but, seeing that these refusals always annoyed her mother, and made her tenfold more anxious and inquiring about her health and spirits, she finally came to the conclusion that it was better and safer to accede whenever she could secure the services of some kind neighbour to replace her by her mother's side. One condition, however, she made, and strictly adhered to, namely, that she was to be permitted to continue without let or hindrance the labour upon which her daily bread and, far more so, her mother's comfort, depended.

This Flora at first valiantly opposed. She could not or would not understand the necessity for such unremitting exertion. Nursed in the lap of affluence, she had no knowledge of the real value of money, or conception of daily work for daily sustenance, and declared that Alice had no right to wear herself out by such perpetual slavery, as she termed it.

"Flora, my love," said the countess to her one day, "you are a foolish girl to try and sow such seeds of discontent in Alice's mind. Rather should you take from her a lesson of sweetness and humility than try to put her off doing her duty so well and bravely."

"Between ourselves, *belle mère*, I don't think humility would sit well on me," retorted Flora, eyeing her own stately figure and sparkling face in a convenient mirror, "and sweetness is ever mawkish to me, except yours," said the affectionate girl, stopping to kiss the countess. "As to industry, I have no need of it, and like butterflies better than the ants to whom we are recommended to go for instruction in wisdom. Alice is too proud, rather than too humble; she will take nothing, even from those who have a right to offer it."

"A very worthy pride, which beseems her well, Flora, and sorry should I be to see her without it. God grant, my dear daughter, that if ever it be His will that ye should come to low estate, ye may do as she has done and is doing still. I will see Madam Scott myself, and if we can render her any friendly service in all neighbourly kindness I will not be backward; but, Flora, let Alice do as seemeth her best; she is a better judge than we of her own affairs."

Flora only pouted her red lips and tossed her pretty head, vowing that it was a crying shame Elsie should do nothing but sew her whole life long, until a visit which she paid with her mother to Madam Scott a few days after converted her, as far as she was convertible, to a comprehension of her friend's merits and admiration of her modest devotion.

We need hardly say that the astonishment of old Janet Rutherford the portress was great on beholding two richly-dressed ladies of such rank and appearance mount the narrow, dark staircase which gave access to Madam Scott's humble apartment. Nor were they less surprised and delighted at the exquisite neatness of everything that apartment contained. The floor was as clean as hands could make it, the simple furniture tastefully arranged, a half-open door gave glimpses of the little bed-room beyond, with its white linen; each corner showed plainly that delicate care which gentle breeding will bestow in the midst of poverty. To the credit of old Janet it should be remarked, that she was a ready and willing helper to Alice in whatever she thought beyond the girl's strength, for she had been touched to the quick of a very warm heart, disguised beneath a crabbed temper, by the girl's ceaseless industry and excellent conduct.

"Hout awa, lassie!" she exclaimed, when Alice first offered to remunerate her for services which were a great relief to her own overtasked energies, "hout awa, I say! div' ye think I'm a heathen, to take the hard-earned gear o' the fatherless? Pit up yer coins o' gowd and coins o' siller, Alice; deil be in Janet's fingers if ever she touches ane o' them!"

"But then, Janet, it is I who will rob you," said Alice smiling. "You work hard enough already."

"Prut tut!" retorted the energetic old woman; "haud yer clavering tongue; what's in an hour's work ilka day for ye to mak sic a fash about? It's just a ploy for a teuch auld carline like me; but it beseems na a bonnie lassock like yersel', that suld be a leddy by name as ye are by nature, to file yer dainty fingers wi' sic like turns. Na, na; bide by yer ain callin', the makin' o' a' thae bonnie dies and whigmaleeries for lords and leddies and gentles; and, if maybe ye'd do a bit scrap o' sewin' for auld Janet when ye hae naethin' better, I'se hauld mysel' as weel feed as if ye had gien me a gowpen fu' o' caroluses. I was aye gey gleg at the spinnin' and knittin' work, but white seam I never could abide, forbye that my een is waxin' a wee dim noo, ye ken."

Alice could find no more appropriate way of thanking her humble friend than by kissing her heartily—a proceeding which so touched Janet that she immediately began to fulfil her share of the bargain with a zeal which gradually absorbed all the heavier and more disagreeable details of Alice's frugal household occupations. She now ushered the countess and her daughter to Madam Scott's room, with many a reverential courtesy, and retired, to be interrogated in turn by all the other lodgers respecting the quality of these unaccustomed visitors, and to enjoy the important privilege of mentioning "my Leddy the Countess o' Glencarrig, and my Leddy Flora," an indefinite number of times.

The widow was reclining in her accustomed place by the window, warmly wrapped up, although the weather was beautiful and sunny. Lady Glencarrig was shocked at the change which her husband's sudden death and several months of illness had wrought in one whom she remembered a comely and pleasing matron. Her hair was almost as white as the coif which covered it, her features drawn, her eyes faded, and, although she spoke cheerfully and did not seem in pain, the hard short breath and dry cough were distressing to hear. She greeted her noble visitors with sincere pleasure, not with the fawning servility of a low mind, but the quiet respect always shown to superiors by those who truly respect themselves. Madam Scott was not proud, but she never forgot that she had gentle blood in her veins.

Alice was absent, and, after many mutual inquiries concerning what had passed during their separation, the conversation naturally fell on her. On this subject the widow was never tired of expatiating, and Lady Glencarrig watched her daughter's countenance as the fond proud mother told of all that Alice had done for her, with a tender enthusiasm which she well deserved.

"Oh, my leddy," she said to the countess, "ye are a mother yersel', and hae a bonnie and winsome daughter, that I doubtna ye would gie yer heart's drap for, and a noble young son that is the vera apple o' yer e'e, but gif ye had feifty sic, and feifty mair to the back o' them, they never could be to you what my Alice is to me! Do ye mind Ruth in the Scripture, Leddy Flora? Weel, I'm just convinced in my ain mind that Ruth was the picture o' Alice.

"But, Madam Scott," said Flora, "surely Alice need not work as she does from morning till night. Nay, now, mother, do let me ask this! Need she, madam?"

"No, Leddy Flora, she *needna* just," replied the widow with a strong emphasis on the word.

Lady Flora looked triumphantly at her mother.

"Wait a wee, Flora, you have not heard all," said the countess. "Say on, Madam Scott, say what is on your lips, and convince this silly bairn of mine."

"Dinna ye see, Leddy Flora, that it's no for hersel', but for her puir feckless mother, that my Alice wears hersel' awa—and what can I do? My auld e'en are just bleared out wi' greeting, my hands have lost their cunning, my heid is weary and weak, and my Alice winna see me want for aught. Sae she rises up airly, and late takes rest, and when I flyte at her and pray her not to do't, she kisses me and says 'Dinna fash yersel' about me, mother, I'll do weel enough.'"

"It cannot be for herself, certainly," said the young lady, "for Alice eats and drinks, as she sings, like a mavis."

"Ay truly, my leddy," said the widow smiling, though tears of mingled joy and sorrow stood in her eyes. "Ay, truly, it's no for hersel,' but to keep togither wer sma' plenishing and the bonny white napery that I spun mysel' lang, lang syne, and that she thinks I would be wae to want; it's to gie me the white manchets, and the sweet butter, and the wine posset, and mony an orra thing that's hard for the like o' us puir folk to come by, and to pay the doctor his fee in hand. I canna bear to see it, madam; in truth I canna—and yet what am I to do?"

The poor woman was weeping now, and even the gay Flora's eyes were full of tears.

"It is a grief to me, even while I thank my God for having gi'en me sic a blessin' as she is, but my heart is dowie to see my little doo, sae blithe and sae fair, growing wan and sad—to think o' her, sae young and tender, wearying awa' her life for me. Oh, my leddy! human nature is a frail thing, and maybe I am committin' a sin to say sae, but I would be content to lay me down in the kirkyard, if Alice could be released frae the burden she has to thole for me."

"But you will soon grow strong, dear Madam Scott," said Lady Flora kindly, "and then she will be happy again."

The widow's mild face grew paler as she answered,

"Na, na, my leddy! that will never be—never again! The doctor bids me hope, and the kind neighbours would fain cheer me, but my ain soul tells me a truer tale—an ower true tale, that I daurna mint to Alice yet. Puir lassie! Didna I say even now that I would be blithe to lay me doun and dee; and that maybe it was sin to say sae? It was sin and folly baith, my leddy, to wish to leave my sweet bairn her lane in this world o' dool and evil—not but what God can guide her better far than I, but a mother's human heart cries out at thought of it. I am in a sair strait betwixt twa, having a desire to depart since he died that was my dearer life—but then——oh, madam, my Alice!"

"I promise you," said the gentle countess, deeply moved, "that if your presentiments come true, which God forbid! Alice shall never want a home—she shall be my child."

"And my sister, dear Madam Scott," added Flora, who was crying like a child: "but you must try and hope."

"Hope is a sweet thing, my bonny leddy," said the widow, wiping her eyes as she spoke—"but whiles it is a cruel and beguiling folly, and sae would it be to me, gif it garred me fear to look death in the face. Heaven be praised, it has nae terrors for me, nor the grave a victory."

"You are a happy woman," said the countess with gentle gravity.

"Ay, madam, and it is a happiness man taketh not awa'. I thank Him above that Alice hath it likewise. She was aye a pious, God-fearing maiden——Whisht, dry your tears, Leddy Flora! I hear her foot on the stair!"

The step came up, a hand turned the latch, and there entered—not Alice, but her brother Norman.

He was about one or two-and-twenty, of slight, spare stature, and resembled Alice in the small features and fair complexion, but his hair was of a sandy brown and his eyes blue, of that cold pale blue which is often the index to a cruel and ferocious temper. His lips were thin and closely shut, his cheek more haggard than became his years, while the whole expression of his face was such as to render a very regular set of features positively disagreeable. His general aspect presented something colourless and inanimate, an impression which was particularly heightened by his plain suit of grey cloth, such as was then commonly worn by persons in his station.

"Norman! how came ye hither the day?" exclaimed his mother in surprise.

"I had a spare hour, and am come to see you and Alice. Where *is* Alice?" he asked sharply, looking round.

"She's gaen up the street a wee; but, Norman lad, dinna ye see my Leddy Glencarrig—ye'll mind her, sure?"

Norman Scott only acknowledged the presence of his mother's noble friends by a stiff salutation, scarcely even polite, and, withdrawing to the opposite corner of the room, sat down without seeming to heed their presence any further than to wish them away.

The countess and her fair daughter felt uncomfortable, they hardly knew why; all conversation languished, and, after a very short interval, they rose to leave. By tacit consent neither spoke any more of Alice—but the countess's affectionate pressure of the hand, and Flora's hearty, expressive kiss assured the poor mother, that in the event of her own death her child would never be friendless.

Norman listened to their retreating footsteps, then

rose and stood near his mother, with a look of cold displeasure.

"Mother," he asked, "who are these that I find here, bringing the follies of the world into the sanctuary of pure religion—into the heart of a family who have sworn to lead a godly life in all good conversation?"

"They are your father's friends, Norman," said the widow, her pale face flushing with pain and annoyance—"your dead father's friends, and gude anes hae they been to you and yours."

"*Good* friends!" retorted the young man contemptuously; "how can good fruit come from an ill tree? how can a poisonous fountain send forth sweet water? Say rather false friends, whose kisses are deceitful, snares of the evil one to gild over with fair words and looks the curse of prelacy and popery—abominations in the sight of the Lord. Is it not true that they are followers of the carnal Luther—of the sycophantic bishops who bow the knee to Baal, and pay allegiance to the idolatrous tyrant whose hands are dyed in the blood of the saints? And are such as these, children of the world, whose thoughts are of lying vanities, who cannot cease from sin, fit to be the chosen companions of those who call themselves Covenanting Christians?"

"Oh Norman, Norman," remonstrated his mother, "when will ye learn charity, my son? why will ye aye be seeking evil instead of good? God forbid I should not shun the errors o' prelacy even as ye do yersel', but He forbid also that I suld condemn them that visit the widow and the fatherless. Never hae they said or done aught to turn us frae the gude path, and wha kens but in his ain gude time the Lord may bring them in as stray sheep to his fauld?"

"Alice sees them, I suppose?" asked Norman with a half sneer.

"Ay, and Norman, hearken till me! ye maunna say a word to Alice against them. D'ye hear me, Norman?" pursued Madam Scott, with an energy her feeble frame seemed incapable of exerting. "I am content to be wearied wi' yer hard judgments o' those that hae been a blessing and a pleasure to your ain folk, but I winna bide to hear ye vex my sweet doo, or speak again as ye hae whiles spoken before her, anent evil she never ha' thought on but for your daft speech. Ye hear me, Norman, and again I charge ye as ye heed my blessing to please yer sister and be tender wi' her; she will sune hae nane left but you here below."

A violent and exhausting fit of coughing put a stop to further exhortation, and in the midst of it Alice came in, with her little basket on her arm, and on her face a glow of that April gladness which always cheered her mother's heart to behold. She started and changed colour when she perceived Norman, as though he could have read in her heart the secret cause of that thrill of happiness which had made it bound a few minutes before. She went up to him and kissed him, to hide her momentary embarrassment.

"I thought you were in Holland," she said; "are you long returned?"

"Since the day before yesterday."

"And you did not come to visit us before—fie!" said Alice, trying to assume an air of playfulness, in spite of the atmosphere of depression which his presence brought with it to a spot where such an influence was little needed.

"I had no time," he replied coldly.

Alice retreated into herself, and, after arranging such little household matters as her absence had left incomplete, sat down in the window-sill to pursue her customary work—outwardly at ease, but inwardly anxious to discover whether anything had passed between her mother and Norman to account for the unusual colour on the cheek of the former, and the sullen silence of the latter. She was never able to divest herself of a nervous dread, lest by some unforeseen accident or imprudence he should be informed of her *rencontre* with Claverhouse on the night of Lucky Wilson's death, and this alarm, doubly great since his violent expostulation with her, was so vivid as to render any event probable if it tended to produce this result. Perhaps she felt conscious of its importance in her eyes, and that this burden of a secret, beyond even that entrusted to her mother, rendered her morbidly sensitive on the subject; but certainly the idea of Norman's learning the particulars of the case, in whatever manner, or from whatever quarter, was a nightmare to her. She could hardly think without trembling of what might ensue if he were ever to hear her name coupled with that of Colonel Grahame, and when Norman was by she forced, as far as she could, *that* one name from her mind, lest in some inexplicable manner he should divine that it dwelt there.

This was no easy matter to accomplish, however, for Alice had but just met its owner, and every nerve was yet quivering with pleasure. She worked away with double diligence, to conceal the involuntary smile which would contract her lips, and stooped her head until the glossy curls of her long hair quite hid her face. Unobservant of anything but her own thoughts, she had gradually begun to forget her brother's very existence, when his sharp voice nearly startled her out of her seat.

"You take strange pleasure in that work, Alice."

"Strange! why strange?" she asked, not lifting her head, but turning it a little towards him, whilst their mother glanced nervously from one to the other."

"Strange in this—that one to whom more light has been granted than to the blind followers of blind leaders, should devote her days and nights to such gewgaws of soul-enticing folly."

"Is that all?" said Alice, quickly. "Ye speak coolly, brother; but I do what I can—beggars maunna be choosers."

"And can you do nought but minister to worldly lusts?" asked the uncompromising young fanatic—"nought but waste the precious hours vouchsafed ye for repentance, for grace, and usefulness, in adding fresh beauty to the luxurious devices of Satan for ruining more deeply those already sunk in sin? Is this labour for a Christian maiden, I would ask?" he concluded, scornfully, taking up and flinging down a beautifully fringed and embroidered riding-glove, of which Alice was finishing the fellow.

"I have never heard that the use of such things was forbidden to those who only put their true value on them," answered Alice. "And as to my working hard at my employment, do we not read that we are to be diligent in business, serving the Lord in all matters, small as well as great?"

"Aye, the enemy can quote Scripture for his purpose, and give ye both law and gospel for any transgression. But woe unto them that put bitter for sweet, and sweet for bitter; that cry peace, peace! when there is *no* peace! What peace can there be as long as the abominations of Babylon pollute the land? pomps and luxuries, the lust of the eyes and the pride of life, even as in the days of old, before the Flood, when they ate and drank, and laid by great store, and married and were given in marriage, saying in their hearts 'There is no God.' As it was then, even so is it in this untoward generation; soberness and godliness, reverence and chastity, are things out of mind, and, in place thereof, broidering of garments, and braiding of hair, and putting on of apparel, gold, and jewels,—revelling, dancing, and jesting, which is not convenient,—the daughters of disobedience with the sons of sin, the women of vanity with the men of wrath and bloodshed; while the servants of the Lord groan aloud before Him—Oh, Lord! how long, how long will thy wrath burn like fire—for ever?"

"Is all this caused by my poor bit of broidering?" said Alice, half provoked out of her usual gentleness by her brother's absurd intolerance. "I would you had never seen it; but, as I have no other means of earning our mother's bread and our own, I am fain to continue in my own way, even though it chance to be sinful in your eyes."

"And in those of all sober men," said Norman; "well may my soul be moved to wrath when I find my own flesh and blood made a slave of such wantonness. I repeat, that this is no work for one who would serve the Lord in spirit and in truth; the blessing can never descend upon such unlawful gain."

Alice only smiled; she was very much annoyed, but self-command had become easy and natural to her long ago, and she did not feel disposed to afford Norman any fresh advantage by losing her own temper.

"Laugh! ay laugh!" said he, gloomily, "laugh *at* sin rather than weep *for* it; that is the creed of these days; scoff at those who cry aloud like the watchman on the tower, that night is far spent and day at hand; shut thy ears to the words of soberness, like the deaf adder that refuses to hear the voice of the charmer!"

"I cannot say ye are meikle like a charmer, brother Norman," retorted Alice, with a demure malice that was a sparkle of her old gay wit. Her mother was so pleased with the girl's patient good humour, that it half disarmed her displeasure against Norman for his disregard of her injunctions; and this little speech betrayed her into a laugh.

"Norman! Norman!" she said, as the young fanatic's face grew terribly dark, "I'm sair afraid that, for a' ye speak o' godliness, the spirit o' meekness is no in ye, nor the charity that covereth a multitude of sins. Ye will never be half sae wise a man as yer blessed father, that never spake a hard or cruel word o' ony living soul."

"And thereby made to himself friends of the mammon of unrighteousness," said Norman, in his bitter tone.

"If you're meaning my Leddy Glencarrig when ye speak o' the mammon o' unrighteousness, I maun just say ye're no sae ceevil as ye might be, Norman," remarked Madam Scott, rather sharply, "and, gif ye hae naething pleasanter than thae observations to make, I'm muckle o' opeenion that ye might as weel let alane coming to see us. We're no just that owerladen wi' glee—Alice and me—that we suld be deaved wi' a' these clashes anent lying vanities and pomps and luxuries and sic like. Gude kens, there's few eneugh o' them comes up as high as this."

"I will not compromise the truth, and be a consenting party to any pact with the world, for fear of displeasing a child of man," replied Norman, no way abashed at his mother's rebuke. "The time is at hand, yea it is even now upon us, when all things that are old shall become new, and principalities and powers, and spiritual wickedness in high places, shall be swept from the face of the earth like chaff before the stormy wind—like stubble before the fire; when the righteous shall shine forth as stars, being girt with vengeance as their armour, with zeal as with a cloak. Then shall they who have put their faith in the great ones of this earth find them as the staff of a bruised reed, upon which, if a man lean, it shall pierce his hand—then shall they who have served the Lord with half a heart, and bowed the knee with the followers of priestcraft, dealers in soul-destroying forms and ceremonies (which is as the sin of Naaman the Syrian, when he bowed down in the house of Rimmon, the god of his master Benhadad)—then, I say, shall they cry unto the Lord, and he shall not hear them; they shall call aloud, and he shall not regard it; swift destruction shall compass them round about, and the voice of the avenger shall be heard in their streets. 'They have forsaken that which I had appointed unto them; they have chosen evil, knowing the good; they have cast in their lot with the people whom my soul abhorreth—Ephraim is joined to idols —let him alone!'"

Nothing could be more singular and painfully impressive than the contrast between the speaker's youthful appearance and the passionless, unfeeling fanaticism of his language. His whole being seemed to have no sentiment or faculty distinct from the one master passion of mingled religious and political bigotry, which had hardened into precocious ferocity a character that the most graceful and softening influences could never have rendered amiable. He was the type of a sect and class, common then and for long afterwards, whom no charity could touch, no kindness subdue—no oppression could crush, but also no toleration conciliate—whose religion was self-righteousness towards themselves and Pharisaic hatred of others; whose tenets were the narrowest and dreariest that ever bore the name of Christianity—that faith of light and love, and whose principles, had they triumphed in all their austerity, would have reduced Scotland to the yoke of a belief as exclusive as ever was Judaism.

The silence remained so uninterrupted for a few minutes after the conclusion of this harangue, that Alice hoped the discussion might end there, as a fire expires for lack of fuel; but the widow, who had her fair share of the argumentative qualities peculiar to her native country, irritated, too, by Norman's harshness to his sister, took up the word again.

"And I say again, Norman, that for a' yer preachings and threatenings, I winna believe that my Leddy Glencarrig isna a gude Christian; and sae thought and said yer father, wha was a discreeter and mair learned man than his son, and a better, I fear, than ye will be, if ye dinna strive to love them that love ye—leastways yer ain flesh and bluid."

"The wisdom of the world is foolishness with God, and the friendship of the world enmity towards God," replied Norman's impassive voice. "And in this matter there is scantly even carnal prudence. Know ye not that these women, these daughters of Moab to whom your hearts cleave, know ye not that they are kith and kin to the destroyer of the saints, the tyrant over Israel, to John Grahame of Claverhouse? If the servants of God fling themselves into the lion's den, by what right can they hope not to be devoured?"

"I'm sure I dinna ken. I'm no sae weel acquaint wi' the ways o' lions as some folk," retorted his mother, provoked by his imperious manner into defending a cause which she might otherwise have been induced to leave to its own merits. "An' what if they are as ye say, wherefore should we care? If there's ony body has reason to fear Claver'se, it's just yersel', laddie, that has sae mony braw sermons on yer tongue, and sae little discretion to hinder ye frae uttering them in season and out o' season; and mair aften out than in. Certes, I canna comprehend wherefore ye suld ca' my Leddy the Countess, an' the winsome Leddy Flora, sae sweet and kind, 'daughters o' Moab,' and ither ill names, just for a' the warld because they are sae unlucky as to hae been born sib to an evil doer. Indeed if ye kenned a', ye wouldna, perhaps, be sae gleg to speak ——"

"Mother," interrupted Alice, pale with anxiety at the turn the conversation was taking, "dear mother! pray let this end at once. Norman!" she turned to him imploringly, "all this does mair harm than good; indeed it does. I canna think as you do—I canna, for scruples which are not my own, give up the friends I have loved ever since I remember, who are dearer to me than any but my own kindred—kinder, perchance, than *one* of those is now. Forgive me for my seeming disregard of what I know is sincerely, what I *hope* is kindly, meant, and dinna look angrily on me for seeing worth and goodness where you cannot."

"It is well, sister Alice," said Norman, rising in sullen anger, and with an emphasis on the endearing title that was not affection. "Is that all you have to say?"

"It is; but oh, Norman, dinna part from me in anger! Take your path, and I will take mine; but, for our loved father's sake, let us at least meet in peace when they cross."

"Twice have I spoken, twice have I warned—you will forget and despise the second warning as you have forgotten and despised the first."

"I have *not* forgotten it," said Alice, in a low voice; "the wound was too deep and too needlessly inflicted,—but I have forgiven it, as I do this."

"Beware, lest you despise a third; and when you call there be none to deliver! Farewell; God bring you to a more sober frame of mind. Mother, farewell! it may be long ere I see you again."

He kissed her with the same motionless aspect, and left the room without paying any attention to the outstretched hand and wistful face of poor Alice, whose heart had sunk, beneath his freezing influence, from its flutter of innocent joy into the slow monotony of its daily beat. She sat quite quiet for awhile, but her young spirits had been too harshly checked—she was not prepared to encounter such a contest, at a moment when her usual armour of patient self-retraint had been weakened by unhoped-for pleasure, and soon the large tears began to roll fast over her cheeks.

"Dinna greet, my love Alice," said her mother,

soothingly; "come hither and kiss me—and dinna greet for a' that fule's talk o' Norman's."

Alice obeyed; and, kneeling down with her head on her mother's knees, cried intensely, but so quietly, that not even that mother's anxious ear caught half the grief hidden in this fit of long-suppressed weeping. It was, in truth, her brother's intolerant harshness which had unsealed the fountain of her tears; but their primary source lay deeper than any stab his hand could deal, and she poured them forth with a sense of unspeakable relief, in the certainty that their origin would not now be so much as suspected by one, to secure whose peace and repose was her chief earthly aim. The widow, troubled by the young girl's unwonted emotion, could find no way to console her—she could only pass her thin hands over the beautiful curls of dusky gold which were scattered over her lap, and repeat, "Hush, dear! hush, my little Elsie! Dinna greet, my lamb!"

For some time her sobs would not be stifled; they had been too long kept down to be easily conquered. At last, however, she lifted her fair face, and said, in a voice which belied her attempt to smile—

"Never mind, mother dear! but I was happy when I came in, and Norman troubled me. I canna help being afraid for him."

"Ye're right there, Elsie; he is a sair trouble and vex to mysel'. What was that he said anent a second warnin', that he told ye not to forget as ye had anither?"

"It was only—only—" and the little head drooped

again; "once, when you were not by, he spoke slightingly to me, and insisted to know what I had done that night—the night—you mind, mother?"

"The night ye met Claver'se? Aye, surely, Elsie."

"And I would not tell him," continued Alice, the rose-red colour creeping over her whole face. "I *could* not, mother. And he flyted at me sadly." Her voice failed again.

"Dinna ye think now, Elsie, that if he kenned how Claver'se spoke to ye, and guided ye weel, Norman might——"

"Oh, mother! no, no!" cried Alice, lifting her clasped hands eagerly; "for mercy's sake, no! he would never believe it; he would think—he would slay him—I *know*."

"Aweel, dearie; there is nae mair to be said then. I would cut my ain tongue out sooner than vex ye."

"Promise me again, mother, promise me," said the girl, gazing fixedly into her mother's face.

"I promise—I promise, my doo—ye canna ask what I wouldna do for ye, Alice."

The poor child threw her arms around her mother's neck, and the two lonely women—the one whose sorrows were drawing to an end, the other whose trials were just beginning—clung together with a love neither had fully understood in the days of their prosperity, but which was their richest consolation now.

CHAPTER XVII.

THE FOSTER-SISTERS.

She gazed upon a world she scarcely knew,
As seeking not to know it—silent, lone,
As grows a flower, thus silently she grew.

THE five or six weeks which followed these incidents were a period of great tranquillity and comparative enjoyment to Alice. Her mother's health, although fluctuating, was not on the whole seriously worse; and the kind attentions of the countess afforded many an alleviation to the straitened circumstances of her old acquaintance. Alice was not one of those perversely independent people who *will* be poor, nor one of those unhealthily-minded people who *will* be unhappy; her honest pride would always have prevented her allowing her mother to become a pensioner on any human being's bounty, but she did not consider herself obliged to refuse the delicate gifts and thoughtfully-contrived comforts that were showered upon the invalid—she accepted them as heartily as they were offered, and felt doubly gratified that her mother, and not herself, had been chosen as the object of generosity.

Neither, we repeat it, would she be wilfully unhappy, although, often after spending a couple of hours with her friend, poor Alice would droop miserably, from the very violence of the reaction.

Flora's merry gossip, her bright hopefulness and exuberant life, jarred most painfully on the tender nerves, which, bruised and aching with a constant strain, shrank sometimes from the most delicate touch. Often would her young heart, laden not only with her secret cares, but with the additional burden of her parent's declining strength, and Norman's unloving conduct, have fain relieved itself by a flood of bitter tears; but that could not be—she must bear up until—until when?

Alice dared not yet ask herself that question; the loss that was too surely coming upon her cast its shadow before, and darkly that shadow fell, deepening the twilight of a life scarcely yet in its early morning bloom and freshness. But, until what was now a transient pang of anticipation became a real living grief, she would endure all resignedly, nay, cheerfully: then if the voice which summoned her mother away should call her too, how gladly would she answer, "Here am I, Lord! thy servant heareth."

If anything, however, could have restored her spirits, it was the unfailing kindness which cherished her at "the Earl's Lodging," for so the mansion of the Glencarrig family was familiarly designated. The position she held in reference to her aristocratic friends was one which would hardly be understood at the present time. In no country of Europe were the privileges attached to gentle birth more scrupulously defined, or more rigidly adhered to, than amongst the higher ranks in Scotland at that period. Money there, as elsewhere, and as in all stages of the world's progress, had its full share of influence; but such was the value attached to birth and descent, that no amount of wealth was able fully to atone for a deficiency in this particular; while the possession of such advantages, even by a simple soldier in the ranks of the more aristocratic Scotch regiments, constituted him in every social respect the equal of men infinitely above him in fortune. Such being the case, it is very possible that Alice's claims to good, if not noble, blood may have had some effect in procuring for her the attention and respect with which she was treated by those so far removed by every adventitious circumstance from the humble station to which misfortune had reduced her; certain it is, that never by word or deed was she reminded of an inferiority which she scarcely forgot herself. The countess's affection for her was as much heightened by similarity of temperament and feeling as Flora's was by contrast. The elder lady had never recovered the shock of her husband's untimely death in the first days of their wedded happiness, and, although her piety and sense had taught her submission to the will of God, she had sunk beneath the blow, and for many years led the life almost of a recluse. Since her children had begun to grow up, she had indeed exerted herself more, and so far broken through her habits of retirement as to visit Paris and London (where Flora had been presented at both courts), and afterwards to inhabit for a time the family residence in Edinburgh, in the hope of securing a suitable establishment for her daughter.

But even there she rarely went abroad, save on some errand of benevolence, and left Flora a good deal to the chaperonage of Lady Dunbarton, who, although scarcely of an age to play duenna with effect, was a person of whose discretion and experience Lady Glencarrig had a high, and deservedly high, opinion The countess herself spent much of her time in her own apartment, or in a little room which, if we were not speaking of a staunch Protestant, we should be tempted to style an oratory—save when, now and then, a few intimate friends and connections met to enjoy a quiet evening with one as much admired as loved by all who knew her sense and gentleness.

Flora loved her mother dearly, and had for her far more deference than could have been expected from the young lady's lively and impetuous temper; she trusted her too, with all the simplicity of an unsophisticated heart, to which any sort of deceit was utterly foreign; but this latter merit had its inconvenient side, she was entirely wanting in reserve and self-command. What her heart thought her tongue spake unhesitatingly—a weakness which rendered the prospect of enjoying again the society of a friend into whose affectionate, and as she hoped sympathising, ears she could pour out all her news, her little troubles, her hopes, disappointments, and flirtations, something exquisitely delightful, especially when that friend was one whom she had known from childhood to be true as steel. So, on the very first day of their re-union, Alice found herself installed into the responsible office of *confidante en titre*, and depositary of the thousand little mysteries which gave so great a zest to Flora's pleasures in the gay circle to which her rank, wealth, and beauty, gave her an undisputed *entrée*.

The general scene of their conversations (if such be the word by which to describe a state of things wherein Flora talked and laughed, while Alice smiled, worked, and listened) was Lady Flora's dressing-room, or wardrobe as it was then called. This apartment was divided on the inside from her sleeping-chamber by three or four steps, and on the opposite side from the countess' oratory, by a private door and a long passage. The indulgent mother had fitted it up anew for her use; the hangings and furniture had been chosen by Flora herself, with coquettish reference to her own style of beauty—they were of yellow damask; the carpet had been expressly matched to them; the large mirror, in its broad carved frame, was almost tall enough to reflect the whole person of the fair occupant: every trifle about her showed the double influence of wealth to purchase and affection to lavish on a beloved child all the comfort that riches can obtain here below. The room looked out into a small court, containing a grass-plot and some fine old trees—a poor substitute for a garden—but, such as it was, few houses within the town could boast a similar possession. Here, whenever Alice could spare the time, or consent to leave her mother, the two girls would sit; Flora, luxuriously extended in an arm-chair, which, with its upright rigidity and uncompromising angles, would probably seem a stool of repentance to a modern fine lady; and Alice seated on a low cushion or ottoman by her side, her nimble fingers flying through the satin, velvet, or leather on which her skill was just then displaying itself, and which she rarely relinquished during her visits to the countess.

It was a considerable time before Alice could accustom herself to the sanguine lightheartedness of Flora; her own little world of ideas had closed in and darkened so steadily and imperceptibly, while Flora's had as steadily expanded and brightened, that they found themselves at an immense distance from each other. Alice felt this deeply; and the contrast of position, added to the difficulty of forcing her mind from its now habitual channels, rendered all communication with her new-found foster-sister rather painful than agreeable at first. But the great lesson of self-denial which her life had taught so well had not been wasted, and the unselfish gentleness with which she strove to banish her own pre-occupations to enter into Flora's pleasures profited her unconsciously. The weight of care might fall back as heavily as before when the short forgetfulness ceased; but momentary relief prevented its becoming overwhelming, and gave the quivering nerves time to gather strength for a fresh effort. Even in this world, the least of our good deeds never goes quite unrewarded, to those who can see and value the recompense.

Alice, when she had at last succeeded in partially turning her mind to a train of thought so unfamiliar, could not help confessing that Flora had grown a most amusing companion. She had, during the last two years, travelled a good deal, as travelling went in those days; and her observations, although rarely deep, were always lively and characteristic. Alice would listen with half-surprised amusement to the flood of gay talk, mingled with many a flash of wit and good feeling, in which Flora described her residence at Paris, the splendours of Versailles and Fontainebleau, the luxury of the French court, then in the apogee of its grandeur; or, coming nearer home, expatiate upon the beauty of Mary of Modena, the wit and grace of the noble English courtiers, and all the thousand attractions of the southern metropolis. But in these descriptions and anecdotes Alice only took such a dim, languid interest, as we feel for those things and persons with whom we have nothing in common, and whom we never expect or care to see. She waited and listened for one single name, to drink in the praises of one single being; but she was constantly disappointed—and the rest had but a poor savour to her longing ears.

We should have mentioned that the young Earl of Glencarrig was a very frequent guest at these conversations; and, after the first two or three hesitating approaches, had succeeded, as he phrased it, "in effecting a lodgment in the body of the place." At the beginning of their renewed intercourse, his visits to Lady Flora's boudoir had been confined to a ten minutes' chat, while comparing notes for the day's engagements and occupations; then, kissing his sister's hand with the chivalrous politeness required by the etiquette of the day even between near relations, and performing the same ceremony to Alice with an additional dash of warmth and gallantry, he would cock his beaver, arrange his ruffles before the mirror, give a glance at the tie of his cravat, a becoming twist to his hair, and betake himself to his amusements, leaving the two girls to their own devices. But very soon this short apparition extended itself to half an hour, then to an hour; and at last the very presence of Alice in the dressing-room seemed to acquire some marvellous faculty of summoning him from wherever he might happen to be, to the precincts of the pleasant, luxurious little sanctuary in which the friends wiled away their spare hours.

The earl was very fond of his beautiful sister—very fond and very proud: it was pretty and graceful to see the resemblance between the gallant young stripling and the handsome, warm-hearted girl, as well as the strong affection which united them. Both had the same sunny, exciteable temperament, inherited from their father, the same happy faculty of seeing things *couleur de rose*, the same childlike open-heartedness and sincerity which made every emotion transparent, the same rather petulant temper and little goodnatured vanity, which so many advantages of nature and fortune might well excuse. But these latter faults, although common to both, were more conspicuous in Flora; and there were also other differences very discernible to so quick an observer as Alice. Flora was shrewd and rather satirical, the earl blunt, unsuspicious, and earnest; her careless speeches, amounting frequently to imprudence, were the result of gay *nonchalance* and overflowing spirits, while his straightforwardness arose from that boyish *naïveté* which no acquaintance with the world ever quite destroys, when inherent as in his case. Both were affectionate, but Flora's affection, especially to Alice, had always a spice of playful patronage about it, rather perhaps in manner than in feeling; the earl's, on the contrary, resembled the eager yet submissive vehemence of a caressing child who will be loved and noticed at any price. But, in whatever points they might be unlike, they agreed marvellously well in spoiling each other, and seemed much disposed to follow the same course towards Alice, who, poor child! had so long been deprived of any such gratification, that she rejoiced at first in the tenderness which showed itself willing to smooth, as far as might be, her rough and solitary road through a world that was so full of friendly warmth to them.

"At first," we said, and not without reason for the qualification, for matters were not always destined to run so smooth a course. The first ripple on the quiet stream was a most disagreeable and perplexing consciousness of a marked change in Lord Glencarrig's manner towards herself.

Alice had no taint of coquetry in her disposition, and as little vanity as it is possible to imagine; but her perceptions were exquisitely delicate and keen, and, as in some finely organised natures, amounted at times to an infallible instinct. She neither disliked nor feared the young earl; on the contrary, she bore him all that frank, trustful attachment which arises naturally from the remembrance of childish companionship in happy days gone by, and, as long as his feelings merely reciprocated this, she had not scrupled to show *hers*. But as soon as he changed, even by a hair's breadth, the perfect simplicity of their brotherly and sisterly intercourse was marred; the more he advanced, the more Alice drew back, for she knew, with the unerring quickness of her sex, sharpened too by the new experience which had come upon her, that the boy friend was rapidly becoming the lover.

Of all unwelcome knowledge this was, perhaps, the most painful to Alice—not merely from a sense of the unlikelihood of anything but sorrow resulting from it—not merely from the proud humility which, situated as she was, made the very suspicion of such an attachment a sort of treason to her confiding friends—not, certainly, that she suspected him yet of evil which did not enter her innocent mind—but chiefly from this, that she loved another wholly, utterly, entirely, and shrank with a true woman's sensitive repulsion from any homage but that of the one beloved. She alternately hoped and feared that Flora might notice and speak of that which to her was so plain; she would willingly have consented to stand self-accused of the most outrageous vanity if she could thus have obtained the certainty that she had been mistaken, and that the fits of depression, caprice, and wayward passion which had replaced his wonted glee, and unclouded enjoyment of every passing hour, could be traced to any other source than one which was adding a fresh perplexity to her varied troubles. She tried to shut her eyes upon the fact, she tried to refer it to any cause but that which *would* not be driven from her mind; but blindness and indifference were both equally unavailing; the conviction remained, and, what was worse, its correctness became every day more apparent. And, as if some adverse fate had laid a spell on all that concerned our gentle heroine, the last poor remnant of doubt to which she clung was torn from her when she least expected it.

She had gone one morning to visit Flora, who had been slightly indisposed, and was standing waiting at one of the dressing-room windows, looking down into a narrow lane which ran into Peebles Wynd, and formed one side of the house. Flora came softly in, and took her friend round the waist.

"What, Elsie!" said she, kissing Alice's fair cheek with an air of protection that was very pretty and appropriate from the tall, stately beauty to the slight, modest, tender-eyed girl, "What, Elsie! art *thou* watching for them? Fie on thee, my little Puritan! these are worldly vanities, thou knowest."

"What are, Madam Flora?" asked Alice, surprised.

"The soldiers. Hast thou not heard that there is wild work again with the clans in the north, and that some of the Scots Musketeers, and three companies of Wauchop's Foot, are under orders to march this morning? 'Twill be a pretty sight—I love the brave scarlet and flashing steel;—and there is to be a review before they leave, at which my cousin of

Claverhouse will attend with a troop of the Guards, and many noble gentlemen besides—the Duke of Queensberry, the Earl of Dunfermline, and Gilbert Hay——"

"Does Colonel Grahame go north also?" said Alice, timidly.

"No; but Glencarrig does," replied Flora, "and I know not what I shall do without him. My mother has been urging him to this for a month past; his presence is needed at the Castle, but still he lingers here as if he were charmed to the spot, as, indeed, I doubt not he is."

"How so, Flora?" said Alice, with nervous anxiety for the reply.

"Don't look so startled, Gowan; hast thou not yet ceased to believe in the sprites, and bogles, and worricows that scared our babyhood? The only enchantment in the matter is the handsome face and bewitching eyes of Mary Charteris; at least so I guess, for she was the first dame who fired his susceptible breast, and he consorts over much with her brother Walter, a graceless youth! If indeed this be true, why then woe is me for my poor Glencarrig! she is the most heartless coquette that ever beguiled an unhappy mortal to his misery, and will fling him off like a soiled ribbon at the first caprice."

They continued silent for a space, both looking vacantly below, where the earl's servants were in attendance with his horses and baggage. Then Flora resumed, turning to her foster-sister,

"I hope a short stay at Glencarrig may help to cure David of this infatuation."

"He does not accompany the troops then?" said Alice.

"Only so far as their roads lie together; but the country is so disturbed that the countess was glad of an escort. I wish, Alice—I wish that I were going too, there is no place so fair to me as my dear home; and yet I should most likely be weary of it in a week, and impatient to return here," added Flora, laughing and blushing with charming embarrassment.

"I would that I had never left it," murmured Alice."

"Ay, Gowan! and wherefore?" asked Flora. "But hark! here they come! Oh, how my heart dances to the trumpet's call! I am a true Scotswoman and soldier's daughter! We shall see them bravely, for Colonel Grahame promised to stop, and meet David here, on their way. Come to the other side of the house, Elsie, they will pass down the wynd—come, quick!"

And without waiting for Alice she darted off to seek a better point of view for her own especial attraction in the gallant train which already began to fill the narrow wynd, with noise, and music, and military splendour.

Alice, still more deeply interested, was preparing to follow, when the glitter of steel caught her eye; the trampling of horse, which had stopped for a moment, was renewed; and Colonel Grahame of Claverhouse, followed by several other officers and gentlemen of rank, rode into the lane, and reined up his impatient steed under the window from which Alice, half nestled in the curtains, leaned to watch him.

He was mounted on a superb bay charger, whose sinewy limbs, small head, and arched neck, showed a strain of Arab blood; his scarlet uniform and brilliant cuirass, his golden gorget and jewelled sword-hilt flashed back the sun-rays in a glow of dazzling radiance. He looked magnificently handsome, as he bent gracefully from the saddle to speak with Lady Glencarring at the open window below; the snowy plumes on his polished head-piece, drooping over his shoulder until they mingled with the rich dark hair, which, lifted softly by a light morning breeze, waved back from his flushed cheek and noble face, usually so calm, but sparkling now with unwonted gaiety and interest. No wonder was it that Alice should stoop, with parted lips and quick-drawn breath, to gaze on him; no wonder that her soul passed into her soft eyes, as if by the electric passion of that glance she could stir to life one spark of responsive fire in his; no wonder that she strained her ear to catch the faintest sound of the voice, which rose, clear and full, through the mingled noise of man and horse; but better far for Alice had it been that her spirit had passed away on that never-to-be-forgotten night—when her head lay on that mailed breast—when those dark eyes looked down on her with such fatherly pity—rather than that the voice, so fatally dear to her now, had ever aroused her from her dream of placid childhood to this knowledge of a woman's love and a woman's despair.

A hand stole into hers and lifted it from behind; a breath came upon her cheek, and a voice said in her ear,

"Alice, dearest, I *must* go. Farewell."

Blushing deeply, Alice hastily, though quietly, withdrew her hand from a clasp which spoke unutterable things.

"Farewell, my lord," she answered; for the speaker was the young earl himself, equipped in travelling gear, booted and spurred.

"How coldly you say it, Alice," he answered sorrowfully; "have you no share in my regret at parting? have you not a kind word for me?"

"Indeed, my lord, one would think you were bound on a ten years' journey," replied Alice, trying to hide her double embarrassment by forced playfulness.

"It will seem a lifetime to me, away from you, Alice," he murmured.

Alice set her lips with almost painful force, and said nothing. The young man's eyes followed hers jealously; fortunately, from where he stood he could not see Claverhouse.

"Say, adieu, and God speed me, dear Alice," he said, almost imploringly.

"With all my heart," replied Alice, frankly. "See, my lord, they are waiting for you below. Let me call Flora."

"It is needless; I have already seen her. Your hand, Alice—nay, you will surely not refuse me!"

Seizing both her hands in his, he kissed them repeatedly—lingered an instant—turned back once at the door, and disappeared.

Alice saw him mount and prepare to start—she

saw him give an upward glance at the window, and involuntarily drew back; a cold chill of miserable presentiment crept over her; but it was not until Colonel Grahame had ridden off—not until the last outline of his figure had vanished, and the clatter of horse-hoofs died away on the pavement, that she allowed herself to think of any other mortal being. Then she sat down, and, covering her face, gave way.

She did not shed a tear—she dared not, for at any instant Flora might return; but she wrung her hands in very shame at her own helpless weakness. For weeks and months she had striven so honestly, so firmly, to quell this passion—she thought she had, at least, schooled herself to calmness and courage—and lo! in one single moment the whole fabric of her boasted self-reliance had fallen lower than ever. And, as if that were not enough, she now saw herself destined to become to another the origin of the same suffering as she experienced—she, a victim, was to become the tormentor of a friend!

The first sound that startled her out of this perplexity of contending emotions was Flora's voice; and that fell in the midst of her secret thoughts so suddenly, that she indeed turned pale like a guilty thing. She looked so unlike herself, that Flora anxiously asked if anything ailed her.

"Nothing that you or any one else can help, dear Flora," she replied. "But I am weary of the town—the air is so thick and stifling—I think I cannot live long here." Her voice was trembling, a very little.

"Oh! Elsie, what an idea! my little Gowan, what

folly!" exclaimed Flora, laughing: "thou art tired, that is all—I always said thou did'st work too hard. Why, the bugles and trumpets just now might have scared away the darkest vapours: if I were but a man, like David, I would turn trooper myself. Did'st thou see my cousin Grahame, Alice? Is he not handsome? But, I forgot; Glencarrig vows that thou and he are old acquaintances—tell me all about it, my little gossip."

"Indeed, I cannot, Madam Flora," said Alice, decidedly. "Do not ask me."

"Not ask thee! faith but I will, and I do! such a tale must be worth hearing. My shy little Gowan acquainted with so terrible a person as Claver'se, and I am forbidden to inquire how it came about! Come, Elsie—love—tell me."

But all Flora's caresses and teazing were thrown away for once: Alice was firmly resolved not to commit the keeping of such knowledge to any chances of discretion. She was sure that Flora had no secrets from her brother—she more than suspected that the earl's curiosity had stimulated his sister's; and the mere idea that all her precious memories might become public property made her shiver. And then, if the story came round to Colonel Grahame's ears, with what contempt would he learn that she, who in that mute appeal had so earnestly implored his silence, had been the first to betray her own confidence! She only shook her head, replying to Lady Flora's playful though half-annoyed entreaties by the same words as before.

"Do not ask me, Flora—I dare not."

She spoke the truth in this; for, indeed, she dared not trust herself to tell that tale—to utter his name, lest she might be carried away to say that which she would bitterly repent before the words were spoken.

Flora grew quite angry.

"He must either have injured you deeply, I conclude," she said, when she had exhausted all her powers of persuasion, "or else, what is far more likely, Alice is grown such a coward as to put faith in every silly old wife's fable that has stained the fame of a noble gentleman."

"No, Flora, no, you are unjust!" said the poor girl, and could say no more—her friend's temper pained her too much.

Flora coloured, and, turning sharply away, took up a large black bound volume from her dressing-table, and sat down with her back to Alice, feigning to read. But the pages were passed over a great deal too rapidly for the ponderous nature of their contents, which, being the last new romance of Scudéri, exceeded all previous ones in incomprehensible and dreary absurdity. Throwing that down, she next fetched a piece of such needlework as fine ladies are wont to dawdle over; but her silk knotted, her needle broke—nothing went to her mind; and the young lady, feeling herself thoroughly in the wrong, grew completely out of patience. A quarter of an hour had elapsed in these various little manœuvres, until Alice, who had been watching for an opportunity to address her, rose, with a stifled sigh, to take leave. That sound, and the sight of her sweet, patient face smote Flora with a sense of her own ungenerous behaviour, and her heart melted. She threw her arms round Alice, and exclaimed, petulant in her love as in her anger:

"My own sister! kiss me! forgive me! how cruel I have been. Keep thy secret, and fifty more, for aught Flora cares!"

Alice looked up, and laid her cheek against Flora's, but her throat ached so intensely with suppressed emotion, that she could not utter a syllable. Flora fondled her like a child, and kissed off the large drops which hung heavily on her brown lashes.

"Is it peace?" she said, with an arch smile—and the reflection of that smile on Alice's face assured her that it was.

The friends sat side by side for some time, quite silent.

"How could I be unkind to thee, Gowan?" said Flora, remorsefully: "but I was chafed to think thou could'st be weak enough to believe all the idle falsehoods that are told of my cousin Grahame. Thou mayest have seen him, Alice; but thou can'st not *know* him, or thou would'st surely have forgotten them at once."

"Indeed, Flora?" said Alice, only too glad that her friend's fancy had taken a wrong direction, and quite willing to leave her in error.

"Ay, indeed, Alice," said Flora, smiling; "but I was not always so brave. Dost thou mind how, years ago, at Glencarrig, news came down that Claver'se was expected on a visit to my mother—and thou and

I, our heads filled, I trow, with thy good father's stories of Drumclog and Bothwell, fairly wept for terror, like silly moppets as we were; and how we prayed that we might go to the manse, and stay there until he had left? My mother said that for thee it mattered not; but that I was half a Grahame, and must meet our kinsman."

"I mind as if it were yesterday, Flora; and how Lord Glencarrig mocked at our terrors."

"Telling us that we were mistaken—that Claverhouse was no *mangeur de petits enfants*—no rude soldier—no noisy, fire-eating trooper; but young and gay, fair in face, and mild in speech—a gallant and winsome gentleman. It was all true, Elsie, and so I acknowledged, when four months syne I met my kinsman for the first time."

Alice raised her face, in which the colour had begun to dawn again—for, to a woman's ear, there is no sound so exquisitely sweet as the praise of him she loves—and Flora spoke so rarely of Colonel Grahame as to make the delight all the greater from its scarcity. She smiled brightly at her friend's reminiscences.

"Thou may'st smile, Elsie, but it is no jest," said Flora: "and, by my faith, I wish I could see thee face to face with him—my pretty Puritan dove with the Cavalier falcon. I would never forgive thee, could'st thou think evil of him after that."

"Why then is he called cruel and cold?" said Alice, driven to speak words her heart disavowed by that wretched love of self-torture which sometimes prompts us to drive the sting of a hated idea deeper and deeper into our own minds, as if to try how much we can endure.

"I cannot tell," answered Flora: "cold, indeed, he seems to pleasure, and with little interest in the common trifles that surround him: but I know him to be a true and stedfast friend, deeply loved by those who have been with him for years—who have fought by his side, and read his innermost heart; and, if he be harsh, it is only to such as by their crimes and rebellion have driven him to sternness. I admire him much, and like him well; he is a valiant soldier and true Cavalier, as spotless in repute, as devoted in loyalty, as ever was knight of old—*sans peur et sans reproche*. They say the King is about to create him a viscount. I hope it may prove true, for never, surely, was coronet more gallantly won or more worthily worn.—But, Alice," she added laughing, "you will fancy I am in love with my handsome cousin, to hear me speak thus warmly of him, I suppose."

"No, Madam Flora, I know better than that," replied Alice.

"I should hope so, Gowan. But I *am* proud of him, as is natural to one in whose veins runs the mingled blood of Grahame and Bethune. I am little of a heroine, I trow, yet if aught could make me so, that surely might."

"I am no heroine either," said Alice, "and yet, Flora, for a good cause, for right and truth, for the sake of one I loved, I could die; nay, more, I could *suffer*."

"Is suffering worse than death, then?" asked Flora in great astonishment.

"Ay, madam, death is short and life very long, and sorrow is hard to thole—it is a daily death."

"Thou art strangely grave, my darling Elsie, and thy pale cheek and trembling lip tell me thou art speaking from thine own knowledge, and not from other folk's fancies or experience. Thy fate is a dull and lonely one, and I swear to thee that I feel almost guilty at times, to live so bright and careless a life, when I think of thy patient goodness. I could, I *know* I could, fly to meet danger and death on a battle-field, for my heart leaps up, and my blood stirs hotly, at feats of devoted daring, but I should soon fade and pine away were I in thy place, Alice."

"As is thy day, so shall thy strength be," said Alice. "I cannot ask more than that promise; I have many blessings, and, when I repine, it is not His fault who denies me what I wish, but mine that cannot see my own good: and indeed His ways *are* dark sometimes, very dark."

Flora put her arms round Alice and held her close, with a generous admiration of that quiet heroism which she herself would have been incapable of exercising. Alice did not pursue the subject; it was too tender and dangerous a theme, for, whenever it recurred, the multiplied difficulties which surrounded her would crowd back upon her heart, and impel her with almost resistless force to pour out her troubles and fears in words. The temptation was so strong that she would again and again have given a kingdom to discharge her overflowing feelings; and, debarred as she was from home confidence by the dread of distressing her mother, find, if not consolation, at least relief, in the tender affection of one whom she regarded as a sister.

Alice was very young, not eighteen yet, and, much as she had learned and suffered during the past year, the frankness of youth, and the natural trustfulness of her disposition, struggled hard against the imperious necessities which bound her to silence. How could she tell the haughty girl that her brother was in all human probability on the verge of a declaration of love to the humble friend whom *she* chose to treat as an equal? How could she, by betraying her anxiety for Norman's future, accuse him of participation in intrigues for which death was then regarded as too easy a punishment? And how, most wildly impossible of all, could she avow her unsought, despairing love for such a man as Claverhouse, and that to his own kinswoman? The energy with which she repelled this temptation only increased its fascination, and, if Flora never knew what was passing in her friend's mind, she never knew either how often the confession had risen to her lips, had actually begun to take voice, and died away from the impossibility of putting such thoughts into language, as well as from dread lest she should thereby alienate the only friends she possessed. Her modest and delicate nature, strong as it was to bear pain, shrunk from shame or shadow of reproach with morbid sensitiveness; she longed for sympathy, yet by no effort could she have brought herself to risk what might, or as she thought *must*, ensue upon any attempt to obtain it. So she turned to her patient waiting again, and, communing with her own heart—sadly enough, God knows, for one so young and fair—was still.

CHAPTER XVIII.

THE COURSE OF TRUE LOVE.

> **A subtle, sudden flame,**
> **By veering passion fanned,**
> **About thee breaks and dances.**
> **When I would kiss thy hand,**
> **The flush of angered shame**
> **O'erflows thy calmer glances;**
> **O'er thy black brows drops down**
> **A sudden curved frown.**
>
> **TENNYSON.**

IT may perhaps seem strange to those who have never remarked the incredible, inexplicable fatality by which certain persons are surrounded, or how in real life the most apparently improbable circumstances are combined in a manner that would be condemned as unpardonably absurd in fiction—to such, I say, it may appear strange that so little mention should have been made by the Glencarrig family of their kinsman, or that the subject should have been so seldom broached. But if all the details of their connection, too long to explain, and uninteresting to the reader, were brought into action, the singularity would vanish at once, and appear in no way inconsistent with the relation in which he then stood towards them.

His early friendship for the countess had been so long broken off, that upon its renewal at the time of her arrival in Edinburgh they had met almost as with morbid sensitiveness; she longed for sympathy, yet by no effort could she have brought herself to risk what might, or as she thought *must*, ensue upon any attempt to obtain it. So she turned to her patient waiting again, and, communing with her own heart—sadly enough, God knows, for one so young and fair—was still.

the dissipation and excitement of the capital, Colonel Grahame's duties rarely permitted him to enjoy the pleasure of her society, and, as a wood-lily hangs its fair bells at the foot of a stately oak, she lived placidly in her sweet seclusion, overshadowed by the renown and importance of her husband, hardly remembered or regarded by the world, or by those who perchance resented her marriage as an intrusion on the exclusive purity of their Cavalier blood. She was unknown to Flora, except by name, and in all probability the young lady hardly cared to recall her existence.

The fact is, that Lady Flora might, perhaps, have had more thought to spare for her cousin's concerns, and been induced to take more interest in his proceedings, but for the attachment she had formed to Lord Gilbert Hay; and Alice had not conversed twice with her friend before she became quite initiated into this little romance. Flora made no direct confession; indeed, she generally pretended, as is the fashion of some damsels, to feel a carelessness about him, which, being over acted, defeated its own purpose. The matter was tacitly understood between them, and Flora, in complete defiance of her feigned indifference, would talk to Alice by the hour together of all that had occurred since first they met, and the various lights and shadows which had flitted across her prospects. It was a very honest and real affection; but Alice, poor simple child! used often to marvel in the secret of her heart whether this summer-day love, with its yet untold but mutual preference—its bright future, its pretty jealousies, only another and almost as delightful an adoration—its tender quarrels and ready forgiveness—its thousand graceful incidents of pleasure, and of pain almost as sweet, could indeed be the same feeling as the untameable passion which was slowly drinking her life-blood—whether she herself were a creature of the same mould and race? If Flora's were a true love, what could this be which she experienced?

The intercourse between the young friends was somewhat interrupted by the sudden illness of Madam Scott. In this emergency, Alice was very glad to be able, by the countess's assistance, to devote herself solely to the task of nursing her mother, and for many days she scarcely left her an instant. Meanwhile, the unwearying kindness of her noble friends seemed to redouble. Every appliance of comfort and proof of sympathy that tenderness could bring to bear upon their troubles was freely showered on Alice and her parent. Lady Glencarrig was a constant visitor in the widow's sick room, where her light hand, her sweet voice, her sincere kindliness, and, above all, that exquisite refinement of feeling and manner which personal experience can alone bestow, rendered her presence as soothing to the weary sufferer as it was cheering and delightful to Alice. Lady Glencarrig kept Flora carefully away until all immediate danger was over, for she knew only too well that her daughter's high spirits were the last thing likely to raise those of Alice under the pressure of such alarm and anxiety; but when the crisis was past, and Madam Scott began at length to speak and move freely, which for some time she had not been permitted to do,—when a little rest and quiet had restored Alice to something of her usual self again, the countess allowed her daughter to spend much of her time with her foster-sister, in the double hope that her gaiety would amuse the invalid, and that the sight of sickness and patient resignation might temper Flora's superabundant, almost reckless, animation. So many a day the noble young lady would come to her friend's humble lodging—only too glad to see her darling Alice again, and rejoicing in the warmth of her honest heart at being no longer excluded from anything that could serve or please her.

Madam Scott was excessively fond of Flora, whom she had once helped the countess to nurse through a long and dangerous illness; nothing delighted her more than that the young lady should sit beside her bed and amuse her by the hour together with lively tales of the world's gay doings, with anecdotes of great folk (for Madam Scott, like most of her country-people, had an immense and childlike reverence for ancestry); stories of her brother's goodness, courage, and amiability; and especially with minute accounts of their own life since the two families had been separated. When, as sometimes happened, the invalid was too fatigued or too excited to bear this, Flora would retreat into the little sitting room, and drawing Alice along with her, hold deep consultation on innumerable girlish difficulties—nearly all of which, as may be imagined, related to her own love affairs.

One sunny evening towards the close of July, Flora made her appearance as usual, but with an air of semi-depression on her radiant face that was something quite uncommon. Madam Scott, too weak yet to rise, was fast asleep, and Alice in the front room intently busy with some work which had been long set aside and was now urgently required. Flora, who possessed to a singular degree all the instincts of coquettish luxury inherent in those whose whole existence has been passed in elegance and ease, took possession of the wide window seat, arranged the stuff curtains so as to make a cushion to lean against, and sat there coiled up in an attitude perfectly graceful, because perfectly natural, looking sometimes out of window—no very extensive prospect—and sometimes at Alice, who worked away with her habitual steady diligence. She never did anything by halves.

Ten minutes might have elapsed before Alice came to a pause, and resting her hands for a minute on her lap looked admiringly at Flora.

"Well?" said that young lady, interrogatively.

"You are quite a picture, Flora," said Alice, for her tasteful eye caught at once the whole beauty of her friend's appearance—the evening sunlight tinting her thick raven curls with a purple glow, heightening the fresh crimson of cheek and lip by the reflection of the curtain against which she leaned, and suffusing her polished neck and round white arms with a rosy flush.

"You are bonnie the night, Flora—I never saw you look so beautiful."

"I don't care!" retorted Flora, with an odd laughable mixture of affected sullenness and decided gratification, "I don't care a straw! What good does it do me or any one else? I would not care if I were as ugly and wrinkled as old Madam Rachel."

Alice rested her elbow on her knee, and her chin on the palm of her right hand—asking no questions, for she was quite sure that now the ice was broken Flora would go on spontaneously—but showing sufficient interest in her face to encourage her exasperated friend to unbosom herself, and follow up this remarkable speech by something explanatory.

"I might as well be so, for aught anybody cares!" said Flora, with a fresh pout.

"Anybody or somebody?" asked Alice, with a little smile.

"Somebody if you will, it is all one to me!" was the sharp reply, emphasized by an indescribable motion of the head, and a toss back of the shining black tresses which promised nothing pleasant to the offender.

"How long is it since you saw Lord Gilbert Hay?" said Alice, perceiving that Flora desired nothing so dearly as to be asked.

"The day before yesterday—and oh, I wish I had not! I wish I hated him!" said poor Flora, impetuously, and with a sort of sob; "he's cruel and insolent, and I *do* hate him."

"Hush, hush!" said Alice, who was pretty well used to such little outbreaks, although this seemed more serious than the generality of Flora's quarrels with her liege vassal. "Speak lower, dear Flora, you will awaken my mother."

Even this very modest request seemed a fresh offence to the irritated damsel; she held her tongue abruptly, and looked studiously out of window; but presently the flood of vexation boiled up afresh, and she began again, half muttering to herself,

"If his lordship dreams that Flora Bethune is his devoted slave, forsooth! to be put on or flung off at pleasure like his glove, he shall rue the day he thought so. Good faith, I'll make his life a burden to him! Now, Alice, you shall judge between us."

"I'll be a sad partial judge, I fear, dear Flora."

"No, no; you know not what it is to be in love; shame fa' on me that own it! So listen; nay, your mother is sound asleep—come closer, or I shall repent having said I would tell you."

Alice did as she was bid, wondering what great offence had occasioned this mighty tempest.

"It happened at the Duke of Queensberry's," began Flora, trusting probably to her auditor's penetration to discover the fact to which this vague impersonal pronoun referred. "We were trysted, Alice; he was to meet me there, and I had promised to him every dance for which I was not engaged beforehand. I went with Lady Dunbarton and the earl."

"Was your mother not with you?" asked Alice.

"My mother, dear innocent soul! was at home; and do you think I weary her with this sort of thing? Well, but he was *not* there; no sign nor shadow of him to be seen! I took patience, and danced with every one who chose to ask me; but I was growing furious. Ay, Alice! you may look at me with your dove's eyes, I was! Eight, nine, ten o'clock came, and no Gilbert. I heard Anne Laurie and Magdalen Carnegie whispering and mocking behind me: Annie was saying, 'Poor Lady Flora! she has lost a night.' 'Ay,' answered Magdalen; 'and, what is worse, to-morrow she will have to wear the willow!' *I* wear the willow! I just happened to look round, and there stood my cousin of Claverhouse, close beside me, with his eyes fixed on me; he had heard their talk, and knew all, I am convinced."

"Why do you think so?"

"By his face; by the expression of those strange eyes of his, which I never could fathom, nor any one else, I fancy. They are as clear and dark as the great pool of the Carrig-burn, beyond the stepping-stones where we used to cross to the Greenshaw-bank; you mind, Alice?"

"Yes, too well," answered Alice thoughtfully. Too well, indeed, she knew that look in the deep eyes, which, like the heaven-stolen spark of Prometheus, had first fired her woman's soul within her.

"'Colonel Grahame,' said I, 'are you engaged for the remainder of this night?' 'Not in any way that could prevent my being at the orders of the fairest lady in this assembly,' said he smiling. 'You will, then, consider yourself my cavalier until we break up?' said I. He bowed. I took his arm, and began to talk gaily to him, though my heart was sair, for, Alice, I had just seen him—Gilbert, you know—come into the ball-room with a stranger. I was resolved to punish him."

"Oh, Flora dearest, how wrong!" said Alice gently.

"*Wrong!* when he had broken tryst. *I* wrong! nay, Alice, you are not half a woman!" exclaimed Flora with great dignity. "Just hear the rest. He came up to us, and claimed my promise. 'Pardon me, my lord,' I said, 'you have broken *your* half of our evening's engagement; permit me to consider myself as free from mine. I am no longer at liberty.' Gilbert turned as pale as you are now, and his eyes flashed daggers at Colonel Grahame. Had my partner been any one else, I should have been thoroughly frightened lest a quarrel should come of it; but nobody likes to meddle with Claver'se, and for that very reason I cast my eyes on him. None other would have answered my purpose half so well. 'Can I not persuade Colonel Grahame to relinquish his fair cousin's hand in my favour?' said Gilbert very courteously, but his face was working. 'Your lordship must excuse my objecting to any such disposal of my person,' said I, as haughtily as I could. 'I shall follow my own inclinations—under your favour;' and therewith turned my back on him. He called me by name, but I lent only a deaf ear. He stood still, looking dumbfoundered; then deliberately, before my face, went and asked Magdalen for the cotillon! What was my anger to him? He knows I cannot bear her, and intended that for a fresh insult. All the rest of the evening I danced with Claverhouse; and, although I feigned to be gayer and more lighthearted than ever, and flirted and jested with all comers, I was sick with disappointment—I could not have suffered more from the thumbscrews—for I could see him talking and laughing with Magdalen; not once coming nigh me, not even looking towards me; and she, the vain peat, triumphing in her prize. And, oh! I hate him!" sobbed Flora, quite breaking down, and apparently not in the least aware of her own inconsistency. She was a great deal too much in love to be reasonable or logical.

"Go on, dearest," said Alice, much interested, but quite unable to conceive the feelings which had prompted her friend's line of conduct.

"He passed me as I went out, and looked as though he would have addressed me, but I was utterly blind and deaf to him, with no eyes or ears but for my cousin. Yet he, like you, thought me in the wrong!"

"Let me listen one moment," said Alice, laying her hand on Flora's arm, and raising her head to listen intently; "my mother called me!"

"No, no," repeated Flora impatiently. "As we went down the stair to join Lady Dunbarton, my cousin said to me, 'Pardon me, Lady Flora, if I tell you that you have not acted a wise part to-night.' 'I want no one to teach me how to act,' said I, for in truth I cared not to be so schooled; it was my affair, not his. 'And,' he went on, 'as I have helped you to torment some one else, as well as yourself, most assiduously to-night, give me your permission to assist in setting this slight variance straight again.' '*I* have not been tormented,' said I—(oh, Alice love, it was false; but I was angry to think how well he read me!)—'and if Lord Gilbert Hay cares for my favour, and has suffered under its loss, let him come to seek it again himself.' 'You are wrong, Lady Flora,' said my cousin Grahame; 'believe one who has had reason to know; men's hearts are not to be won or kept so lightly, even by the lode-stars of your bright eyes.' 'If he chooses to be jealous, let him please himself,' answered I. 'That, my fair cousin, you must know is impossible,' said he very seriously, and so the matter ended. I forbade him to interfere; so now for four days I have not caught a glimpse of Gilbert, except once in the Lawn Market, when he just lifted his hat and passed me by like a stranger; and I am wretched!"

Therewith Flora wept afresh; then pretended she did not care in the least—a pretence which could not hide a very plain prick of conscience; and finished by vowing most vehemently for the third time that she detested her truant lover.

"Flora, Flora, you are to blame!" said Alice gently, but decidedly. "You know nothing of his reasons for delay; you were hasty and unjust—wherefore should you have tried to make him jealous?"

"Jealous! absurd!" retorted Flora petulantly; "what call had he to be jealous, I ask you?"

"I know not," replied Alice in a low voice, for the effort to speak was very great; "but, from all I have heard of your cousin—of Colonel Grahame—I should not have thought him a rival to be despised, even by my Lord Gilbert Hay ——"

"Claver'se!" exclaimed Flora, laughing outright in the midst of her tears; "jealous of *him!* is any one jealous of the Bass Rock, or of Benarde, or ——

Besides, my silly little Gowan, remember, I pray you, that Colonel Grahame ——"

"Is married," would the next moment have left her lips, but Alice had already disappeared. A faint call from her mother's room had already twice reached her ear, and that sound had overpowered even the echo of the loved name.

Ten minutes or more elapsed ere she came back, and Flora had by that time subsided into a fit of passionate crying, which quite extinguished every trace of what she had been about to say. Alice tried very hard to comfort her, but Flora refused to be comforted; and, instead of submitting to be shown her error, and the best way of repairing it, wandered off into a half-angry, half-regretful description of all the happiness she had hoped to enjoy, of her jealousy and despite, of two other assemblies where she had failed to meet him—until, at last, her sorrowful stories were cut short by the arrival of her servants and the necessity for departure.

Alice kissed her affectionately; and, telling her that the darkest hour is always before morning (an assertion which Flora received with a mournful shake of the head and a fresh burst of tears), went back to sit by her mother's side, to watch her troubled slumbers, and to wonder whether *her* darkest hour was come, and when her morning star would rise.

Oh, Alice, not in this world—not here, nor yet, sweet Alice! But the light that ariseth in darkness was thine; and, feeble though its ray might sometimes be, it was never extinguished, but shone on more and more brightly until the perfect day.

CHAPTER XIX.

ATTACK AND DEFENCE.

This sport, well carried, shall be chronicled.
If you have any pity, grace, or manners,
You would not make me such an argument.
MIDSUMMER NIGHT'S DREAM.

ALICE was really somewhat anxious for Flora—the more so, that three days elapsed without her coming near them; and the young girl felt certain that, had any favourable turn taken place in the ruffled current of her true love, Flora would have been only too eager to communicate it. She had been thinking of this a good deal, and watching her mother as she reclined near the open window of their little sitting-room, when the light, hurried sound of steps, and the rushing of silk and brocade along the narrow passage, announced the advent of Flora. In she came, breathless, flushed, with sparkling eyes—looking perfectly enchanting.

"Dear Flora! how glad I am!" exclaimed Alice, springing up; "is all right?" she added in a lower voice, holding her by the arm.

Flora held her peace for an instant, struggling between smiles and tears; then, with an April face of showery laughter, she cried—

"Alice! Alice! kiss me! I am too happy—happier than ever I deserved to be! Why do you look at me so? Cannot ye guess, my doo? He has spoken to my mother—to David—and I am to be his wife!"

"Come hither, my bonnie leddy," said the kind widow, stretching out her hand to Flora; "God's blessing be on your betrothal, and mine too, if it's on'y comfort to ye, and on yer husband that is to be; I mind him weel."

"You! dear Madam Scott?" said Flora, in a tone of some surprise and pleased curiosity.

"Ou aye! if he's the same Gilbert Hay I kenned years syne at the Howe o' Angus; he was there wi' his wee brither Richard and his dominie Maister John Strachan—a gentle auld body, but ane that the young lords behoved to obey. Isna he a straight and buirdly youth—fair and tall, wi' blue e'en, and a winsome face, and hair like Elsie's yonder, but mair reddish like?"

"It is 'nt red!" replied Flora, laughing.

"Aweel, na, it isna precesely; but its na sae brown an' gowden as Elsie's. Oh, I mind him weel, my Lord Gilbert; and he's no that ill-conducted as wer young generation gaes. I'm weel pleased that it's him, and no his cousin Sir John, that ye are trothed to, Leddy Flora, though he's richer than Lord Gilbert; but he's just a vera deil for rioting and godlessness."

"I know that," said Flora, nodding sagaciously; "but I cannot stay to talk now, David is waiting on me below. He begged hard to be allowed to come up with me, but I forbade him. I thought you would like that better—eh, Alice? Come to me soon, my Gowan; I shall need you so much now."

"One moment, Flora," said Alice, stopping her; "is it to be soon?"

"In the latter days of September," said Flora, blushing; "he would have it so, and I was willing."

She had brought sunshine into the room with her, and it departed when she was gone. There was no touch of envy in Alice's heart; but she would have been either more or less than woman not to feel the contrast between Flora's destiny and her own. She would now, in all probability, lose her friend; for, once married, the numberless cares and interests of wedded life must inevitably diminish the attraction of their girlish friendship, even if Flora did not leave Edinburgh, which seemd very likely, as Lord Gilbert's property lay much further north. All this was quite trouble enough, but the rapid and premature return of Lord Glencarrig was for the time her great and pressing discomfort.

And it was one not to be got over or done away with—one which closed round and hemmed her in every day; for the gradual improvement in her mother's health, and Flora's eagerness to profit by the short time they had to spend together, forced Alice into constant communication with the young earl. Nothing could Flora do without the conjoint advice and assistance of her brother and her friend; every purchase that was made, every arrangement that was agreed upon, every proposal that was started, found no favour in her eyes unless Alice and David were unanimous in their approval; and Flora, most innocent of the evil she was forwarding, absolutely rejoiced in the affection (restrained by her presence into *brotherly* affection) which the earl betrayed in every tone and gesture. Alice could hardly bear it. In the sickening anxiety and weary irritation which possessed her, she was sometimes tempted to accuse Flora of selfish unkindness, that she should be so obtuse to what had been from the very first clear and manifest to her; and to take any step, however desperate and unaccountable, that might rid her of an admiration which, although in no wise disrespectful, was rapidly turning her old affection for him into positive dislike. His voice, his eyes, his whispered words, his broken sentences, the intense tenderness of his manner when he found himself for an instant alone with her, his pertinacity in contriving these occasions, which sometimes no prudence of hers could defeat, all told an unmistakeable tale; and that Flora was ignorant of his passion can only be attributed to her knowledge of the affection which had always existed between them, her conviction of the earl's unrequited attachment to another, and, above all, the absorbing interest of her own prosperous love, the sudden and fortunate crisis whereof had been brought about by the friendly mediation of the Countess of Dunbarton. That lady, being perfectly cognisant of Flora's penitent distress, as well as the confidant of her mortified lover, had assumed the part of peacemaker, and, with the assistance of Colonel Grahame, quietly achieved the desirable consummation which we have described.

So things went on, and no change worth mentioning came to pass in the relative situations of the personages of our tale. The fiery July burnt itself out, the mellow August weather set in, and Alice began to look forward with no pleasant anticipations to Flora's wedding-day. She had succeeded, by an amount of manœuvring which sorely taxed her ingenuous temper, in keeping clear of the young earl for several days; but every time she had been compelled to meet him had only proved more distinctly the fruitlessness of her endeavours to persuade him, by such avoidance, of the pain his addresses gave her. She had heard nothing of Norman since his last visit at home, and therefore concluded him to be absent on one of his usual journeys—so on one point, at least, she was tolerably tranquil.

"Alice," said Lady Flora one day, when Alice had been sitting some time ostensibly watching the progress of her toilet beneath the hands of her fidgetty tirewoman—"Alice, if you can bring down your mind from the sublimities it is contemplating, and heed any such mundane speech as mine, I should be glad to talk to you."

"I am listening," said Alice, whose mind had, indeed, been straying far from the scene before her eyes, flitting like a bird to its nest, backwards into the past. She looked up abstractedly.

"Umph!" said Flora, drily, "that's a question, I'm thinking. What is the lassie dreaming about?"

"Of what suld she be dreaming but of her jo, Madam Flora?" said the attendant Marian, no pert soubrette, but a staid elderly woman, who had been Lady Flora's maid ever since her birth, and loved Alice almost as much as her own young mistress. "Of what suld she dream but her ain true love? Ye needna blush like the red rowan berries, Alice hinnie, for ye'll no be denying it, I'm sure."

"Whisht ye, Marian," said Flora, "Alice yonder is not like other folk; *she* has no true love, and looks down upon poor me as one sold to the empty follies of this world, to wit, marrying and giving in marriage. Be done, you weary woman! am I to sit here and be worried like a witch at the stake until set of sun?"

"Bide a wee, bide a wee, Leddy Flora! Eh, my darling, dinna start and fidge aboot that gate or ye'll just ruin a'. Bide still, dearie, and I'll gie ye the last touch in the blink o' an e'e. But, Alice, ye needna be ashamed o' an honest man's love. Alack! young lassies feign to be sae now-a-days, as if wer auld mither Eve had never been wedded by God's ain hand to wer gude-sire Adam."

Flora's clear, hearty laugh was as pleasant a comment as could be desired on this odd illustration of the worthy old servant's position.

"Leddy Flora, ye are nae better than a bairn!" exclaimed Marian with some irritation, as the young lady's hilarity occasioned the sudden downfall of an elaborate edifice of curls and braids which she had just brought to a satisfactory elevation; "if ye dinna be still I'll just hae to begin 't clear ower again frae the foundation."

"Heaven forefend!" exclaimed Flora, with comical

gravity, and settling herself into an attitude of resolute endurance.

"Eh, eh! it's easy enow to see that my Lord Gilbert's no coming hither the night," said Marian, nodding at Alice from behind her young lady's chair, "or we shouldna be sic a steer to get quit o' puir auld Marian. There's mony a day, Alice, whan I can scarce win through in twa mortal hours, what wi' frizzlin', and curlin', and perfumin', an' kamin', and a wheen maggots o' my leddy's, that nae mortal ever fancied before. My conscience! she's ill to please then."

"I really did not know it was so much trouble, Marian."

"Trouble! na, that it isna, Leddy Flora; ye ken vera weel that it's my dearest joy to dress yer bonnie locks, tho' it's little o' *my* help they need. The bonnie locks," repeated the affectionate nurse, passing her hands over the girl's black, glistening tresses, "as mirk and saft as the corbie's wing, or my leddy the countess' satin goun. And I maun e'en say, to my Lord o' Hay's credit, that he thinks as meikle o' ye as ye deserve. He's a leal and true lover, my darlin', and weel he may be, for a fairer face than my ain Flora's the blessed sun never shone upon."

"A *fair* face!" retorted Flora merrily, glancing at her own reflection in the mirror; "why, ye false woman, I am black as the corbies ye spoke of a minute syne."

"May be sae; but ye are like the bride in Solomon's Sang—if ye're black, ye're comely," answered Marian sententiously. "An' I dare swear ye'll be the bonniest jewel o' a bride the house o' Beatoun has seen this mony a year, in yer robe o' the white and siller taffeta and three-pile velvet, and yer fine Flanders lace."

"Alice holds all these pretty things for vanities, Marian," said Lady Flora, demurely.

"Not for such as they concern," replied Alice, as quietly.

"And dinna they concern yersel', my doo?" asked Marian. "Od, lassie! whatna gate is yon for ye to speak, sae dowie and laigh, wi' tears in yer voice if they arena in yer e'en. Tuts, Alice, look at me; I never was half sae bonnie as you, and I hae had twa husbands, as braw and stalwart lads as ony in the Mearns—wae's me that I suld ha seen them baith laid low before me! And ye're gentle and fair and weel born eneugh to be an airle's leddy—isna she, madam?"

"A duke's," replied Flora, unhesitatingly.

"An' if yer jo disna luve ye as he ought—aweel, I ken it's a weary time to dree; but hearts is no that easy broke, and ye'll just content yersel' wi' a better. There's never a Jill but got a Jock, and yours, Alice, maun certes be a gentleman born, or he'll not sort wi' *you*. Eh! look at her, Madam Flora!"

Alice was, indeed, blushing deeply under the influence of these well-meant but most unpleasing consolations; yet, in spite of the nervous irritability which almost mastered her, she answered quite simply, "You are so utterly wrong, Marian, that I will not even try to set you right."

"Then he'll be a learned student body, eh?" asked

Marian, busily putting the last touch to her young lady's dress. "Ay! and we'll see ye some bright day mistress of a manse, as yer mither was before ye—the gentle creature she was and is! Ye are just her vera moral an' image, Alice."

"When you have settled Elsie's wedding day to your liking, you may go, Marian," said Flora, laughing; then, sitting down again in her arm-chair, she took Alice by both hands, held her fast, and made her stand before her.

"Now, Elsie, I am determined to know whether Marian guesses truly."

"About what, madam?"

"Is it true that your lover is unkind? nay, tell me! What are you afraid of from me, who have confessed so often to you, my little mother abbess?"

"No, Flora, it is not."

"Oh, Elsie, Elsie! I sadly fear the truth is not in ye! Let me guess, as we used to do in our baby games, and that will spare you telling tales outright. Has that learned student body Marian talks of, asked you yet to be the mistress of his manse? It would be the very life for you, my white rose."

"Oh, Flora, Flora! ye are just absurd!" said the girl, dreading lest she might guess nearer the truth.

"Or has no sturdy armourer, whose trade makes him half a gentleman—no valiant Henry of the Wynd, yet wooed and won the fairest damsel in Edinburgh to lighten his labours, and bring all the wealthiest cavaliers to his shop? Why ye might become a Provost's wife, Alice—think of that! What!

no word, no smile; nothing but that quick little frown? I see I must try again—for, in sooth, thou art too delicate a blossom to flourish in the air of a forge. Some gallant soldier? as I live, I have it now! Hist, Alice! whisper it to me; does he wear the black corslet of the Scots Royals, or the white plumes of the Life Guard, or the —— No, there is no other choice—for, as Marian said, Alice's lover must need be a gentleman. I don't ask his name, give me that hint to satisfy my cravings and —— What, tears!"

Tears, indeed, not of girlish bashfulness, or tender emotion, but of sharpest pain and annoyance, filled Alice's soft eyes; she tried to stifle them, and, fixing her clear, honest gaze on her beautiful tormentor, said firmly,

"Flora, this is the idlest of nonsense. I never told a falsehood in my life, and now I say, from my heart, that never has any man spoken of love to me; and lover I have none."

The sounds had hardly been formed, when the remembrance of Lord Glencarrig's unvaried admiration stung her with a sense of most involuntary deception—she stopped short, while Flora laughingly took her up.

"No affianced and plighted lover, like myself, I can well believe; but wilt thou tell me—*me*, little Gowan! who boast of as much experience in such gear as e'en another of my age—that there is no secret closet in thy soft heart where lies some well-beloved image and semblance—that, when all the world's asleep, and thy minnie not by to see, thou dost not take the key, like Bluebeard's wife in the nursery tales, and go to gaze at thy hidden treasure?"

Alice had been patient enough until now, but this thrust was too keen; she forced her hands from Flora's, and turned away, her face and neck one scarlet glow, and every feature trembling with pain. Thoughtless as she was, Flora had too much good nature and good breeding to press her further, or even pretend to understand the real cause of her confusion.

"There, there! don't blush so angrily, dear Elsie!" she said, "I'll say no more, but wait thy pleasure to confide in me—well do I know that my own Gowan is too good and discreet a lassie to love imprudently or unworthily."

She seated Alice in her own place, and quitted her for an instant, to search among her innumerable ornaments for something she wanted, saying to herself, "A soldier! my poor little Elsie! who can it be? alack! she is not fit for a soldier's wife."

She came back to the toilet table, and, deftly unfastening the black snood which Alice wore, began to bind up her beautiful and glossy curls with a broad purple ribbon, deeply fringed with silver, which had once belonged to her own dress. Alice, seeing in the glass what Flora was about, exclaimed—

"Dear Flora, what is this for?"

"Bide a wee! bide a wee!" said Flora, smiling archly, "have patience, you'll know by and by."

Alice submitted placidly, as she generally did, to her friend's pretty caprices, and, when the matter was settled to Flora's complete satisfaction, the latter took her by the hand, saying, "Now, Elsie, come with me."

Alice looked at her inquiringly.

"I am going to present you to a friend of mine, Gowan."

"Impossible, Flora! what have I to do with your friends? Indeed, indeed, I cannot."

"Gilbert says nothing is impossible that I command, and I think he ought to know. I command ye, Elsie!"

The charming little air of mock imperiousness with which she spoke, and set down her foot on the floor, made Alice smile—but she shook her head again.

"Nay Flora, what new freak is this! I neither ken nor care for your great friends, and who am I to mix wi' them.?"

"If, as old Marian said, and as I say too, ye are good and bonnie enough for an earl's wife, ye might well be good enough to meet a countess's guests. Come, my mother is below."

"No," said Alice.

"So I'll need to spend the whole evening alone," said Flora, pouting; "for Gilbert's away to Perth, and my lady-mother will not let me go to the Countess of Leven's assembly, because, forsooth, she says I dance too much, and will wear away all my bloom"—and Flora took a good long look at the reflection of a face which certainly did not justify Lady Glencarrig's assertion.

"But Lord Glencarrig, and this friend of yours, are not they company sufficient?"

"Small comfort will I have of them!" replied Flora, despondingly, "for David and he are both bidden to Lady Leven's, where I ought to have been also—and I shall be left at home with no one but my mother and Madam Rachel."

"Well, well," said Alice, smiling at her melancholy tone, "I'll do your bidding. But indeed I cannot see mickle pleasure ye'll have from me either, Flora. I would far rather wait for you here until your friend's away."

But Flora had already taken her at her word—and they were beginning to descend the staircase hand in hand.

"What is his name?" asked Alice, stopping, struck by an unaccountable flash of suspicion.

"Eh, Gowan! 't would not enlighten you much to be told—you never heard it before, and I only knew it a very short time syne."

CHAPTER XX.

LOVER AND BELOVED.

> **Oh, that I were beside her now!**
> **Oh, will she answer if I call?**
> **Oh, would she give me vow for vow,**
> **Sweet Alice, if I told her all?**
>
> **TENNYSON.**

LADY Glencarrig's drawing-room was a large apartment, rather narrow in proportion to its length, which had once formed part of a gallery occupying the entire frontage of the house. It was newly and richly fitted up in the French style; indeed a drawing-room or *salon* was quite an innovation upon Scottish fashions, and regarded by many staunch old matrons as an unwarrantable introduction of outlandish habits, tending to mar the homely simplicity of their native manners and customs. The prevailing colours in its furniture and decorations were grey, gold, and light crimson, which the westering sun-rays, streaming in through windows deeply embayed in the massive masonry, lighted up to great advantage. These windows were now open for air, and, as they looked out upon the grassy court and large trees before described, and were consequently neither barred nor grated, the aspect of the room was as cheerful as it was elegant.

Flora pushed open the door and entered hastily, dragging with her Alice, who, with a fluttering heart and eyes dazzled by the brilliancy into which she had just emerged from the dark staircase, kept them bent on the floor. Lord Glencarrig, who was conversing with his mother at the opposite end of the room, sprang towards the two girls as they appeared, and, kissing Alice's hand with a suppressed tenderness, which increased her slight discomposure to positive agitation, murmured in a voice only meant for her ear some lover-like reproach at her not having given him a chance of seeing her for so long. Alice was already beginning to repent having yielded to Flora's wishes, when a shadow came between her and the light—Flora pressed her hand to attract attention, and said aloud, in that curious tone of sly amusement and assumed gravity which had puzzled Alice from the first,

"My Lord Dundee, allow me to present to you Mistress Alice Scott, my foster-sister and very dear friend, with whom I think you are already acquaint."

The name and title awoke no echo in the girl's mind—the voice which answered was that which made her soul plant itself in her ears.

"True, my fair cousin; and I hope that Mistress Alice will honour me so far as to remember it."

Alice's head absolutely grew dizzy as, at the first syllable, she raised her eyes to meet under this new designation the dark, serious glance and thoughtful smile of him whom she had only known until now as Claverhouse.

She faltered out some answer, she knew not what, and Flora, seeing her grow very pale, and feeling the fingers she held turn quite cold and limp, was almost sorry for the success of her little scheme. She drew Alice into a window-seat, and placed herself beside her.

"Thou art not angry with me, at least, dear Alice?" she asked, looking affectionately into her face.

"Angry? dear Flora, wherefore should I be?"

"I can't tell; I did fancy that the sight of a certain person might, perchance, be too much for thee;" and Flora cast an arch, significant look after her kinsman.

The countess here came up, and fortunately closed this embarrassing interrogatory. She expressed great pleasure at seeing Alice, inquired particularly after her mother, kissed her with great affection, and then retired to renew her interrupted conversation with Viscount Dundee.

Lord Glencarrig had been watching these comings and goings with an expression of countenance that hovered between vexation and impatience; but now that the coast was clear he began slowly, with the slowness of lingering boyish timidity, to make approaches towards the centre of his hopes and wishes, the nook where the modest treasure of his heart was enshrined. He felt that evening more desperately in love than ever; he was raging to repay himself for the sufferings he had undergone from the almost total eclipse of her presence during the last ten days, and moreover had determined to avail himself of the first opportunity to express more unequivocally than he had yet ventured to do the whole extent of his passion, to which, with all the self-confidence of youth, rank, high spirits, and tolerable good looks, he entertained no doubt of receiving a favourable reply, there being, to use a homely phrase, none so blind as those who will not see. He did not in the least reflect whither such a conclusion might lead himself or her; he only thought, poor boy! how delicious it would be to win one shy look of love from those modest eyes—to feel her hand close, if only for one second, on his—to see her colour come and go in that exquisite flitting shadow on her cheek—to hear her perhaps say his name in that soft lingering tone which seems to caress every separate letter. Again I say—poor boy!

And so, uneasily hovering round and round, drawing his circle closer every time, like a wretched moth that *will* burn its wings, he finally settled down beside Alice at the open window. As he did so, his sister sprang gaily up.

"Since *you* are here, my lord," she said with a profound curtesy, "I think I may safely abandon the delightful task of entertaining our foster-sister into your hands, and crave your permission to absent myself. I hear my Lord Dundee speaking anent a matter which, if I mistake not, interests me a little."

Poor Alice, thus forsaken by her only defence, felt at the moment a desperate impulse to rise and accompany her, in order to escape the perilous conversation which she saw ready and waiting in every line of the young earl's face. But she was far too timid to put any such step into execution, and could only remain passive, quiet, and, by a great exertion of self-command, outwardly indifferent.

The earl looked at her with his whole heart in his eyes, and in truth his admiration was not ill bestowed. Sober and plain as was her black dress, with its close, high bodice and sleeves only edged with a deep fall of the same stuff, its small plaited ruff and puritanical fashion altogether, there was that about Alice which needed no adornment to make her beautiful. Her figure was scarcely so rounded as became her years, but it was perfectly proportioned, and full of that unconscious grace which makes every attitude and line harmonious, every motion attractive. As she sat, leaning back in the corner of the deep window-nook, her hands loosely folded on her lap, and her small head bent a little forwards, there was something in the very atmosphere which seemed to surround her with a halo of simplicity and goodness—in the intent, sorrowful gaze of the clear hazel eyes; in the wistful droop of the fringed lids; and especially in that touching shadow of grief about the lovely mouth, with its delicate lips of palest, most transparent red—something there was, I say, in all this which a coarser eye might have passed carelessly over, that smote upon the young man's generous heart. He saw not only her exceeding loveliness, which thrilled every nerve in his frame, but he saw too with deep regret that she was unhappy, he knew not why. And if at that instant the fancy flashed across his mind that this unhappiness might arise from a secret and repressed attachment to himself, and if that fancy made him almost rejoice, who shall cast the first stone at him?

"It is a very, very long while since I saw you,

Elsie," he began, using shyly the pretty name of endearment, "and longer still since you spoke to me."

"I spoke to you only three days ago, my lord," replied Alice, trying to laugh carelessly, although her heart was fluttering with apprehension of what inevitably ensued upon their being alone together.

"Yes; you said 'I wish you a fair day, my lord,' when I met you in my mother's room, and never a syllable more."

"Pardon me then, but most likely I had nothing more to say."

"You have always plenty to say with Flora," replied the young man in a tone of some vexation, "but you do not think me worthy to share your conversation. You have transferred all your old love for me to her, I suppose."

At the word *love*, Alice cast a hasty glance at him, and, seeing very plainly that it had not been used without design, bit her lip and coloured.

"Is it not true, Alice? You know it is."

No answer.

"If it be not, why should you avoid me so? Why," and here, lowering his voice, he drew still nearer to her, "why do you shrink from me? Nay, see now, you will not so much as let me touch the tips of your fingers! Oh Alice, how easily you forget old times, old pleasures, ay, and old troubles, we have seen together!"

"My memory of *pleasures* has been sadly ill-furnished of late," said Alice, "and daily labour, and daily sorrow, and many a bitter hour of tears and loneliness have left no trace of a bairn's thoughtless happiness behind them, my lord."

"Call me David, Alice, as you used to do, that I may fancy myself living over again those glorious years we spent at dear Glencarrig, when I was but a headstrong laddie, and you and Flora the prettiest buds that ever blossomed on our fair meadows and grassy holms."

"Pardon me, my lord, but we are not at Glencarrig now—nor yet are we bairns still—fancy and memory have led you far a-field."

The calm repulse disconcerted him infinitely more than the harshest speech could have done. Anger, pride, scorn, these he could have met—conquered, perhaps, for he felt strong in the real though unreflecting sincerity of his love, but this gentle indifference was beyond his grasp. He could make no more head against it than a drifting vessel against a perpendicular wall of polished ice. Yet, confident in the winning power of those childish recollections which had such sweet interest for him, he resumed,

"Do you mind, Alice, the first time I left Glencarrig for Aberdeen, how sorely you and Flora wept? I can see you now, standing side by side on the moss-grown terrace-steps, each with an arm round the other's neck, watching me as I rode away on Black Douglass, with Dominie Todd ambling beside me, and old Willie Grey, Marian's husband, behind. My heart was as heavy and my eyes as moist as yours."

Alice bent her head in acquiescence, and, resting her cheek on her hand, looked steadily out at the moving green trees in the little garden, whose slender boughs cast a flickering network of gleam and shadow on her fair face and golden brown hair.

"And how," continued the young earl, "you and Flora worked for me my first scarf when I grew tall and manly enough to wear a sword. Little had Flora's hands to do in it, I trow; it was all wrought by these pretty fingers, and I loved it the more for that thought. You put it round me yourself, Alice, on my fifteenth birthday, was it not?"

"I have forgot—I cannot tell," murmured Alice.

"Forgot! can you forget what is so precious to me? Alice, I have that scarf yet. When you were gone it was the only gift I had left of my darling foster-sister—my little sweetheart."

The tender accents of his voice brought no flush of gratified pride or womanly pleasure to the cheek of the poor girl he was so unintentionally tormenting—only an expression of deep sadness, partly for herself, partly for him, and of confusion how to meet these declarations, intimating as they did a present passion which veiled itself so thinly beneath reminiscences of the past. She could not find any reply sufficiently decided to check his advances, without betraying thereby her consciousness of a love which *he* had not yet explicitly confessed.

"Oh, Alice, I never guessed until now that you were heartless and cold," said the young man mournfully, after listening in vain for some encouraging word, "I did not think that a few years' absence and change would have altered my sweet, affectionate little Alice into a proud, capricious, unfeeling woman."

"Oh, Lord Glencarrig, by what right speak ye thus to me?" said Alice in grave reproach. "If ye had known what it is to struggle with sickness and death, with grief and poortith—to see the present bare and cold, the future mirk before ye, to be trysted with sorrow as I have been—ye would not seek to wake up sae cruelly the ghosts of lost happiness and joy."

"Are they no pleasure to you then, dear Alice?"

"No, my lord, none," she said faintly, turning again to her silent watching of the restless trees.

"None, Alice! is that possible?"

"Speak to the prisoner in his dungeon of the green fields, the whispering waters, the blue lift—speak to the widow and fatherless of their departed ones—speak to the blind of their lost light—but never, never to a weary riven heart of the peace it has lost, never to win back again," said the girl in a trembling voice. "And ye break my heart by reminding me of the sweet past."

"Dearest Elsie, I know that you are unhappy; tell me then why you fling from you the——the friendship which could make your lot so different."

She only half understood him—indeed he scarcely understood himself—and to that half she could offer no answer.

"Why are you so altered? why cannot you be to me as you are to Flora? why ——"

"Because, my lord," interrupted Alice, driven to speak plainly, "you do not behave to me as you do to Flora."

A brilliant light broke from Lord Glencarrig's eyes

as he made another ineffectual attempt to possess himself of her hand.

"True, true—most true," he murmured, sinking his voice still lower, "you must have guessed, that, much as *they* love you, they could never hold you half so dear as I! Alice, pardon my boldness—I would give the noblest estate in my broad earldom to soothe one sigh that breaks from your lips, to dry one single drop of the tears which even now are starting to your dear eyes. Ah, Alice, believe me ——"

"My lord, my lord, cease this foolish talk which beseems neither your tongue to utter, nor my ears to hear. You have lived ower long abroad, Lord Glencarrig, and have learned too well the art of speaking those false words which are soft to the ear, while the heart is not in them, although now, I am thankful I can believe them hollow sounds. You forget, my lord, that a simple Scots lassie has little taste for the fleeching that sounds sae sweet to a court lady."

"Now, upon my soul, you wrong me, dear Alice,—I swear it!" exclaimed the impetuous youth. "Never was truer word spoken than those I say to you; never was a more constant heart than that which beats in my breast. You will not trust me? You will not have me for your —— friend?"

"I cannot believe those my friends who delight to grieve me, my lord."

"Have I offended you? How? why? I that would die this hour to make you happy!"

"Again!" said Alice, lifting her head firmly, "you ask me why and how you offend, and marvel that I am pained, while you repeat over and over the same empty clashes that should never pass from you to me. My good will is not to be won thus."

"Unkind! cruel!" muttered the earl, rising in bitter mortification, "I will displease you no longer. Since my very voice seems odious to you, it shall not offend again. I leave you—for as my heart thinks, my tongue must speak; I cannot remain beside you and seem of marble while that heart is swelling with an affection as pure and true as ever man felt."

As he uttered these reproachful sentences, he moved away with no very rapid step, for he expected that some sign of relenting or regret in Alice might yet embolden him to return; but none appeared. Quiet as a statue she sat, with her cheek on her hand, and her drooping head, and the sunlight playing on her long, bright locks—no sound save her quick breathing, no motion save the almost visible beating of her heart. The young nobleman's spirits sunk all at once with a presentiment of failure, and for a moment he despaired; but youth, in its flush of pride, knows little of such dejection; and again anger at her supposed coquetry, and a triumphant anticipation of conquest, sparkled in his eyes as he quitted the room, presumptuously imagining that Alice would suffer from his absence almost as much as he endured to tear himself from her.

The door closed behind him, and Alice, released from the constraint of his presence, at length suffered her senses to wander towards the spot where her thoughts had been ever since her entrance—the group at the lower end of the long drawing-room. It was a complete picture, and one which would have charmed a painter's taste.

Dressed in a long, full, flowing skirt and bodice of dove-grey brocade—one of those splendid antique brocades which few of the present generation have seen even in their grandmother's wardrobe—her hair drawn up and covered with a beautiful lace kerchief, matching the rich garniture of her sleeves and stomacher, the countess was seated in a tall elbow-chair, with her little feet in their high-heeled embroidered slippers resting on a red velvet cushion. She had been a celebrated beauty in her day; and even now, although nearly forty years of age, and bearing about her the marks of early and long-continued grief, she still retained more than traces of her charms. The secluded life which she had led ever since her widowhood had preserved to a singular degree the delicacy of a complexion naturally most pure and fair; her eyes were blue like Flora's, but their sapphire hue had a velvety softness, and often assumed a violet shade, which imparted to them a look of melancholy sweetness that her daughter's never wore; her features were regular and delicate, rather slightly marked than otherwise, and her hair of a light *cendré* brown. In fact, had it not been for a fleeting glimpse of family likeness which now and then appeared when the countess grew animated, or Flora serious, two women more absolutely dissimilar than this mother and daughter can scarcely be imagined.

Flora, with her chin resting on her pretty dimpled hand, her bright face all a-glow with interest, and her black curls falling in clusters over her mother's aërial-looking coiffure, stood behind the countess's chair, with her eyes fixed on Lord Dundee, who was speaking.

He was leaning against a carved ebony cabinet, close by the two ladies, and directly facing one of the windows—his head a little thrown back, one hand resting on his side, one foot lightly crossed over the other, in an attitude which, careless, easy, almost indolent indeed, yet conveyed in some strange way a clear conception of the strength and activity which lay beneath that slight outline and elegant exterior, as some indescribable vibration in his soft voice did of the suppressed energy latent within.

His costume was nearly the same as that in which Alice had first seen him, save that, being in full gala dress, he wore a gold sword-belt and jewelled rapier, the gorget and sash of a general officer, and the regulation military peruke, which, ugly and cumbrous as it was, could only half conceal the haughty grace of his noble head and finely-moulded throat, or the luxuriance of his own natural locks, which escaped from amongst the stiff artificial ringlets in glossy, abundant waves. Every line in his figure was instinct with life and meaning, every shadow that crossed his features seemed to give a new and more striking attraction to their grave yet passionate beauty.

Alice held her breath, not to lose a word..

"Yes, at Dudhope still. I know that it is best

for us both in every way; yet here am I, tied down—impossible to leave for one hour. I must, however, find some means of absenting myself, if for ever so short a time."

There was grave concern in his manner.

"Have you any reason to be alarmed?" asked Flora.

"No, not at present, I am growing only too uneasy," replied the viscount, with one of his old looks, so far away into some unknown region of possibility. "But things are in that state that, from day to day, the worst tidings may be expected; then, if the faithful and loyal be not found at their post, what *can* we hope from others?"

"The *worst* tidings!" repeated the countess thoughtfully. "Tell me, Lord Dundee, what do you understand by such tidings? Speak frankly; I am no coward."

"True, my cousin; I know few women so coolly brave as your gentle self. The tidings? They might, nay I fear they *will*, be these—that William of Orange has landed in England, and that our unhappy King is dethroned."

"Impossible!" exclaimed Lady Flora.

Lord Dundee made no answer but by a sarcastic and most melancholy smile.

"Surely, my lord, your fears make you exaggerate," said the countess; "Too well do I know the danger of unfounded hopes, but unfounded fears often prove as pernicious."

The same smile replied to her half-entreating question.

"But why—why—tell us why?" exclaimed Flora, impatiently; "Is this Prince of Orange, this Stadtholder of Holland—I mind him well enough, pale-visaged, long-nosed, sour looking fellow—is he such a mighty potentate, I would crave to know, or is England so far fallen from her old chivalry that he should swallow her at a mouthful thus? Faith, my lord viscount, the gallant English gentlemen owe you small thanks for the light account you make of their valour!"

"*Ma belle cousine,*" said the viscount; "you reason like a woman; and, as most women reason, rather from a warm heart than a clear head. None more than I can esteem the courage of English gentlemen and soldiers, which we Scots learned of old to rate at its true value on many a tough and well-fought field; but how many of these, think you, will draw the sword on behalf of their lawful monarch when the hour of adversity comes? Not one in a hundred."

"I do not believe it!" exclaimed Flora.

"And therefore—for your disbelief cannot weaken my conviction—therefore, I say, this valour becomes a fresh and terrible element in the storm which lours darkly around. I am prepared for the worst."

"What say your advices?" demanded the countess.

"From London, that the discontent is ripening fast; that that discontent is not, as here in Scotland, the rancour of any separate civil or religious party, which the iron heel of authority can crush, but a swelling of the whole nation, the uprising of one great torrent, which, unless our king should make concessions to the universal clamour which he never *will* offer, must too surely overwhelm his throne, and land the Prince of Orange at Whitehall."

"But what *could* he—*can* he do?" asked the countess, clasping her hands; "Who is to blame in all this?"

"His advisers, madam, those accursed Jesuit priests, whose bigoted absurdity is driving him to destruction, and whose hold on him is now too fast ever to relax. It is not in England as in our unhappy Scotland; there no provinces are in armed rebellion or secret conspiracy—there no fanatical madmen rave and shout, setting forth treason and sedition as godly zeal—there is no call for the stern arm of military justice, or the terrors of martial law. What *here* is only needful severity for the preservation of the lowest degree of public security, *there* becomes ——"

"What?" said Lady Flora.

"Folly," concluded Lord Dundee, with a stern glance; "suicidal folly."

"Your pardon, my cousin," said the countess; "but these are hardly the sentiments I had expected to hear from you, whose upholding of the royal prerogative hath been accused of verging on greater severity than is consistent with humanity."

"I am a soldier, madam, and, as such, have a soldier's duties to perform: what they command, I without scruple or hesitation obey. I love no half-measures. But these proceedings of the court have been dictated by nought save a blinded zeal for the Catholic form of worship on the one hand, and, alas, that I should be forced to confess it! as blinded a trust in false leaders on the other. Confident in the wisdom of counsellors who see not an inch before them, in the honesty of statesmen who betray him before his very face, our unfortunate prince is sowing the whirlwind—God grant he may not reap the storm! He will not weather it."

A short silence followed this gloomy prediction.

"But surely, surely," said the countess anxiously; "the army might be relied on in case of an insurrection, still more of a foreign invasion."

"That invasion, madam, will not come as a *foreign* one," replied the viscount with the same deliberate calmness; "half of the men who serve under William's standard and direct his measures are English or Scottish renegades—Burnet, Carstairs, Melville, Dalrymple——"

"He of the wry neck?" said Flora, laughing. "Oh, comfort yourself, cousin Grahame, he will of a surety be hanged!"

"Hush, Flora," observed her mother, "such foolish jests are out of season!"

"And these are men especially to be feared and guarded against, for they represent the hereditary disloyalty of our worst and darkest days. But I thank heaven," he added with gleaming eyes, "there *are* yet hearts and hands left in Scotland to do and dare whatever man may—ay, and heads too!"

"Think you that the English troops would not stand, then?"

"I can hardly say. The troops might shrink from open desertion of their leaders and standards, but, when those leaders set the example of treachery, why should we expect the followers to remain true?"

"I have heard much praise of my Lord Churchill," said the countess inquiringly; "he is spoken of as a gallant and skilful soldier, and is moreover bound to the King by no common ties."

"Ay, a *quasi* brother-in-law," replied Lord Dundee, with an odd smile. "Yes, he really is what you say, brave, skilful, ambitious; he has not yet reached the zenith of his greatness. For that aspiration I blame him not, but for the means which I foresee he will take to realise it."

"I remember him perfectly, also," said Flora; "I danced with him at Whitehall on the Queen's birthday. The handsomest man and the gayest cavalier I ever met—saving your presence, *mon beau cousin*," she added, with an arch smile.

"And can any dependence be placed upon this man's fidelity and devotion?" asked Lady Glencarrig.

"Oh, assuredly, madam, every dependence; provided the cause in which he is engaged be strong enough to render their assistance superfluous."

"But *all* cannot be base; I will not believe it!" exclaimed Lady Glencarrig; "The Earl of Feversham?"

"A most doughty carpet-knight," replied the inflexible Claverhouse. "No, my dear cousin, all are not traitors, far be it from me to say so; but it is not among English courtiers or Scottish politicians that true men are to be sought."

"And here?" asked the countess. "Are there none here who would do as Montrose did—dare all, suffer all, lose all, die, if need were, to save their King from exile, perchance from his father's fate—their country from the deep dishonour of foreign conquest?"

"Yes, madam, *I* would," replied the viscount, with indescribable pride and nobleness in those calm words. There was no bravado in his tone, nothing but a simple expression of conscious power and genius, which struck the hearers with admiration, almost with awe.

"Oh, I know you to be loyal and brave as the noblest of our noble race, my cousin," replied the countess, her fair face lighting up with all the glow of ancestral pride and generous enthusiasm; "but, one man against a kingdom, one arm against tens of thousands!"

"Nay, I should not be alone," replied Dundee; "you do deep injustice to our Scottish gentlemen, if you deem that there are not hundreds to be found who would reioice to sacrifice themselves in this cause; and who can say what a handful of resolute men may do, with a sturdy will, fearless hearts, and a united purpose? The mine of power and martial resources which Montrose found amongst our gallant and warlike clans in the North is unexhausted, is scarcely yet understood; there lie the means of shaking England to the foundation; and who knows but what——" He stopped, and—gazing straight before him, as though the steady glance of those large, melancholy, dark eyes through which the fiery soul seemed to look forth with such strange prescience into his fated life could pierce the misty veil of futurity, and bring its secrets back to him—remained for several minutes, meditating or dreaming profoundly."

"These are very sad anticipations, cousin," said lady Glencarrig, breaking the silence.

"And they *may* be erroneous—would that I dared to hope it!" replied Dundee. "In Scotland I can hardly imagine but what authority and right must prevail, in spite of the ferment of intrigue and fanaticism which for years past we have been so sorely tasked to subdue. In the teeth of Dutch gold, and Scottish greed, and Whig rebellion, I have still some faint hope that our adversaries may have learnt the lesson we have so assiduously taught; but as to England (and that reminds me of what I was about to say), William will not have set foot on English ground ere every Scotch regiment will be ordered southwards."

"I would I were a man, to fight by your side, cousin Grahame!" said Flora, clenching her white hand and striking her foot on the carpeted floor. "I feel a giant's strength within me."

"Woe to the English cavalier who met you, Lady Flora," said Lord Dundee, "he would indeed rue the day, my fair Amazon, if you looked then as you do now."

"I hardly know whether to feel joy or sorrow that my David hath never become a soldier," said the countess, her heart sinking at these varied prognostics of evil.

"As yet, it has mattered little; but, if the time came when honour and allegiance summon every gentleman to the field, would you spare him then, madam?" demanded the viscount almost sternly.

"Nay, I say not so," answered the gentle mother, "although my very heart sickens at the prospect of losing him as I lost his father. Oh, Lord Dundee! we women are but women after all; we live in our affections, and husband and children are dearer to us than monarch and state. You men speak very calmly of things that rend our souls asunder."

"I am a soldier and a Grahame, my cousin; did either ever shrink from death?"

"From death, perhaps not; but, when we spoke just now of Montrose, my thoughts flew back, not to his glory and eternal renown, but, alas! to his shameful end—to the executioner's cart—the gibbet, the axe, and quartering-block, to the bloody head and mangled limbs ——"

She shuddered violently and hid her face, while even Flora turned rather pale, for the disgraceful trial and atrocious butchery of that ill-fated hero were no mere matter of history then, but a fresh and well-remembered fact, present to every mind, and witnessed by numbers yet alive.

"On that track my fancy followed yours, madam," replied Lord Dundee, "and, remembering that ere many years have rolled by such may be my own destiny, it behoves me to contemplate it firmly."

"And could you go to meet such a doom without shrinking?"

"Without a sigh; as cheerfully as ever I braved death in the field. On the stainless and true, gibbet and axe can inflict no *shame;* and what can a gentleman and Scottish peer dread but dishonour? Is any other mortal thing worthy one pang of terror? I feel, I know, that my life will not be a long one—and axe or rope, bullet or steel, what matters the trifle which cuts it short, if I die in the service of my King, for my duty, and my country!"

"Alas! alas!" murmured the countess, "would to God that David were safe!"

"Nay, mother!" answered Flora almost impatiently, "say rather, 'I would he were a soldier to do good and leal service to his prince.' That would better beseem our name and lineage, methinks!"

Lady Glencarrig rested her elbow on the arm of her chair and her face on her slight thin hand, the nervous clasp of the fingers betraying no small degree of agitation.

"You are doing yourself injustice now, Beatrix," said the viscount; "no one would credit, to hear you speak to-day, that you are the brave woman I know you to be."

"A mother has twice a woman's weakness, my lord, and you have pressed me sorely on this tender point.

But God forefend that all these horrors should come to pass. I *must* hope still."

"Hope if you can, madam. I would give much to do so likewise; but I cannot disguise from myself that a man standing over a mine, with a lighted match flaming beneath him, is safe compared to us. Of the nobles who have been enriched and favoured by the King, *all* will desert him, save one or two, whom I believe to possess what it seems are rare commodities now-a-days—gratitude and conscience."

"What says my Lord Chancellor Perth and his brother? Do they partake your fears?"

"My Lord of Perth trembles and temporizes. Melfort schemes and intrigues, urging our King on the high road to ruin. Argyle and Hamilton show a smooth front as yet—wait till the tide turns!"

"Nay," said the gentle countess, "I cannot marvel at my Lord of Argyle's enmity; bethink you of how his father died."

"His father was a rebel to his King and a traitor to his country, madam; an accomplice of Monmouth, taken red-hand in arms against his sovereign; for such as he small ruth is needed," replied the stern soldier. "This man is the truest Campbell, the veriest Mac Callum Mohr, that ever drew breath—and I know not which is the deeper-dyed and more consummate knave, he or his kinsman John of Breadalbane."

"Beware!" said the countess softly, and her eyes sought the window where Alice sat apart.

"It matters not!" replied Dundee haughtily. "I care not to speak in a corner. These men know me as well as I know them, and little reck I who hears or does not hear my opinion of them. If they and Athol, Dalrymple, Melfort, and James Douglas of Queensberry, were just now swinging in the Grass Market, I might perhaps venture to indulge a hope of safety, although, God wot, Scotland never yet lacked traitors in her hour of need!"

"Traitors! traitors! oh how fearfully that ominous word recurs at every turn!" sighed lady Glencarrig.

"Because wherever we turn the *thing* meets us, Beatrix—because it is in vain that we would close our eyes to the knowledge of this—because we are sunk, steeped, in it to the very neck, and, as with men struggling in a quicksand, every attempt to reach some firmer footing startles us to a more appalling conviction of the rottenness of what we deemed most sound. Men who to-day seem honest and loyal subjects change to half-hearted, calculating schemers at the very point where they might have been moulded into useful weapons—the bold grow timid, the true false—the very air we breathe appears to engender this corruption—and the few who survive such a universal contagion will be left stranded, helpless, alone! Some there are indeed—the noble Dunbarton, my gallant old friend Seyton of Dunfermline, and the brave gentlemen of my own regiment—on whom I can depend as on myself ——"

"What line will Drumlanrig take?" interrupted the countess. (The Earl of Drumlanrig was the eldest son of the Duke of Queensberry, and Lieutenant-Colonel of the Life Guards.)

"I am inclined to think he will follow his father's lead, whatever that may be, and his grace is a disappointed man."

Another long silence, during which Lord Dundee was revolving some train of thought in which Alice had a share, for, rousing himself after awhile, he said to the countess—

"I am about to beg the favour of a short conversation with your *protégée*, Mistress Scott; a wandering idea has reminded me of something which it would be well that she should know."

Flora was just going to inquire what that could be, but the countess, who perceived that the request implied private speech, signed to her daughter not to follow him, and, bidding her fetch the tapestry-frame which stood near, kept her at her own side.

The young lady, whose chief defect was really not curiosity, obeyed without any great symptom of reluctance, and soon became so absorbed in a conference with her mother respecting the unhappiness of Lord Glencarrig (as attributable to the supposed coquetry of Lady Mary Charteris, and the singularly obstinate reserve of Alice), that she quite forgot to wonder what could be the occasion of any secret communication between Lord Dundee and her foster-sister.

CHAPTER XXI.

A WORD IN SEASON.

Thither, in trust unbaffled, may'st thou turn
***   *   *   *   *   *   ***
Quenching thy soul's thirst at the hidden urn
That, filled with waters of sweet memory, lies
In its own shrine.

ALICE saw Lord Dundee turn from the two ladies and approach her; she instinctively rose, partly from respect, partly from an indefinable nervous emotion which rendered her almost unaware of what she did. The viscount touched her little trembling hand softly.

"Do not disturb yourself, Mistress Alice," he said smiling, "or you will drive me to the necessity of speaking with you standing. Be seated, I pray you."

He led her back to her seat, placing himself in such a position as to have a complete view of her countenance, and yet to screen both himself and her from any observation on the part of the other inmates of the room. Alice was not in the least *surprised* at the courtesy of his tone and manner, but there was nevertheless a charm of almost personal preference and attention in their chivalrous refinement which was exquisitely sweet and soothing to her; too sweet, alas! for it fostered unconsciously the latent hope which, say what we will, *must* lurk, unacknowledged and uncherished, a feeble spark, in every woman's heart. If not, why should Alice have felt so tenderly grateful for his smile of cordial recognition, and his few words of simplest kindness?

Nothing can be imagined more singular than the relation which these two, so accidentally brought into contact, bore to each other. That Lord Dundee was utterly, completely ignorant of Alice's feelings we need hardly say; his mind was not of the order which readily originates or harbours such conceptions, even when suggested far more distinctly than any circumstances had done in the present instance. Proud he might be, and was—self-concentrated, self-reliant, but not self-seeking—his bold nature had no place for the miserable egotism, the pitiful grovelling vanity, which constitute the coxcomb; loving and beloved in the narrow circle which bounded his share of domestic joys, he had no care or interest beyond it. Even at the hands of his most unscrupulous enemies, no charge of vice, or even of irregularity, has been recorded against him; whatever may have been his errors or crimes, no stain of immorality attaches to his name. His fiery temperament transmuted into one stern idol of duty every thought and affection which crossed his path; and, mistaken as was his belief in that false God, ruthless as had too often been his devotion to its worship, it had at least contributed to preserve him from youthful dissipation and the worse vices of maturer manhood. His life of intense thought and restless action left no room for frivolous or sensual pursuits, while his attachment to his amiable wife had been preserved in youthful freshness by the long separations and constant vicissitudes of his soldier's life. Thus it was, that, as he gazed on the fair young girl who sat near him, no suspicion arose in his mind of her innocent but ill-omened passion. He saw and noted indeed, with that quick scrutiny which in men accustomed or destined to lead their fellows is less even a habit than an instinct, all the outward signs and tokens of discomposure, but for once misread those hieroglyphs of the soul, and set them down as the result of natural timidity—the remembrance of the unpleasing nature of their first meeting,—to any cause, in short, rather than the love which burned on her cheek, which throbbed in every nerve, and the exquisite delight of his presence, which, denied all vent by word, glance, or sigh, was growing almost painful in its intensity.

And yet he certainly felt no small degree of interest in this modest, high-minded girl, an interest almost paternal, for as far as years went she might have been his daughter. It was a very compound sensation, derived partly from the high esteem in which she was openly held by his noble kinsfolk, but infinitely more from the remembrance of a benefit conferred—an influence more powerful in binding us to our fellow-creatures than gratitude itself—added probably to an unacknowledged impulse of romance, inherent in one form or another to all genius, of which it is an essential element, and which pleased his fancy with the certainty that in this child of a man who had doubtless abhorred him, in this votaress of a sect which regarded him as little short of the Arch-enemy himself, he had a sincere though humble friend. Few friends had he been permitted thus to win during the relentless career of warfare and bloodshed to which his nature and his destiny had committed him; and the hope of being kindly regarded and leniently judged was perhaps more delightful than he would have cared to acknowledge even to himself. And thus it was that his proud lip relaxed, and his dark eyes softened, whenever he addressed her—that mingled pity and respect gave a gentleness to his voice and a conciliatory accent to his language, all unneeded to win her good-will, and only calculated to add fuel to a fire which, had he conjectured its existence, would have struck him with something very like dismay.

He was the first to speak.

"Mistress Alice, I trust you will excuse me for starting two very unpleasing subjects, but I wish to inquire——Nay, do not look at me with such frightened eyes, or I shall believe that you have not kept the promise you gave me the night we parted at your own door."

"Oh, sir, I have, indeed; how *could* I fail?" she answered timidly, and with a half glad, half reproachful look of affectionate gratitude, that made him smile, so child-like and artless was it.

"Easily enough, Mistress Alice; the request was so unreasonable on my part, and so hastily—nay, so generously, granted on yours, that I should not have been hurt had you repented of it later."

She shook her head, and smiled in turn.

"No? Then I thank you all the more for not

deeming it so, and may proceed at once. You have not, I presume, been further molested by your enemy?"

"By Mr. Drummond? No, my lord."

"I was pretty certain that you would be fairly quit of his importunities; within a fortnight after that occurrence he left Scotland, and will not re-enter it in a hurry, I rather think," observed Lord Dundee in a careless tone.

Alice looked up quickly. She guessed instinctively that this departure was more than a lucky coincidence, and something in the viscount's expression confirmed the supposition.

"Oh, my lord, my lord!" she exclaimed, clasping her hands; "and was it for my sake ——"

"Gently!" said the viscount, raising his finger, "you will be overheard. *They* have learnt nothing—from me at least."

"How can I ever thank you?"

"No thanks are needed on your part, Mistress Alice," he replied. "I would fain leave you in an error so gratifying to myself, and accept them as honestly merited, but truth must be told. Drummond did not leave Scotland on your account; even my influence, which is not perhaps insignificant, could not have compassed that. Other interests demanded his absence; others than yourself had a desire to see him put out of the way. Now to my second question. Pardon me again if I pain you. Have you seen your brother of late?"

A thrill of fear shot through the girl's heart, piercing it like a poisoned arrow—the first real pang of her long-cherished dread. What could Lord

Dundee know of Norman? What did this question presage?

"Why do you not answer?"

"My brother, my lord? I never told you that I had ——"

"That you had a brother? Certainly, you did not; but I know it."

"How?" she began faintly, her agitation increasing rapidly, in spite of the kindliness of his manner.

"Ah! that is another story, too long to enter upon. I hear strange things now and then, Mistress Alice, and in strange ways. But, I pray you, answer me without further delay, and be frank with me: I pledge you my word, as knight and gentleman, that I have no intention of forfeiting one single jot of your friendship and good will."

"I know not in the least where he may be, unless in Edinburgh or Holland, my lord," she replied; "nearly three months back he was here: but neither I nor my mother have seen him sinsyne. He never confides in us."

"But can you not guess? Do you receive no news from him through any channel?"

"One scrap of writing came to us a few weeks ago; but that bore no mark nor date of inditing."

"Extraordinary!" muttered the viscount. "Now, Mistress Alice, hearken to me, for this matter tholes no trifling. Your brother's name has been before the Council."

An inarticulate sound died on Alice's lips—she tried to speak, but failed; and, drooping forwards, as if bowed by some heavy load, covered her face with both hands. Then followed a minute's pause, during which the clear mumuring voice and gay laughter of Lady Flora, as she chatted with her mother at the other end of the saloon, were alone to be heard. But, feeling at last that Lord Dundee was steadily regarding her, and awakening to the pressing necessity for exertion, Alice gathered herself up, and met his fixed unswerving glance with one which was a most eloquent appeal for support and assistance. The face on which she looked, in its pensive calmness, with its noble brow and sad fathomless eyes, was so exactly, in every line and shadow, the same as that which had bent over her on the night of their first meeting, that a gleam of faith and hope warmed the deadly chill at her heart; he surely could mean her no injury; he had only spoken of this disastrous event in order to advise and help her—it must be so. He laid his hand upon her arm, just as he had done once before, and again the firm, composed touch seemed to calm and strengthen her as by magic.

"Tell me all; I can bear it," she said in a low voice.

"There is very, very little to tell; you are too easily alarmed."

"Too easily! oh, my lord!" she said reproachfully.

"Not too easily for what *might* result from what I have to relate, but for the immediate peril. Your brother is in no danger at present, as you might infer from our ignorance of his abode. I should not certainly have asked *you* thereanent, had he been a prisoner of State."

She drew in a long breath, and laid her hand on her bosom, still looking at him.

"Let me hear," she said more quietly; "cruel, unloving as he is, Norman is yet my father's son."

"Norman—ay, that was the name—Norman Scott. I thought I could not be mistaken. During the examination of a prisoner at the Council-board yesterday evening, it was discovered that some papers and pamphlets of a most treasonable and incendiary tendency had been brought over from Holland, by one Norman Scott, known to be, or to have been, in the employ of Andrew Kerr the bookseller and printer, who (contrary to his wont, I must admit) does not seem to have been implicated in this particular affair. But, whether your brother was acquainted with the nature of his charge—where he has since taken refuge—or, indeed, anything further on this head, is for the present wrapped in complete obscurity: our researches have as yet proved fruitless—the prisoner utterly refusing, even when put to the question, to admit any connection with him. An order for his arrest was nevertheless issued last night before we separated, and will be carried into effect without delay."

Alice bent her head despairingly. The first large drops of that black cloud which had so long loured over them were beginning to fall, and this distant crash was but a prelude to the storm she anticipated. Her temples throbbed with a desperate effort to grasp the real extent of her brother's peril, and the readiest means of warding it off; but all was so dark and vague! How could she do anything to the purpose without her mother's knowledge; and yet, how venture to communicate this new misfortune? In her perplexity she still clung, with a woman's true instinct, to the very man whose acquaintance with Norman's situation was most fraught with danger.

"My lord, tell me more, tell me all! how can I save him? My mother is dying even now, and, if my brother were to come to any violent end, it would kill her at once—the shame, the horror ——"

"My sweet mistress," replied Lord Dundee, "I have already told you all I can—all that I have a right to disclose. I am willing to hope that your brother may escape; he is still young, and if by his sister's influence—the power which such a sister must have over any brother—he can be made to see the predicament into which he has thrust himself, so much the better, and, what is more, the sooner the better: for, unless he consents to forsake the folly of his ways—hiring or giving himself to aid and abet treason, he will most certainly entangle himself in a position from which I should have neither the power, nor indeed the wish, to save him."

He spoke these last sentences in a very serious tone, and seemed to leave them for her consideration, for he added no more just then, and sat playing with the silk and gold tassels of his splendid sash, yet without once losing sight of her pale, troubled face.

"What *can* I do? what will I do?" she murmured. "I know not where to find him. Oh, Norman! oh, mother!"

"He had better be in any spot than Edinburgh, I assure you, Mistress Alice," said Claverhouse. "I do not intend to create in your mind any exaggerated idea of the present peril, but any one who has ever been attainted with such an accusation, and come under the ban of the Privy Council, is a marked—I had well nigh said a *doomed*—man for ever after.

"I know it, I know it too well," sighed Alice.

"And most justly," added Lord Dundee; "we sleep on a powder magazine, and cannot afford to allow amongst us men whose every word is a fire-brand."

"But, my lord, if this be true—nay, what am I saying?—if he were guilty—alas, he *may* be! what danger—what punishment ——?"

"I cannot decide, that must depend entirely on the extent and importance of his offence; imprisoment at the Bass for life—transportation to the plantations—death, it might chance."

"Or worse, torture," said poor Alice, shuddering.

"You are right, it is—ten thousand fold worse," said the viscount; "and, stern as men hold me, never have I been able to reconcile myself to the sight. I would rather, and with a clear conscience, order twenty men to execution than one to torture."

Alice shuddered in every limb, but said nothing.

"Men *must* die sooner or later," pursued Lord Dundee; "in the struggle between authority and rebellion blood must inevitably flow, and if by the death of ten the lives of thousands can be protected, or good service rendered to the State, false mercy would be the sheerest cowardice, and so-called cruelty the truest mercy. If a traitor had a dozen lives, and order and public safety required that he should lose them, take them all and welcome, to put him out of mischief, but, for heaven's sake, while he hath human sense and life, leave him his human form! Kill him without pity, if needs must—a shot, a groan, the pang is short—not crush, and rend, and mangle, and deface, until the miserable wretch would not be recognised by the very mother that bore him."

A sudden quiver of disgust and pain passed over his whole countenance, like the rippling of a breeze on a still, clear pool, contracting the smooth brow and curved lip, and dilating the arched, open nostril; but it melted away almost before the eye could mark it, and he continued, with a rather forced smile,

"I hate them all—boot, rack, and caspie claws; but most especially the thumbscrews; I always feel as though they were crushing mine own finger-ends. Times out of number have I witnessed such scenes, and never could do aught but marvel at their purposeless atrocity. For what avails it, I would ask, to extract revelations, confessions, betrayals, by such means? Men who would encounter death without a moment's tremor will often crouch and shriek for mercy, at the first sight of those accursed instruments. Ay! the stoutest will lie and invent—accuse innocent and guilty indiscriminately—violate the very ties of nature—to shun that horrible anguish. I repeat it, nothing worth winning can be gained by such gratuitous inflictions, and I scarcely understand myself that I should have sat silently by to behold them so often. But this is most unseemly speech for your ears, Mistress Alice," he added; "you have more than enough with your own fears, without my darkening the picture by any such sombre shadows. What say you? have you decided how to act?"

"My lord, I intreat you, help me, advise me," said Alice, imploringly. "See how I rely on you."

"I cannot advise you beyond what I have already done, my poor child. With all my regard for you, I cannot promise to shield your brother from the consequences of his own acts, should they prove to have been what I most sincerely hope they will not. Your best, indeed your only plan, is to communicate with him as speedily and as prudently as may be, and warn him solemnly of the probable results of his weakness or worse, in mixing himself up with the crimes of the lawless men whose fanatical treasons have already drenched Scotland with blood. Show him all this as I have showed it to you—nay, use my name, if you find it expedient, to prove that you speak upon good authority. Why do you look so pale?"

"*Your* name—to him! it would be madness, my lord."

"Ha! and how so—has he any special enmity towards me? But do as you please; you have my counsel and information, make the best of both; right glad shall I be to learn that you have been able to profit by them, for I am selfish enough to consider that I shall thus escape the unpleasantness of sitting in judgment on one who is dear to you—little as he seems to deserve it. If he will not repent and turn from his wild errors for such pleading as yours, I should think him but scantly worth the tears you shed for him."

"Do you know him, my lord?" faltered Alice, whose tears were indeed falling fast; not more for Norman's peril, than for the grateful emotion aroused by the viscount's kindness.

"Not I, fair mistress! and for your sake, as well as his, I trust we may never become personally acquainted," replied Lord Dundee. "I could scarcely venture to answer for the result of our mutual communications. And again, I beg you to remember," he added, more seriously, "that we *may* very probably meet under such circumstances as will render it impossible for me to afford him the slightest countenance By his own deeds he must stand or fall; and even for the sake of his gentle sister I neither could nor would interfere with the course of justice. The reasons of State rise in such cases above all merely private feeling, as I have had but too good cause to know. However, let us hope for the best."

"Oh, that I could repay you for your goodness!" murmured Alice, tenderly, her lovely face one glow of blushes—"but I never can."

"You can, by never speaking of such service as deserving requital," replied the viscount, smiling. "Your good opinion, and the pleasure of contributing to your happiness, would repay any reasonable man an hundredfold for such trifling assistance as I have rendered you."

"But that night, when you so generously——"

"When I did not even unsheath my rapier in your cause—when I did not lose even a drop of blood—when I had not even a scratch, a pinprick to show! Why, mistress Alice, would you put me to the blush, by offering thanks for such poor championship! But I suppose I am invulnerable, in virtue of that profitable compact on the subject of which you obligingly enlightened me. I hope it may prove a valid one, for there are stirring days at hand—and I foresee a tempest ready to burst which will bring a leaden shower about our ears, heavier than the rain drops in summer, mistress Alice."

His gay laugh and pointed glance, as he rose to depart, disconcerted poor Alice—she was confounded at finding how exactly he had repeated her own expressions on the night of her rescue.

"Oh, Lord Dundee, pardon me such folly!" she said, very humbly.

"Most cheerfully, sweet mistress; your error was not greater than that of thousands who should be wiser, and I am happily convinced that you hold me in better esteem now than to suffer such absurdity to disturb your good-will towards a very sincere friend. Certes, if I *have* sold myself to Satan, the Prince of Darkness hath dealt most scurvily by me, for I have met all through my life with injustice, ill-luck, and hard fortune enough for the greatest saint that ever, like the good St. Anthony, did battle with him until he fled. And now, I must really wish you farewell—time runs on and I should be away; I trust to hear of your complete success with your brother the next time I have the pleasure of meeting you."

He bowed, and turned to cross the room, with a graceful inclination of the head, and a kindly look in his brilliant dark eyes that set her heart throbbing almost as much with fear as pleasure, for Lord Glencarrig was standing by. He had entered a moment before, and, moved by that aimless jealousy which men are apt to feel, on small provocation, or on none at all, had hastened to the window embrasure, but only in time to catch the last insignificant sentence.

"It is wearing somewhat late, I think," observed Lord Dundee.

"I am waiting your pleasure, my lord, and have been so this last half-hour," replied the young man, with as much ill-humour as he could venture to inflict on his kinsman, who, by the sheer weight of character, possessed very considerable influence over him, divested of any external attempt to exercise it, for, even when the application of this power was most irresistible and apparent, the viscount was, or more likely chose to appear, unaware of it. Glencarrig kissed his mother's hand, and, after bestowing a few taunts of provoking pity on Flora that she should miss the evening's entertainment, the two gentlemen took their leave.

Alice sighed deeply, sadly, as the door closed—the happiness she had enjoyed had been great and unforeseen; but it had left a cruel sting behind. She now began to realize in all its magnitude the distressing perplexity in which she was involved—ignorant of her brother's abode, of any channel of communication with him, afraid of some fresh worse discovery taking place before she could succeed in warning him, perhaps to have the warning flung back with sullen obstinacy and insulting suspicion. But *that* could only grieve herself, and she would encounter anything to save him, to preserve her mother from the agony of seeing him fall into the hands of the relentless Privy Council.

To find him first, to obtain an interview—that once attained, all the rest would be, must be, easy!

The bright evening was fading fast into twilight; Flora, who had been loitering about the room since her brother left, sauntered slowly up, and, throwing herself down into the place which Lord Dundee had vacated, laid her head on Alice's shoulder with a sigh.

"My little quiet Gowan! would I had half thy patience! Gilbert hath not been absent four days yet, and I am wearying for him already."

"He will very soon be back," said Alice, kissing her.

The two girls sat locked in each other's arms, neither caring to speak. The twilight deepened fast—the countess had already left the apartment; and, as they looked from the window, the faint white lustre of the coming moon was just visible on the summits of the tall trees, whose darkened branches made a trembling pattern against a space of amber sky. The soft loveliness of the autumn evening, the fresh perfume of the moist leaves and grass, the low hum of the surrounding city which alone came across the stillness, or rather seemed to make a part of it, touched every sensitive and wounded nerve in Alice's heart. She passed her arm round Flora's neck, and hid her face there, and soon a few large unwilling tears, a few ill-concealed sobs, betrayed that patience itself might be too hardly tasked.

"My poor bird!" said the startled Flora, who was so accustomed to her friend's sweet cheerfulness that such emotion quite disturbed her; "my bonnie bird!" she said again, like a child fondling a pet dove, "oh, that I could see thee as happy as myself! I would be content to part from thee then! Has Glencarrig vexed thee? He is rough and careless sometimes, too like myself, and his temper has been sadly soured of late, but I am sure he loves thee dearly at heart. Do not be angry with poor David, Alice; he has his sorrows to bear as well as thyself. My darling sister, trust me! I would let myself be torn in pieces sooner than breathe a letter of thy secrets to any living soul!"

It was so earnestly and truthfully promised that Alice resolved to give herself a little relief. She dried her tears and said in a cautious voice, "Norman."

"Aha!" said Lady Flora, raising her head as a light struck her, "I am not astonished. So it was of *that* my cousin wished to speak with you?"

"Oh, hush! yes."

"What mischief has he done? Oh, I always said he would be a heavy trouble to you all!" exclaimed Flora, angrily.

"Dearest Flora! speak laigh, if you love me!"

"Did not my cousin tell you what it was?"

"Alas, very, very little; and that I must not repeat—I know not whether I have the right."

"Can I not help ye—nor David?"

"No; you must not tell him—nor even your dear mother, Flora."

"But, since Lord Dundee could bring you to the knowledge of the difficulty, he could surely find some way to get over it," said Flora, thoughtfully. "Alice, I know him far better than you—he is generous and noble—he would gladly —— "

"Hush, Flora! he can do nothing; he *ought* not to do anything," replied Alice, with singular comprehension of, and sympathy with, his stern sense of duty, even where, as now, it told most heavily against herself. "Whisht, dear madam! say no more; the very walls seem to me alive with greedy lugs and open eyes —— No, no! I will strive and strive until the end; but God will surely help me, for other help I have none."

"If Gilbert were here?" sighed Flora. But Alice only shook her head very decidedly; and thus in silent sorrow on the one side, in silent sympathy on the other, they remained until nine o'clock rang from the cathedral spire, and the moon rose round and bright in the purple sky, lighting up the two fair motionless forms as they leaned against each other in their sisterly embrace—Flora dreaming of her absent lover, Alice in a turmoil of anxious thought, gilded it is true by that ray of dazzling joy which the presence of him she loved with such distant adoration could shed over the saddest hours of her difficult and wearying pathway. Then, with an affectionate kiss, she left her friend, and went home to seek, through what seemed likely to prove a restless night, the means of saving one who had never been aught but a drag on her best energies, and a gnawing sorrow to her right-minded and pious spirit. Her mother was already quietly asleep, and, as Alice lay down beside her, tired out with excitement, the slumber of which she had despaired stole kindly to her pillow, and brought to her aching head oblivion at once of love and of sorrow.

CHAPTER XXII.

A DOUBLE DILEMMA.

> She is a precious jewel I have found,
>
> . . . .
>
> I'll stoop for it, and when I wear it here,
> Set on my forehead like the morning-star,
> The world may wonder, but it will not laugh.
>
> THE SPANISH STUDENT.

THE long and deep rest which succeeded the varied excitement of this evening acted favourably upon the perturbed feelings of Alice, for she rose the next morning not less impressed with the urgency of her brother's danger, but ready and decided to take some step for communicating with him—resolved, now that her mind was made up, to act without even allowing her mother to suspect the evil. Her first proceeding was to apply to Maister Andrew Kerr, bookseller and imprinter.

This worthy lived in a narrow wynd leading from the Cowgate to the North College Street—a favourable situation for one of his craft, as he was well known and extensively patronised by the University students. He was a hard-featured, grim-visaged individual, with a face about as destitute of expression as a man of wood; and this command of countenance, whether natural or acquired, had repeatedly stood him in good stead during his conflicts with the authorities, of which he was, in truth, not a little proud, as they conferred on him a sort of brevet rank of martyrdom, causing him to be regarded as "ane persecuted sanct," without entailing on him as yet any of the weightier inconveniences usually annexed to testifying. These *demêlés*, and the constant stretch of every faculty of caution they superinduced, had given rise to a popular legend, that good Maister Andro had never returned a straightforward answer in his life; and the more irreverent gossips amongst the college youths openly affirming that, "sanct" as he wished to be thought, this excellent disciple would not have felt himself "free to confess" that he had ever been baptized, had the inquiry been propounded by a macer of council.

The subject of these disparaging remarks, attired in a plain doublet and hose of sober grey, with a flat blue bonnet, much the worse for wear, on his bald crown, was busy in his shop arranging and ticketing his store of books and pamphlets (a musty, yellow, scanty assortment it would have seemed to modern eyes), placing some on shelves, others, probably of a more exceptionable and dangerous description, in large oaken lockers, with fastenings strong enough for a jail door, when Alice entered with an eager, inquiring expression of face which made him prick up his ears.

"Is my brother here, Master Kerr?" she said, after a polite greeting.

"An' wha may he be?" was the response.

"Norman—Norman Scott," was the surprised answer of Alice in turn. "Is he not here?"

"Na, he isna." And therewith Master Kerr turned him to his books once more.

"Will he be here soon?" asked Alice.

"I canna just say."

Alice stood confounded at the *sang-froid* with which the bookseller denied all acquaintance with his assistant's movements; but, calling to mind the worthy man's proverbial reputation, she persevered in her inquiries.

"I want very much to see him, Master Kerr; couldna ye just tell me where he is, or where I could find him?"

"Ye are his sister, said ye, maiden?" asked Master Kerr, who had seen Alice before, but had either forgotten or chose to forget her on this occasion.

"Ay, sir, his sister; and I must needs see Norman. I pray you tell me where he is."

"And what for need ye him?"

"For an important matter—for my mother's sake, as well as his. Can I find him?"

"It wad be easy, doubtless, if ye kenned whar to seek," said the bookseller drily.

Poor Alice looked miserably disappointed; and her blank face stirred the compassion of Dame Marjorie, the printer's wife, who, sitting in a square massive chair of oaken boards, which looked as if no mere human agency could have moved it, was busily knitting a pair of thick woollen hose for her husband.

"Eh, Andro!" said she in a low voice, catching hold of his sleeve, "dinna speak sae to the puir bairn; dinna ye see she's like to greet? Is your mither sick, hinnie?" she inquired kindly.

"Yes, very," replied Alice abstractedly, without, however, intending to convey the impression of that being the cause of her visit.

"Eh, Andro! hearken to that!" whispered the good-natured dame, pulling him again by the arm; "and she nae doubt come to seek her brither to bring him hame; wherefore canna ye answer her mair discreetly?"

"Dinna you pit yer fingers into ither folk's pies, Lucky," retorted her spouse rather grimly; "they'll do weel eneugh without you, I'se be caution."

"But tell her, Andro; what matters it?" persisted his wife.

"Naething to you, dame, ye may swear; take tent to yer knittin' work, or I'll be getting a bout o' the rheumatiz the winter that's comin'; and beware o' fashin' yersel' anent things that's aboon yer comprehension. Aweel, maiden?" (to Alice, who still remained, patiently expecting some information).

"Is he not in Scotland?"

"Ye'll ken, whenever ye see him."

"But I ask whether you are likely to see him soon; you surely must know so much as that?" said Alice, with tears of anxiety and mortification standing in her mild eyes.

"May be sae, and may be no; I'm no that certain," replied Andrew in an oracular tone, and with a solemn action of the jaws that would have been ludicrous if it had not been hideous.

Alice sighed, hesitated; then said,

"Would you give him a bit letter from me, when you see him?"

"I canna say when I'll see him," repeated Andrew, as the girl drew carefully from the bosom of her dress a neat little case of her own work, and extracted from it a small billet tied with a thread of green silk waxed over the knot. Another slip of paper dropped out by the same movement, upon which Master Kerr's hawk-eyes fell instantly; but Alice sprang on it, and, putting it back into the case, restored that to its hiding-place, and stood with her hand pressed to it, as if to guard the valuable contents.

Master Kerr took the letter, and twisted it round and round in his knotty fingers.

"Aweel, maiden, if yon holds treason, your head will need to pay for't, and no mine, I would wuss ye to comprehend," he said with the same oracular intonation. "I'm laith to hae aught to do wi' strangers: in these kittle times it's no angels that ye entertain unawares, my certie!"

"Only give it to Norman as soon as you possibly can, sir; that is all I ask," replied Alice; and, getting no answer beyond a surly grunt, she wished the old dame good day, and departed, very uneasy at the secret ways and extreme rudeness of Norman's employer, which seemed to betoken a fear of involving himself in some suspicious affair; but comforted at the thought that she had done her best, and must leave the rest to Providence. They had no friends or acquaintances with whom her brother was likely to be in even casual communication; so Alice was forced to school herself to patience, and await the result of her letter, for she could not doubt that Maister Kerr, in spite of all his evasions, was either perfectly informed of his assistant's whereabouts, or in actual correspondence with him, since it appeared that he was not in the capital. She found her mother full of questions as to how she had spent the previous evening, and, anxious to divert the invalid's attention from herself, Alice gratified her curiosity to the uttermost, dilated on the elegance of Lady Glencarrig's new withdrawing-room, on Flora's affectionate kindness, on every point, in short, except the two subjects which engrossed her own thoughts, answering the good dame's exclamations, queries, and shy curiosity regarding Lord Dundee with that quiet indifference which far more often covers an interest only too fond and deep than the carelessness it seems to assert.

She had not expected any immediate result from her missive, but as five, six days, a week passed, and no token was received from her brother, her suspense grew almost unbearable. Still she had enough to divert her thoughts, for the first week in September had begun, and rather more than a fortnight would bring Flora's wedding-day. It had originally been fixed for the twenty-sixth of that month, but, Lord Gilbert Hay having been chosen to proceed to London on political business which admitted of no postponement, the marriage had been hastened in order that his young bride might accompany him. From thence they intended to visit Paris, and thus the separation which both the friends so much regretted was likely to prove long and wide. The necessary preparations were hurried on, and Alice became more than ever indispensable to Lady Flora. Very often, indeed, she refused to leave her mother, but Madam Scott almost as often overruled the refusal. She was grieved to see the quiet melancholy which was now the settled expression of her child's face—she knew how dearly the young Lady Flora prized her, and how doubly hard the parting would be to Alice now that so many other cares weighed upon her—she therefore constantly insisted that no consideration for herself should interfere to prevent Alice from spending as much time as her necessary occupations would permit with the friend whose society she could not expect to enjoy again for so long a period.

It is probable that all her persuasions would have been unavailing to induce Alice to quit her had the young girl not found for her a companion as careful and trustworthy as she could desire, in the person of old Janet Rutherford. Madam Scott liked her, and she in return had gradually grown much attached to Alice and the invalid, to whose slightly condescending manners she submitted with perfect good faith, as feeling them to be only a proper indication of the distance existing between herself and the "weel born and weel educate" women, who had a countess for their friend and a born lady as a foster-sister. Janet was considerably above seventy years of age, and had gone through many sorrows: her father had been killed on his own hearth-stone by some marauding English troopers during the troubles of Charles the First's reign—her husband had fallen while in arms for the King at the battle of Alford,—her son-in-law had been shot by the Covenanting general Lesley after the fatal day at Philiphaugh, and her daughter had died of a broken heart, leaving an infant of three months old, which soon sickened and died, so that the lonely woman was without a near relation in the world. But all this had failed to damp the vigorous spirits and strong energies of Janet, and she had contrived to live ever since her widowhood by the labour of her hands, if not in comfort at least above indigence. She was gifted with a prodigious memory, and could recall, with vivid distinctness, events which were almost history to Madam Scott and remote tradition to Alice; so that the former could well spare her daughter, and the latter depart in comfort, when old Janet volunteered to transfer her spinning-wheel or knitting-work to the lodger's little sitting-room, and pass her evening there, pouring out for the invalid's amusement the accumulated experiences of threescore years and ten.

We have already described the first evening which Alice spent in the drawing-room of Lady Glencarrig—it was not the last. Her good taste and good sense enabled her to resist all Flora's blandishments whenever she discovered that company was assembled, but at other times she yielded more easily; and such was the effect of Flora's unremitting attention, of Lady Glencarrig's kindness, and the young earl's respectful homage, that she soon took her place there naturally and gracefully, though always with a retiring simplicity which never sought to advance a step beyond it. Lord Gilbert Hay, a frank, warm-hearted, polished gentleman, soon began to appreciate and like his promised bride's foster-sister, and always treated her with a courteous consideration that greatly increased the esteem in which Alice held his character. It was all the more agreeable that even Lord Glencarrig could not condescend to feel jealous of his sister's devoted lover and affianced husband, while the presence of a stranger restrained him, in a great degree, from those demonstrations of his passion which so often distressed Alice. But during the hours she spent thus, one single idea could be said to have real existence in her mind —the presence or absence of Lord Dundee. In his presence she *lived*, in his absence all else seemed the shadow of a dream—confused, dark, and hardly interesting enough to be worthy of a thought.

The exquisite happiness which she enjoyed on the occasions when this secret desire was gratified was so intense and all-sufficing, that in it she forgot how soon those occasions must cease. She did not even calculate upon the probability of his addressing her; it was only too much happiness to hear his step on the stairs, his voice in the room—to listen, in wonder and delight, to the long, and to her partially unintelligible, conversations which took place upon affairs of State and foreign policy—to watch his dark, liquid eyes light up with their passionate, tremulous fire—to see his haughty brow and pale cheek flush—to mark the stern enthusiasm which often thrilled on his tongue, and which, little as she understood its purport or could sympathise in its fiery daring, seemed only to elevate him the more above the level of ordinary beings. Alice could hardly credit that the fierce warrior and the experienced politician, who at one moment inspired her with such distant awe, should become the next her *friend*, who, with smiling lip and gentle glance, came to her quiet nook to speak of her mother's health, to inquire as to her own well-doing, and, whenever opportunity served, ask news of her success with Norman. News of that kind, unfortunately, she had none to give, and her silent, desponding shake of the head was answer enough to the question which she divined in his face whenever they met.

This was oftener than she had ever dared to hope, for Lord Dundee rarely passed many days without visiting his relations, either to communicate some fresh advices from the metropolis, to discuss the news of the day, or enjoy the conversation of his cousin, Lady Glencarrig. He remembered her a young and lovely girl, for whom, in his boyish days, he had experienced a real though fleeting attachment, speedily dissolved by the interference of parents and Lady Glencarrig's happy marriage; and he still retained towards his widowed kinswoman something of the chivalrous affection he had once vowed to Beatrix Grahame. He valued highly both her character and intellect, and, reserved as he was with most persons, trusted her to a degree which equally surprised and gratified the countess.

She, on her side, was much pleased at this renewal of an intercourse discontinued since early youth, for she hoped that his kinsman's influence might preserve her son from some of the follies and vices of his companions—nor was she disappointed. David held the viscount in profound respect, and dreaded his stern glance of contempt and reproof more than anything else; it would have required a very strong temptation to induce him to brave the concise but scathing condemnation which he had heard bestowed upon others, and which naturally carried with it greater weight from Lord Dundee's practice being known to correspond with his avowed principles; so that, although we could not assert that the earl's conduct was absolutely exemplary, it was infinitely superior to that of the generality of his youthful contemporaries, and happily not such as to cause any serious uneasiness to his pious and excellent mother.

The state of public affairs at this time absorbed so much of the attention of Lord Dundee as to relieve David in some degree from the unerring scrutiny which was wont to read as in an open book the varying fancies which passed through his unsophisticated brain. He was glad to be miserable without observation save that of his mother, who dreaded lest in his moody and restless condition he should yield to the influence of Viscount Dundee's fiery nature, and plunge into all the dangers and misfortunes of the civil war which seemed so fast approaching. She longed to obtain his confidence, but longed in vain, for he kept his troubles entirely to himself, and left her under the belief that he was the victim of an unrequited passion for Lady Mary Charteris, while in truth his whole soul was yearning to Alice.

His difficulties thickened daily. The time was drawing nigh when the departure of Flora from Edinburgh would deprive him of his only opportunities of meeting her friend in quiet and security, and the prospect of losing Alice's society almost distracted him. Some decided step must be taken, that was evident, but at first the necessity alone presented itself to his mind unaccompanied by any means of satisfying it. What step *could* he take to possess himself of the treasure he so ardently coveted, and on which he seemed as yet to have no hold? As this question daily recurred, ever more pressing and harder of solution, he began to see with fresh confusion of mind that only two courses were open, and to do him justice one of these was unhesitatingly rejected.

The tone of morals at the period of which we are writing was not such as to brand vice with shame or reprobation amongst the higher classes. The unrestrained licentiousness of a profligate court had infected every stage of society — abductions, intrigues, every species of excess and libertinism, were ordinary occurrences, especially amongst the arrogant nobility and gentry of both kingdoms; actions which in our more favoured epoch would inevitably lower the reputation of a gentleman, and be considered by all right-thinking persons as a stain upon the unblemished self-respect which should constitute his highest claim to that title, were then passed over with a laugh or a jest, when not positively applauded. But the earl was, as we have said, in many respects superior to the generality of young men of his age; his nature honest, generous, and truthful—and, if the thoughtlessness of youth and the influence of evil example had sometimes betrayed him into venial errors, his heart was far too uncorrupt yet, his mind too deeply imbued with the precepts of an excellent education, ever to originate a base and cruel scheme for the ruin of an innocent girl, his childhood's companion, his sister's friend, his mother's *protégée*. If ever the evil fancy crept into his breast, he thrust it forth with absolute terror, lest remaining there it should strike root and grow, and so wind itself around his heart as to harden him into contemplating without disgust such hateful treachery. He would not even allow the thought to gain ground in his mind that Alice *could* ever become anything less bright and pure than he loved to think her—*could* ever fall from her high estate of modest maidenhood; he almost shuddered at himself when he discovered that this dark and shameful hope had indeed lurked unsuspected in the recesses of his own undisciplined heart.

And yet, how could he venture upon a step so bold, so unthought of, as to bestow his hand and coronet upon a poor, dowerless, almost nameless, girl, the daughter of a humble Presbyterian minister, one who laboured with her hands for daily bread—he, whose ancestors had been known to fame when some of the haughtiest titles in England were yet uncreated, and in whose veins flowed the blood of two of the noblest races in France and Scotland. What would be the displeasure of his mother, who had calculated so proudly upon the wealth and honours which his marriage was to add to the large possessions of their ancient line?—what the wrath of his haughty relatives, the sarcasm of his noble friends and companions, who might indeed think the beautiful embroideress a charming toy to amuse a few idle hours, but would treat with scorn the idea of raising her to his own rank by honourable union? The difficulties seemed insuperable, but, the more evident they became, the stronger and more definite grew his determination to brave them. Something there was of self-will, of a boy's unreasoning obstinacy, in that sudden resolution—something of the spirit of opposition, and of a desire to show that he could think, feel, and act for himself—still more of that chivalrous spirit which had always made him rush at obstacles for the glory of overcoming them—but most of all the ardour of a first true love, which would not admit that its object was unworthy to rank with the noblest and fairest that ever won the coronet of Glencarrig.

Amidst all these fluctuations of passion, pride, hesitation, and resolution, it had never once occurred to him that the one obstacle which no energy of will could vanquish might proceed from Alice herself. In spite of her coldness, and even of the vigorous rebuffs with which his advances had hitherto been met, the natural vanity of youth and rank had combined with the self-deception of a buoyant temperament to insinuate that Alice was only restrained from showing her preference for him by uncertainty regarding his intentions—that it was impossible but what she must appreciate his affection—and that nothing was needed but a distinct avowal of his honourable views to bring to light all the love she had until now so successfully concealed. That she could or would refuse such a destiny as that which he had it in his power to bestow, was beyond his conception.

His lively imagination, once launched on this current, soon bore him away from all contemplation of the obstacles which surrounded his project, to an ecstatic expectation of the happiness he believed to await him. To see her calm face beam, her soft cheek burn with blushes, to receive from her lips a promise of reciprocated love, to press those lips upon his own as he had never done since childhood—all these and a thousand other passionate fancies which had until then been but day-dreams, misty and pale, sprang at once into solid hopes—nay, sober certainties. It could only be a question of time. Reserve, distrust, the fear of irrevocably offending his family, might perhaps delay the acknowledgment of her love for himself; but he would soothe, persuade, plead, encourage, and, sooner or later, prevail. And in the thoughtlessness of pride he asked himself, "Why should she refuse me?"

And why, added Love, growing hour after hour in the atmosphere of these fervid hopes and unchecked aspirations, should he shrink from making her the partner of his destiny? Was she not beautiful as the fairest of the proud and wealthy damsels who openly wooed the heir of Glencarrig? Was she not grace and goodness personified? Had she not all the modest dignity, the refined self-possession which could grace her future station, and which lost nothing even beside the high-bred ease of his own mother and sister? With what triumph he now began to picture the moment when he should place a countess's coronet on that graceful head, and show forth to all men the pearl of great price he had wooed and won!

All this, however, was by no means the result of one deliberate self-examination, but rather the climax and final decision arrived at after innumerable desultory meditations, some of which, we are compelled to admit, were of a tenor almost diametrically opposed to the general current of his resolutions. He was sometimes very much shaken in his steadfastness by some unpremeditated observation of his lady-mother, and much disturbed in his secrecy by the raillery, the coaxing, and compassionate condolences, of Flora, who, having in the course of the last two months assured herself that he kept entirely aloof from the Lady Mary, and seemed scarcely conscious of her existence any longer, very naturally inferred that a quarrel similar to her own with Gilbert had taken place between them, and pitied David with all her affectionate heart—for which pity he was in no wise grateful, and more than once repulsed her caresses with sharp irritability that quite disconcerted the young lady, and sent her to Alice with regrets for the change which disappointed love had made in her once kind and frank-hearted brother.

It certainly cost Lord Glencarrig no small effort to act in a manner so contrary to his careless openness of disposition, but he felt convinced of the absolute necessity for silence. Much as his mother loved and admired Alice, the young man could not doubt that at the first hint of his attachment the countess would find means of preventing this unequal union; his only safety lay in keeping his own counsel until he should have secured the consent of Alicc, after which he trusted to his own ingenuity or obstinacy to break down every barrier that might oppose the fulfilment of his desires. And, even supposing the worst, he could easily wait; in less than two years he would be of age and accountable to no man.

One consequence of his perplexities, and of the minute care with which he adapted his movements to those of Alice, in the hope of finding some favourable opportunity for executing the first portion of his now matured plan, was an absence of interest in his former amusements, which, together with an acerbity of temper never before remarked in him, had for some time past excited the curiosity of all his gay friends.

"What the devil is the matter with Glencarrig?" said young Dalmeny to Fergusson of Craigdarroch as they lounged one pleasant afternoon under the pillars of Hugh Blair's coffee-house in company with several other noted fashionables; "I don't know the lad again, he looks as dowie as a girl that's lost her first love, and as sour as gall and wormwood; he quite turned my claret to-day."

"What would you have?" said Walter Charteris, a tall, fair, dissipated looking young man, glancing round with a disagreeable laugh. "What can you expect? the poor silly fellow is in love."

"*You* need not tell us that," retorted Lord Drummond, the son and heir of the Earl of Perth, who afterwards took no mean share in the disastrous rising of 1715; "we can see and judge for ourselves, and your fair sister makes no concealment of her conquests."

"Tush!" exclaimed Charteris, laughing still, "you have used your eyes to very little purpose, my lord, if you imagine Glencarrig to be still yoked to Mary's car; he hath other and newer game in view."

"He should have pulled off the mourning for his old love then; the rosy god would flee from so tomb-like a visage," replied Fergusson. "Why *I* never was sad because I had mislaid my heart for awhile, and I have been in love a round dozen of times—I always am—I am now—I hope I always shall be. *Vive l' inconstance!* it's the very salt of life! Go on, Charteris."

"Have none of you seen a sweet little craft that follows in the wake of that stately galleon his sister, the Lady Flora, and to my mind takes the wind out of her sails?"

"To *your* mind perhaps, Mr. Charteris," said Lord Drummond, rather annoyed, for he was a professed admirer of the Lady Flora's, and was reported to have received a severe shock from the sudden announcement of her intended marriage.

"Ay, to mine, and to her brother's also," replied Charteris; "I would lay my best hawk to a church-yard rook that he is hunting down that dainty quarry, and no other."

"Who is she? what is her name?" asked several voices.

"Who is she? A sort of humble companion, I fancy," said Charteris, "whom my Lady Flora Bethune, caring for neither pug-dog, parrot, monkey, nor negro boy, hath ever at her side, to pet and caress, to cuff and pinch, as the humour takes her; to dress her hair, to hold her fan, to talk when she is sulky, to listen when she would talk, and to serve as a foil to her gipsy beauty; and her name is Alice Scott."

"I knew an Alice Scott once," said Fergusson, "and sorely my purse had reason to rue it!—an extravagant jade! Can this be the same, think you?"

"Scarcely, Craigdarroch," replied Lord Drummond; "such are not the chosen companions of noble ladies, whatever they may be of well-born gentlemen. What is she like? dost thou know her, Charteris?"

"I have met her twice or thrice with Lady Flora—a demure little nun, with a face fair as a lily-bud, downcast eyes with thick shady lashes and pencilled brows, a rosy mouth set in tiny dimples, and hair of bright pale chestnut in clusters of silky rings; a perfect picture in her Puritan dress and hood, with the little white ruff setting off a throat as white. She seemed marvellously at her ease with Lady Flora—and, by

Jupiter!" added the young guardsman, lifting himself lazily into a perpendicular attitude from the pillar against which he had been resting his shoulder, "I once saw this girl meet and speak to—guess whom!"

The others glanced at each other and laughed.

"Charteris has always some prodigious mystery to disclose, but the mountain generally brings forth a mouse," said Fergusson. "He is a greater gossip and talebearer than myself; but then the ladies will have it so, and I own that he is pretty successful in pleasing *them*. Well! why should she not speak to any one she likes? A pretty woman is the equal of a king—even a coif and short gown have claims on me."

"A hundred—a thousand, to one you don't guess!"

"Long odds! you had better tell us at once, Charteris," said Lord Drummond, with some curiosity. Stay, though—let me have one cast; was it old Geordie Mackenzie?"

"Better still—Claverhouse!"

"Pshaw! you're jesting, Walter!" exclaimed Dalmeny, rather hurriedly, for this circumstance convinced him of what his comrade's description had already made him suspect, namely, that he had better reason to know Alice than even Charteris himself.

"Jesting! not I, in faith; I'd swear to it, for a bodle. I saw her, with my own eyes, in the High Street, some four months back, conversing with him and young Glencarrig."

"A most exquisite jest!" said Fergusson, with extreme amusement. "I always said —— ah! if Ogilvie were but here!"

"What of him? doth he affect this pretty Puritan? A wise man to have two strings to his bow!" said Dalmeny.

"Ogilvie? not he! He is grovelling—soul and spirit—before the feet of my Lady Jean Gordon," said Charteris, not without a sneer. "May I be hung, drawn, and quartered if ever I sink into such a slave to any woman, were she Venus herself. A most sound doctrine that, which establishes that the man is the head of the woman."

"And is it really a fact that the earl languishes for this minion of his beautiful sister?" asked the proud Lord Drummond, contemptuously.

"Nay, gentlemen, do not make me responsible for the statement; if he do not, why the more fool he to throw away what may be had for the asking. But I believe him simple enow for any thing."

"*Aux innocents les mains pleines*," said Fergusson, quoting an old French proverb.

"He must be a greater gomeral than I take him for, to sit thus within the gates of the Hesperidian gardens, and never stretch forth a hand to pluck the golden apples," said Dalmeny.

"And she is always at his house, said you, Charteris?"

"Ay, most often; but she lives with an old bedridden mother, or encumbrance of that sort—a pensioner of the countess, I suppose. Perchance our noble friend hath as yet found the leaven of the Covenant too strong for him, and is considering ways and means. The man is in love, to a dead certainty, and not with any of our belles. He seems proof to shot, and his own old mansion hath wonderful attractions for him. He hath lived too much at home of late to be enslaved elsewhere."

"How do you know all this, Charteris?"

"By mine own good eyes and ears, as I learn most things; and if you keep yours alert, gentlemen comrades, you will see greater marvels than these. I would bet fifty to one that, if no better may be, Glencarrig is the man to marry her."

"Preposterous!" exclaimed one.

"Disgraceful!" said another.

"And wherefore should he not?" asked young Lindsay, who had strolled up to the group a minute previously.

"Wherefore *not?* marry his own sister's waiting-woman!" ejaculated Ferguson; "are you daft, to ask it?"

"Pardon me, Craigdarroch, but five minutes ago I think I heard you say that a beautiful woman was the equal of a king, and I quite agreed with the sentiment," replied Lindsay, who still retained much of his boyish chivalry, in defiance of many an adverse influence.

"And I said truly; but there *are* distinctions to be observed, and such a match would be worse than ridiculous."

"By token too that she is a Presbyterian and the daughter of a Presbyterian, and sister to an ill-conditioned cub of a Whig 'prentice, whose sandy pate I have been half a dozen times tempted to break," added Charteris.

"But," said Lord Drummond, "this does not explain to me what the girl can have to do with Lord Dundee. It seems rather a singular acquaintance for both."

"Not at all singular, in my poor judgment," interrupted Fergusson, maliciously. "The facts are simple enough; he is a handsome man, and she a young and comely lassie—the thing explains itself."

"Ha, ha!" laughed Charteris, "what would Lord Glencarrig say to that reading of the riddle, I wonder? Why, Dalmeny man! you look as sober as old Lockhart when he hath four quarts of claret under his belt. Know you aught of all this, or art thou too smitten?"

"I do know something, certainly," answered Dalmeny.

"Explain, explain!" cried half a dozen voices at once.

"Silence in court, there!" said young Drummond, raising his cane. "Now, Dalmeny!"

A coarse jest trembled on the young laird's tongue when he recalled the scene in which Alice had been thrown, helpless and insensible, into the power of Claverhouse, but a feeling of respect for his commander, of pity for the girl, and some slight doubts of her identity prevailed. He did not respond immediately to the general call, which was in consequence repeated with considerable energy.

"I have nothing particular to say, gentlemen."

His friends looked at each other again, and smiled, for Dalmeny's vacillation was almost proverbial.

"Nothing at least that I wish to say at present,"

continued Dalmeny, a moment of gentlemanly reluctance to injure the fair fame of a woman against whom he really knew nothing, carrying the day over the reckless indulgence of scandal and gossip common amongst these high-bred personages. He took the arm of a gentleman standing by, and the two moved off to a short distance.

"Never mind!" said Fergusson, confidently, "I'll get it all out of him, the very first carouse we have together, for be it known to you, gallants all, that I, your poor comrade and obedient servant, have succeeded to the honourable post of chief Mentor to our facile, soft-hearted friend, *vice* Drummond retired."

"I trust that you exercise it with somewhat more credit to yourself and him than did your predecessor," said the laird of Burnielaw.

"Oh, ay, of course. I am a very phœnix of discretion and sober-mindedness, as all the world knows. But touching this pretty secret which he fights shy of clearing up—I have in my hand some links of the chain, by which I can speedily draw forth the remainder."

"Where is Drummond now?" asked Burnielaw.

"Who knows and who cares?" said his affectionate relative.

"The devil! whose servant he is."

"The latest tidings I heard of him," replied Fergusson, "were, that he had endeavoured to obtain service under old Hugh Mackay, but had been unsuccessful, and was now a volunteer in Count Solms' brigade. I had it on the authority of a gentleman newly arrived from Holland, who had himself seen Drummond."

"I rejoice to hear it," replied Lindsay, impetuously; "I desire nothing more than to encounter him, and, if we march to England, a pistol-shot or rapier-thrust will serve to bear my first greeting to him."

"Burnielaw can't forget his insulted gauntlet," said Charteris, as Lindsay walked away.

So ended this conversation, in which truth and error were mingled in their usual proportions, with perhaps an additional dash of the former in Charteris' statements respecting Lord Glencarrig's designs towards Alice, which were more correct than he had imagined when he put forth his random assertion, intended only to provoke a discussion and raise a laugh. He would have been rather startled could he have guessed how soon the event was about to justify his predictions.

END OF VOL. I.

CPSIA information can be obtained
at www.ICGtesting.com
Printed in the USA
LVHW101944050123
736480LV00003B/112

9 783375 129231